Side Order of LOVE

Tracey Richardson

Bella
BOOKS

2009

Bella Books, Inc.
P.O. Box 10543
Tallahassee, FL 32302

Printed in the United States of America on acid-free paper
First Edition

Editor: Cindy Cresap
Cover Designer: Stephanie Solomon-Lopez

ISBN 10: 1-59493-143-7
ISBN 13: 978-1-59493-143-7

About the Author

Tracey Richardson is a daily newspaper editor who lives in the Great Lakes region of Ontario, Canada. She is the author of *The Candidate*, published in 2008, and wrote several novels in the 1990s for Naiad Press, Inc. In her spare time, Tracey enjoys playing sports such as ice hockey, golf and skiing. She also enjoys the tasty benefits of her partner's wonderful culinary skills (which is why she has to play so many sports!). E-mail the author at trich7117@gmail.com

Dedication

To all those who appreciate a great dish and a perfect golf swing

Acknowledgments

Thank you to Bella for continued support and belief in me. The women in the Bella family are truly wonderful! The readers get my biggest thanks, because without them, so many wonderful things in my life would not have happened. The loyalty and dedication to this genre are remarkable, and it's what helps propel me on. I want to thank my right-hand readers Brenda, Stacey, Cris S. and Barb. Their observations and suggestions were invaluable to me. Brenda is also my dedicated webmistress, for which I'm very appreciative. My editor Cindy Cresap, as always, brought her extraordinary skills to this novel and helped make it (and me!) better. My thanks, as always, to my partner.

CHAPTER ONE

Grace Wellwood leaned heavily against the mahogany-paneled wall at the back of the ballroom and tried to ignore the slightly portentous feeling in the pit of her stomach.

She wished that things in her life were simple, or that at least *one* thing in her life was. Just once, she would love to melt anonymously into the crowd, slip in and out of the room unnoticed, or at least retreat into an unclaimed corner. The idea of getting a little drunk was particularly appealing. It would be just the tonic to get through the grind of pretending to be happy in this room full of strangers and pragmatic bloodsuckers. But Grace was too responsible and much too chained to her obligations to do anything but smile and nod and look far more interested than she was.

"Grace. Congratulations!" It was George Iafrani, one of Grace's main produce purveyors for her Boston restaurant, and he was coming straight for her with his thick, wet lips puckered and looking much like the ripe tomatoes he sold. She turned her cheek just in time.

"Thank you, George. It's so nice to see you."

"No, really, Grace. I *really* mean it."

He had that repetitive, maudlin, sloppy demeanor of having had too many drinks, and he couldn't stop gushing about her new cookbook.

"It's a wonderful book, Grace. Just wonderful. I keep pushing it on all my customers. 'Course, it's good for business when I tell them I know you." He leaned too close to drive home his last point, his alcohol-infused breath forcing her back a step.

George was short and thick and looked like an ex-wrestler. He meant well and was a decent guy, but Grace was in no mood to be cornered by him. He was blathering on now about the poor tomato growing conditions in Mexico this year.

"Grace. There you are." Grace's business partner and best friend, Trish Wilson, swooped in to save the day, a second glass of champagne in her hand like a reward being dangled. "There's someone we need to talk to. Hi, George. Sorry, hope you don't mind me stealing her away."

Trish had her elbow and briskly guided her away.

"Oh, God, thank you for saving me. Another minute and I swear I would have been a rude bitch, and then we'd get nothing but overripe tomatoes for the next two months."

"You, rude? That'd be the day."

Grace gave her a teasing wink. "Still, I could kiss you right now, Trish."

Trish offered her the champagne. "Hmm. I could see that would open up a whole new market for us, wouldn't it? And good 'ol George would probably be first in line."

Grace laughed at the vision. "Straight men getting turned on by two women making out is not a market that interests me, I can honestly say."

"You won't get any argument from me."

Grace sipped her drink thoughtfully. "I guess there's no chance of sneaking out of here early, is there?"

Grace Wellwood and Trish Wilson were America's hottest chefs, also known as the Kitchen Cuties, the Hotties of Haute Cuisine and any number of equally silly monikers the media had anointed them with. They were fiercely popular, thanks to their new cookbook, their ridiculously successful restaurant that was booked solidly two months in advance and their chart-topping weekly television show, *Wellwood and Wilson's Everyday Cuisine*. They were the evening's guests of honor, and so Grace knew Trish's answer before she gave it.

"Never mind," Grace muttered, and cast another furtive glance toward the heavy, double wooden doors across the room. Her heart dropped another unsatisfying notch. If only Aly would show, the evening might actually mean something…

Trish sighed deeply, took a sip of bubbly and studied Grace with dark eyes that could be so brutally frank in their appraisal. "You know, Gracie—"

"Don't say it," Grace hissed. She knew that she and Trish could say anything to each other because they understood one another, even if they didn't always agree. And often they didn't, but they loved each other with a simple clarity that kept them grounded and honest, especially when things got crazy around them as they had the last two or three years. She just wasn't in the mood tonight for Trish to remind her that she was in for another disappointment—that her lover had no intention of showing up. *As usual.*

"Honey, I just want you to be happy," Trish said gently, her eyes softening.

Grace took a long drink of her champagne and took an equally long look around the expansive room, jammed with an assortment of well-wishers, business contacts, journalists, colleagues and people who just wanted to be seen in the right crowd. They talked animatedly in clusters, gesticulating with a tiny crab cake or a delicate canapé of salmon, cucumber and caviar, each one's motivation for being here temporarily lost in the aura of alcohol, music and good food. Laughter and conversation swelled over the string quartet, and Grace longed to feel a part of the lively bonhomie, rather than a spectator. They were all here for her, after all, and she knew she should be basking in the admiration for her and Trish's accomplishments. But it was a role to play, just like every other time she was the main attraction at an event.

Successful businesswoman, popular celebrity. She was about as far as she could get from mucking about in the kitchen, and there were times, like tonight, when she longed for the good old days of just her and Trish and a couple of line cooks struggling to fill orders. She closed her eyes for a moment. If she tried hard enough, she could almost feel the heat of the kitchen, smell the dozen or so different aromas all mixing and competing with one another, hear the sizzling grills and sharply clinking pots.

"Did you hear what I said, Grace? I just want to see you happy."

Grace forced a smile and absently ran a hand over her upswept hair to check for strays. "What's not to be happy about? It's a great night for us," she said without feeling.

"That's not what I'm talking about and you know it." Trish's voice was rigid, though not unkind. "She's not coming, Grace."

Grace reeled a bit at the bluntness of the statement. The two of them, friends and colleagues for over a decade, often spoke in verbal shorthand, so Grace knew exactly what Trish was referring to. Or rather whom. And it rattled her, because Grace had made it clear long ago that talk of her very closeted, very married and almost always absent lover was not grist for the casual conversation mill. Aly was a subject Grace very rarely talked about, and the few times she had, it made her nerve endings prickle. Her mouth automatically tightened and her shoulders straightened, and she hated how it showed that talk of Aly bothered her so much. "I never said she was."

"But you hoped." Trish took a step closer, touched Grace's bare forearm affectionately. "Grace, honey—"

"Look, can we just not talk about this?" Grace snapped. Anguish was beginning to supplant her anger, and she was afraid she might lose it. Going solo to these kinds of events was nothing new, but tonight the loneliness was as sharp as the edge of a knife. While she knew Trish was always there for her, always in her corner, Trish was her friend, not her lover. And tonight Grace needed a lover—someone to look at her with possessive pride, affection and admiration. Someone to go home with, to cuddle

4

with, to rewind the night's events with. Someone with whom she didn't have to be the star attraction.

"Well, there you both are!"

James Easton was their slick, well-groomed business manager with a voice like syrup and a personality as bubbly and sickly sweet as the champagne in their glasses. And while his flaming effervescence could be a bit much at times, James was indispensable to them. He was indefatigable, and not only was his energy boundless, but his contacts, his business acumen and his ability to push them into an ever higher sphere of success knew no limits. He was the engine that drove their success.

"Tsk, tsk, girls. We're not having a little disagreement are we? Now, kiss kiss. C'mon," he trilled. "*Wine Aficionado* magazine is still waiting for that interview I promised on your behalf. Let's not keep them waiting, shall we? Ooh, and then there's the big announcement we have planned." He clapped his hands enthusiastically. "I can't wait!"

He cupped their elbows and began to guide them back toward the crowd, but Grace could not resist another glance over her shoulder at the doors. She caught an "I told you so" look from Trish. Annoyance and embarrassment surged hotly through her until her neck and ears burned.

Everyone had a weakness, Grace knew. Hers just happened to be a bright and beautiful but infinitely unavailable woman who could melt her with just a look or a small touch. Grace drew a deep, painful breath and clutched the stem of her glass tightly. She definitely needed something stronger than champagne if she was to get through the rest of the night.

Her tension had finally begun to ebb. The surprise announcement that she and Trish were opening a second location of their popular Boston restaurant, Sheridan's, in Manhattan was met with immediate and overwhelming approval. After a short speech, a throng of supporters quickly knotted around them, their enthusiasm confirming Grace's private belief that everything they touched right now turned to gold.

Well, except for her love life, which had the distinct tarnish of failure. But it wasn't a total lost cause, she told herself, and began to play the "if only" game—the one she couldn't seem to resist after a couple of drinks. It was the one that let her pretend for a few moments that she was madly in love with Aly O'Donnell and that Aly was madly in love with her, and that any day now the relationship's complications would magically evaporate, like the reduction of a watery sauce. They would be, in her mind's eye, the perfect blend of ingredients, the unique and unforgettable merging of distinct flavors that formed the consummate creation. And if it was not to be, if they were not to make it to the plating up stage, then at least they were sizzling hotly on the grill together. That, at least, was something. *Wasn't it?*

Grace sipped the expensive cognac and let James and Trish hog the spotlight and do most of the talking, as they often did. She let the warm alcohol tranquilize her, and after a while, its numbing effects and the constant well-meaning distractions began to pry Aly from her thoughts. She flashed a long overdue smile at Trish and was rewarded with a wink.

Things couldn't be better. Business was booming. She was a culinary household name in North America. Her peers admired her. Her dog thought less of her because she was almost never home, but what the hell—success did have its price. She was at the pinnacle right now, and it occurred to her that it might never get better than this. Really, what did she have to complain about? Success at work, a hot woman in her bed—even if Aly's presence was infrequent. She sipped the blazing liquid again, her muscles relaxing to the point where she feared she might not be able to walk very steadily. It was good. It was all good, except for that constant emptiness in the pit of her gut. Her mood shifted again, like sand, just as a small commotion drew her attention to the entrance. She caught a flash of that rich auburn hair, and her stomach dropped straight down to her Jimmy Choo heels.

Oh, God. She's here. She's actually here. Panic gripped her for an instant and then gave way to sweet satisfaction.

"Well, well." It was Trish's low and quiet voice in her ear.

She'd disengaged from their supporters long enough to notice the flashy entrance of Aly and her husband, Tim O'Donnell, the Deputy Mayor of Boston. She squeezed Grace's wrist for reassurance, then turned back to her audience, leaving Grace alone.

Why did she have to bring *him*, Grace wondered bitterly, as she watched the power couple move in graceful choreography through the crowd toward her and Trish, stopping periodically for a quick handshake with someone or a private greeting. She didn't know Tim O'Donnell well enough to hate him, but she knew enough about him to know she intensely disliked him. Everything he had done since marrying Aly out of law school was calculated to bring him success and advancement up the social and political ladder. He'd been smart enough to know that the fastest way out of his blue-collar background, besides his law degree, had been to marry the very beautiful and well-bred Aly Fitzsimmons, member of one of Boston's oldest and wealthiest families, whose father was a federal appeals court judge and her mother a Harvard University professor. Now, the forty-two-year-old politician was in the middle of his first term as the city's Deputy Mayor, and he had been making noise that it was merely a stepping-stone.

As the couple approached, Grace stole a quick but sweeping glance at her lover. Aly was as beautiful as ever, and it made Grace's breath catch in her throat. The thick, chestnut hair hung loosely on her bare shoulders. A dark green, off-the-shoulder designer dress perfectly matched the shade of her eyes, which now flicked to Grace and widened with pleasure as they settled softly but thoroughly on her, like a hot summer breeze. Her knees went weak, the same as they had the first time Aly had looked at her like that, almost three years ago at a political fundraiser Grace and Trish were catering. Aly had sauntered up to the buffet table, introduced herself and asked flirtatiously which dish would give her the most pleasure. Her eyes had never left Grace's, and while her motive was completely transparent, Grace couldn't help but be mesmerized by the unspoken promises of carnal pleasure in that solicitous look. Her desire for Grace was red hot and irresistible, and it wasn't long before they were enjoying each other in suburban hotel rooms, in Aly's Mercedes on back roads, even on the tile floor of a mutual friend's oversized, luxurious bathroom once.

"Ah, Ms. Wellwood." Tim O'Donnell shook Grace's hand with the artificial enthusiasm of a used car salesman and gave her a greasy smile. His dark eyes dropped to her cleavage, which she knew her V-necked Halston gown showed off magnificently. She had to suppress a shudder.

"Congratulations on your latest success," he said to her boobs. "My, there's just no keeping you down, is there?"

Did he mean her boobs or her? What she really wanted to do was slap him, but that was sure to be a party killer. *Be good, Grace.* She forced a smile that was every bit as superficial as his. Never knew when she might need a minor variance for major renovations at the restaurant. "Thank you, Mr. Deputy Mayor. It's good to see you, as always."

"Please. My friends call me Tim. And I hope you'll consider me a friend." His smile turned predatory, but he blinked in confusion when Grace's gaze shifted anxiously to his wife. Aly waited serenely beside him, but the intensity of her passion for Grace bubbled just below the placid surface. She could see it in Aly's eyes and in the slow upturn of her pink glossed lips.

Wanting him to move on so she could have Aly to herself, Grace momentarily dragged her attention back to the Deputy Mayor, the muscles in her face tightening as he went on about nothing. *You have no clue I'm fucking your wife, do you, asshole?* Grace made all the appropriate noises and muttered the necessary ego-stroking lies. She hated every minute of this phony crap, but politics and business were natural bedmates, and Grace couldn't afford to let personal biases get in the way of good business.

Finally, Aly nudged her husband along and stood before Grace. She grasped Grace's hand with both of hers and gave a gentle squeeze that shot a bolt of electricity through Grace. They exchanged a brief, longing look, and Aly's smile was charged with a sexual hunger so burningly familiar to Grace. They had not seen each other in more than three weeks, and it was at least two since they had last spoken over the phone. Aly had just returned from a couple of weeks in Palm Beach visiting her parents, and while Grace was used to long absences, they had not gotten easier with time.

"It's so good to see you, Grace." Aly's voice was husky and low with an intimacy Grace knew was reserved just for her. "You look absolutely stunning."

"Thank you," Grace managed, trying to remain cool, even though she couldn't help but stare worshipfully at those soft, full lips, and wishing she could smudge them with urgent kisses. "You look spectacular yourself. I can't believe you came."

"Tim was eager enough when he learned how many people were going to be here, including the press. We just snuck out of a Boston Pops concert."

Grace was giddy and absurdly pleased that her lover had come. "I'm so glad."

Aly leaned closer, lowering her voice to a whisper. "And I'm so proud, babe. I want to see you. Can we meet?"

"Where?"

"At my apartment. Tomorrow night."

Grace smiled her consent, but Aly had already moved on and was shaking hands with Trish, leaving Grace with the intoxicating effects of the quiet buzz of sexual arousal and the warm alcohol.

CHAPTER TWO

They'd barely made it through their first glass of champagne when Aly took Grace's hand, and with a glint in her eyes, led her to the bedroom of the twenty-sixth floor condo along Boston Harbor. The apartment had been a fortieth birthday present for Aly from her parents last year, a place for the hard-working criminal attorney and wife of a busy politician to get away when she needed to. Grace guessed it would be an unbearable shock if the prim and proper Fitzsimmonses ever realized it was a secret meeting place for their daughter and her lesbian lover.

Skillfully, Aly unbuttoned Grace's tight, silk blouse, licking her lips in anticipation, her eyes roaming over Grace's breasts, which were achingly swollen with arousal. Her nipples had hardened long ago at the promise of what lay ahead, and now they stiffened further at the prospect of Aly's hands and mouth just inches away.

"God, I missed you," Grace said anxiously as Aly's lips found the sensitive flesh of her throat. Once together, Grace and Aly could not get enough of each other. Even after nearly three years of secret, intermittent trysts, Grace still hungered for Aly's skilled touch, her presence, her body.

Aly's soft hands caressed where Grace's blouse had been just seconds before. Her touch was cool and butterfly soft, just like the silk, and Grace gave a small shiver of pleasure.

"You're so beautiful, Grace," Aly murmured between kisses, brushing Grace's hair aside to make way for her lips. Grace barely heard her. A moan began deep in her throat and her eyes slammed firmly shut. Her impatience for release was building, and she wanted Aly to take her, quickly. They were often in a hurry to make love—mostly because they had so little time together—and tonight would be no different.

"Oh, God, Aly. Please." It had been weeks, and Grace needed their connection solidified by their habitual hot, hard sex.

Aly growled pleasurably, more than eager to meet Grace's demands. She knew Grace's body intimately, knew just how and where to touch, and she played her body like a master violinist, striking each chord with just the right tempo and pressure.

"Oh, God," Grace choked out as her impending orgasm built like an enormous wave, gathering and pulling, growing more powerful as it approached. Grace bit back the overwhelming desire to tell Aly she loved her, because Aly didn't like ardent proclamations during sex. The physical attraction between them over the years had remained intense. The sex was fast and furious, almost painful at times, and the need for release always acute. Grace pragmatically recognized it as mostly fucking, not lovemaking. It was the way Aly wanted it, and Grace had come to appreciate it too. The orgasms came fast and hard, but when they were over so abruptly, there was always a vague longing that bordered on dissatisfaction—sometimes for hours afterward. There were times when Grace wanted so much more from Aly, and what she got was never enough.

She closed her eyes again, willed away the distracting thoughts and welcomed the growing rumbles of orgasm. Coming was all she needed right now, all she could think about. The trembles escalated, surging slowly through her body until she shook violently and cried out. She clutched Aly's shoulders hard, digging in with her nails, stiffening against her as she came.

Aly smiled against Grace's throat, then kissed her shoulder. "Was that good, baby?"

Grace, still breathing hard, smiled at the question. "As always."

"I've missed this body of yours. Every morning these last few weeks, I'd wake up thinking about fucking you, Grace."

Grace chuckled, but she didn't share the lightness of the moment. It gave her an undeniable thrill that Aly still desired her as much as ever, but just once, Grace wanted Aly to miss her for something other than sex, the way she sometimes missed Aly.

"Grace," Aly murmured huskily against her. "Fuck me."

Propped up on an elbow, Grace watched her sleeping lover. Aly was so beautiful, with that long, thick hair, those flashing green eyes and skin so smooth and taut. She was tall and trim, her legs long and shapely and her breasts still round and firm. She was elegant in the way she carried herself, yet there was the strong suggestion of adventurousness and athleticism. She turned the heads of both men and women wherever she went, and Grace tried to imagine what a distracting presence Aly must be in front of a jury.

Grace smiled and softly caressed Aly's naked shoulder. It had been her good fortune that Aly had chosen her and she'd tried hard not to disappoint. She'd become good at pleasing Aly, though they'd had their rough moments. She'd pressured Aly once to take a vacation, just the two of them, and Aly had finally relented. For a week, they'd gone to San Francisco, where they had anonymously walked the streets holding hands, gone to shows and dinners together, nurtured their bond. They'd slipped away to Provincetown for a weekend once as well, and it had been magical. But the worst times were when Grace had brought up the possibility of Aly leaving Tim. They'd fought and nearly quit their affair three or four times, with Aly imploring Grace to just be patient and to let things ride for a while longer. There were vague promises, and Grace let herself be pacified. In the end, nothing ever really changed. The secret liaisons and phone calls continued while they each went on with their busy lives, and the months rolled into years, each tryst blurring into the next. Somewhere along the line, Grace had stopped wondering what a life with Aly would be like. She'd stopped asking for more.

Grace's fingers trailed down Aly's left arm and lingered on the buttery skin. Aly did not stir. Grace's eyes traveled the length of her arm and came to rest on her white gold wedding band. She blinked at the offending sight and swallowed back the familiar, bitter taste in her mouth whenever she thought of Tim O'Donnell and the poor excuse he and Aly had for a marriage. It was *she* who made Aly happy. It was *she* who turned Aly on and made her beg. It was she Aly said she wanted to be with. But it was The Asshole, as she liked to think of him, who ultimately shared a life with her and the legitimacies and respect the title of marriage so automatically and unfairly bestowed. The fact that he seemed to treat Aly as some sort of handy adornment only pissed her off more. She couldn't understand why Aly stayed with him. Or at least, she didn't *want* to understand why.

Feeling suddenly sick to her stomach, Grace fled from the bedroom. She made herself a cup of herbal tea and curled up on the chocolate brown leather couch, watching the city wake up. Lights faintly twinkled along the harbor, and in the dusky dawn skyline, she could just make out the tall glass building that was the JFK Library with its huge American flag hanging in the atrium. Her soul, too, felt like it was stirring with the first breath of morning.

She sipped her tea and was surrounded by the emptiness that often followed sex with Aly. She knew she wanted more of her, but it had been so easy to just take what was offered and be satisfied with that. And she was satisfied, but she was not *happy*. In fact, she wasn't even sure what happy meant for her, but she knew what it wasn't. She knew it wasn't sneaking around with a married woman for three years, squeezing in what little time and energy they could find for each other, trying to carve out some space for themselves between all the lies and deceit. It was the fast food of relationships, and Grace knew it. She had always known it, and much of the time, it had been enough. But tonight it was not. Maybe it was because she had been anticipating this night together for weeks now, and already it was over with no clear idea of when they would be together again. Nothing about this night had been any different from the multitude of others they'd shared. It'd followed the same script—hot sex, hurried conversation. But this time, it was like fabric unraveling, a coming apart at the pull of a thread.

Grace sipped her tea slowly, until it was cold at the end, and watched the crisp, May sun rise over the city. She knew she needed sleep, and that in just a few hours she'd have to fly to Manhattan with Trish to go over plans for the new restaurant. But she didn't want to lie back down beside Aly and pretend that all was well. Not this time.

"Hey," Aly said softly from the bedroom doorway, hastily tying her robe. "How long have you been up?"

Grace shrugged. "Awhile."

"Why don't you come back to bed?" Aly's smile was suggestive. "We can start the morning off with a bang."

Grace shook her head firmly. "No, Aly."

Aly stepped closer, her face registering that something was wrong. "What's up, darling?"

Grace went to her and threw her arms around Aly's neck, needing a physical connection. She clutched Aly tightly, and Aly clutched her back, pulling Grace in until their bodies merged completely. They maintained the embrace for a long time, until Grace finally whispered into Aly's neck, "I can't do this anymore, Aly." It surprised her to hear the words she'd not really even formulated in her mind yet.

Aly pulled back enough to look at her, concern darkening her face. "What are you talking about, Grace?"

Tears threatened, but Grace didn't want to be a blubbering fool. Didn't want to play the role of the needy, demanding, emotional girlfriend, but she couldn't stop herself, because right now she was all of those things. "I just want to be with you, Aly," she said thickly.

"But I'm right here, baby."

"No," Grace said more forcefully. "I want to *be* with you, Aly. I hate this." A tear slithered down her cheek, then another. She did nothing to stop them from pooling under her chin.

"Is this because of the party? Because I showed up late and brought Tim?" Aly asked.

Grace had been relieved when Aly appeared at the celebration. More than that, she was happy Aly was there to share at least part of the evening. It had almost made their relationship seem like it mattered, like *she* mattered to Aly. But any good feelings had been completely obliterated by the fact that Aly had brought her husband and they'd left after such a pathetically short time. The brief merging of Aly's two lives—her secret one with her legitimate one—had left Grace feeling angry and desolate. Disgusted too, because she suddenly saw how little space she took up in Aly's life.

Grace shook her head again. The party was only a symptom of their problems, a typical example of the inadequacy of their relationship. "No. It's...I just get so *tired* of this, Aly. It just isn't enough anymore."

Grace thought she saw a flash of frustration, even anger, in Aly's face, but the expression quickly smoothed into mild mollification.

"Look," Aly soothed. "You know we can't be together right now. It's just not possible. I hate not being with you too, but..." Aly's voice trailed off. Her eyes grew firmer. "Tim's going to run for a congressional seat next year, and you know I'm expecting to get called to the bench."

It was always something, some excuse why they couldn't be together. It reminded Grace of one of those dreams where your feet are moving but you're not getting anywhere. That's exactly what they'd become, it occurred to her. Motion without movement. She sighed heavily and pulled a little further away until their arms were only loosely around one another. She loved being in Aly's arms, but she knew the longer she stayed there, the quicker she'd give up this fight. And she didn't want to give in.

She couldn't this time.

"I want to be with someone whose hand I can hold in public, Aly. Or go out to dinner with. Someone to spend time with, without watching the clock or looking over our shoulders. Someone who can be there for me, someone to come home to." It sounded so pathetically clichéd, but it was true.

Grace had begun to detest the way Aly made her feel. She wanted Aly, thought she needed her, hotly anticipated the next time they'd be together. But then it was all over so quickly, this building up and crashing down, before the pattern would start all over again. At times, Grace convinced herself that she preferred it this way because it allowed her to concentrate on her work and her demanding schedule. An affair with Aly meant she didn't have the burdens and demands of a real relationship, which left her free to pursue other things, to live life for herself. But she'd been doing that for years and she was just plain tired of the self-indulgence of it. What she and Aly had was hollow and empty, and so was she. Her aloneness had quietly become loneliness.

Aly gently wiped a tear from Grace's cheek. "I know it's frustrating, honey. I want to be able to do those things with you too. But it's a big time in Tim's career right now, and—"

"Screw Tim. What about you? Are you really willing to risk *your* career for us? Would you risk it all for me?" It hurt to think about it, but in her heart she knew that Aly would not risk her future for them.

Aly's silence only confirmed Grace's suspicions. "Grace, don't do this," Aly quietly implored.

"I can't *not* do this, Aly. I mean, what's wrong with wanting us to be together?" It seemed like such a simple concept, but with Aly, it seemed to be the hardest thing in the world.

Aly pulled sharply away, her hands sternly on her hips. The loss of physical contact was almost wrenching to Grace. "Grace, why are you being difficult?"

Grace swallowed hard around the lump in her throat. She would not be bullied. "I am not being difficult. I just want what everyone else wants for once. I want to share my life with someone…" She couldn't stop her voice from shaking. "Who's in love with me."

Aly shook her head slowly and closed her eyes briefly, as though wishing the moment away. "Look, Grace. I know you're under a lot of stress right now. You've got the new restaurant opening, the TV show approved again for next fall, the new cookbook. I understand. I really do."

"No, Aly, you don't understand." Grace wasn't entirely sure she understood, but she knew the ground was no longer sure beneath her. She knew that the loneliness she once feared was no longer abstract, that the void in her life was growing larger by the day. She'd just stripped away the beautifully decorated wedding cake, only to find it was really just cardboard underneath.

"I do understand, Grace. Why don't you just take some time? You know, step back a little. Try to relax for a few days." Aly stepped closer and rubbed Grace's arm affectionately. "Take some time out from us, if that's what you need. I'll be here waiting."

Grace stared at her for a long moment. She was not surprised by Aly's reaction. She'd been foolish to think Aly would agree to change anything.

Without a word, Grace stalked to the bedroom and reached for her overnight bag. It didn't take her long to pack.

Grace stared gloomily into her wineglass. She knew she was being lousy company for Trish—had been all afternoon with the architect and later over dinner. She'd barely touched her duck confit, and now at the bar, she was taking only bird-like sips of her Chardonnay. A despondency had set firmly in since leaving Aly this morning.

"Grace," Trish broke in hesitantly. "I know we don't have a lot of heart-to-hearts, but—"

"Let me guess. You're having the sudden urge for one," Grace said flatly.

Trish sipped her wine and watched Grace with sympathetic eyes. "Gracie, what's wrong?"

"What makes you think anything's wrong?"

"Because you look like shit and you've been tired and distracted all day. And I know it's because you've been with Aly."

Grace looked benignly at Trish, unwilling to play along with the little therapy session. Self-pity, not evaluation, was what she wanted.

"Don't deny it, Grace. You always act weird for a couple of days after you've been with her."

"Weird?"

Trish lowered her voice. "You know I've never said much about the two of you, but—"

"Could that be because it's none of your business?"

"No, Grace. It is my business, because you're my friend and I love you, and I don't think she's good for you." In their younger days, Trish had always been the wilder of the two, yet Grace knew she'd never approved of her relationship with Aly. Trish had her standards, and clearly, Aly didn't fit them.

Now Grace stiffened against Trish's blunt criticism.

Trish looked sheepish for about three seconds. "Well, I'm sorry, but she's not. You deserve better, Grace, than some married woman who treats you like her little closet kitten."

Grace flushed. As right as Trish was, there was a stubborn need to defend her lover and their relationship. It was her life, dammit. She didn't need Trish's approval, nor did she need Trish reminding her that her love life was crap, that she'd made a poor decision three years ago and was paying for it.

"What makes you think she's not good for me? You don't know anything about her, Trish. Or about how we are together."

"All right," Trish said. "Explain it to me, then. Tell me about her attributes. Tell me what it's like between the two of you."

The hours and the distance from Aly had not strengthened Grace's resolve, and now she fought the petulance rising in her. She knew Trish was just trying to help. Her intentions were good, but her comments still came across as harsh and judgmental. If she weren't such a good friend, Grace would tell her to go to hell.

"She's a good woman, Trish." Grace sipped her wine, feeling

worse by the minute. "She's beautiful, smart, ambitious, totally competent in everything she does." Aly almost sounded like the perfect woman. And she might be, if only she'd commit to Grace—make a life with her. *Yeah, like that was ever going to happen.*

"You could be describing yourself, you know."

Grace shrugged. "I love her, Trish. What more can I say?"

"Does she love you?"

Grace knew her hesitation was not lost on Trish. "Yes." *Does she?* Grace couldn't even remember when Aly had last said the words. She didn't know when she last said them either.

"If you love each other, then why are you so miserable? And why aren't you together?"

Grace's composure began to crumble. She shook her head lightly. "Because..." *Because we'll never be together. She'll never leave Tim and the life she has. Her marriage might be a sham, but so is her relationship with me.* Tears threatened. She would never have predicted that she would spend three years being the other *woman.* But here she was, and the picture that was her life was becoming harshly clear. She needed to make a break from Aly, and she had read enough self-help articles in women's magazines on endless airplane rides to know that it would get harder and harder to preserve her self-respect the longer she stayed. To keep on settling for what she and Aly had just meant burying her own identity deeper and deeper, Grace knew. Loving Aly meant not loving herself. It was that simple.

"You deserve more, that's all."

Grace gave a cynical snort. "Don't we all?"

"Grace." Trish touched her hand soothingly. "Why don't you take some time to get away?"

"Funny." Grace laughed bitterly. "You're the second person today who's told me that. Does everyone think I'm insane or something?"

Trish laughed. "Insane is the fact that you haven't taken a vacation in at least two years, Grace. You've been pushing yourself too hard the last little while."

"So have you, in case you've forgotten."

"True. But I don't have the added stress of running around with a married woman."

Grace frowned. "As I recall, you hardly took any time off last year when you divorced Scott."

Trish shrugged one shoulder and studied her drink for a long moment, looking wistful. "Maybe I should have."

"So, am I really that fucked up, Trish?"

Trish raised her eyes, which were kind, but there was a hint of criticism in them. "I'd like to see you get some perspective, Grace. Get some balance in your life. Find out what you really want for yourself. *Who* you really want in your life."

"Let me guess. You don't think it's Aly," Grace said quietly, without the sarcasm this time.

"It doesn't really matter what *I* think."

"You don't like her. Is it because she's married?"

"No. It's because after all this time, she hasn't tossed you over her shoulder and carried you off. That's why I don't like her. Because she doesn't know a good thing when she damn well has it."

Grace wanted to cry over how much Trish loved her. And then she wanted to laugh at the vision of Aly—or any woman—tossing her over a shoulder and carrying her away. "All right. I'll take a couple of weeks off."

Trish's face lit up. "Really? And actually go somewhere by yourself?"

Grace rolled her eyes. "Yes, I'll actually go away, though I'd like to bring my dog. So I won't exactly be by myself."

Trish's expression darkened. "There's one thing, Grace."

"What?"

"You need more than a couple of weeks. I was thinking more like a couple of months."

"What?" Grace nearly slid off the barstool. "That's impossible!"

"No," Trish said calmly. "It's not. Because that's how long it's going to take."

"To what?" Grace said acidly. "Get Aly out of my system? Isn't that what you really mean?"

Trish squeezed Grace's hand affectionately. "Truthfully? Yes."

Grace shook her head stubbornly. "C'mon, Trish. Two months is ridiculous. I can't be away from work that long. There's no way."

"Yes, you can, Grace. I'll pick up the slack. And James is a workhorse, you know that."

"No, I couldn't ask you to do that."

"Grace, you're not asking. I'm telling. And I won't take no for an answer."

"Trish, really. I'll be fine. A couple of weeks, three maybe."

"Gracieeeee. Don't argue with me. You know what happens."

Grace rolled her eyes again, then laughed. "I know, I know. I always lose arguments with you."

"Remember my cottage on Sheridan Island in Maine?"

Grace laughed, the vague sweetness of long forgotten fun floating to the surface like the grenadine in the many tequila sunrises they'd drunk. "The one time I visited you there for a few days, I think I spent the whole time inebriated. So I'm not sure how much of it I actually remember."

"Don't even get me started on the stories from that visit!"

Grace put up her hand in supplication, still laughing. "All right, all right. We swore what happened on Sheridan Island stayed on Sheridan Island."

Trish narrowed her eyes teasingly. "Whew, you had me going there for a minute."

"Don't worry. Your secret's safe with me."

Trish winked. "That-a girl. So, listen. Take the cottage for a couple of months."

"You won't need it?"

Trish shook her head. "I'll be too busy, remember?"

"At least come and visit me?"

"I'll try to squeeze a visit in. Only this time, *I'll* spend the entire weekend inebriated."

"Deal. And I'll have the wild fling!"

Trish stared wide-eyed at her and neither said anything for a long moment. Then Grace's hand flew to her mouth and they both laughed uncontrollably, like a couple of teenagers high on life and all its endless possibilities. And for a few moments, life was easy again.

They enjoyed their wine and reminisced about that lost weekend six years ago and about all the freedom from responsibilities they'd once had. Then Trish affectionately studied her and said, "God, it's good to see you laugh again, Grace."

Grace smiled, feeling the sting of tears of joy—or maybe relief. She blinked her agreement. She wasn't sure what she was getting into, but it had to be better than what she was getting out of.

CHAPTER THREE

Torrie Cannon polished off her third can of Budweiser, rooted in front of the forty-two-inch television and completely riveted on the playoff between her friend and the young upstart who'd been such a pain in everyone's ass over the past year.

Golf was Torrie's life. Literally. It was what she did for a living and it was her reason for getting up in the morning. More than a dozen years of her life had been completely devoted to the sport, and it had been good to her in return. She'd earned millions along with seventeen championship titles on the LPGA tour, including four majors. She was one of the country's best women golfers. Except now, for the first time in her career, she was a spectator, watching the Tour go on without her.

Torrie's mother slipped into the room and joined her on the sofa.

"Hey, Mom. It's Diana and Amy King in a playoff. God, I hope Diana pulls it out." Torrie leaned closer to the TV. "They've both just sent their drives out nicely."

Torrie never referred to the teen golf sensation by just her first name. It was always "Amyking," as if the girl's first and last name were one word.

Her mother chuckled softly. "That girl is still giving the rest of you ulcers, isn't she?"

Torrie ignored the comment, so fierce was her concentration. She wanted so badly for her friend to kick the youngster's butt. Show her that victories were to be earned through years of hard work and not by luck and circumstance and the devil-may-care attitude of the young.

Sarah Cannon moved closer, nudging Torrie's good shoulder. "You've been watching this tournament almost non-stop for the last two days. Can we talk, Torrie?"

Torrie cast her a quick glance that conveyed in no uncertain terms that her mother's timing sucked. "Sure. After this is over."

Torrie could feel her mother's impatience, heard it in her sigh. When she wanted something, she was relentless about it—a trait Torrie could certainly identify with. But right now, she would have to wait.

It didn't take long for Diana Gravatti to take control of the playoff, finishing off the young sensation with a thrilling chip-in birdie. Torrie pumped her fist in the air and let out a victory yelp. If there was anyone she wanted to win in her absence, it was Diana.

"Now. Let's have that talk," her mother said evenly, rising and leading the way out onto the deck without waiting for Torrie's acknowledgment.

Torrie hesitantly followed, sensing a forthcoming lecture. But since she was staying in her family's house, recuperating from major shoulder surgery ten days ago, she would humor her mother. She would not be impolite in her parents' home, and she owed her parents so much, especially her mother.

"How's the shoulder?" her mother asked mildly.

Torrie winced. It still hurt like hell, but she would not admit it. If she could convince herself the pain wasn't too bad, maybe she could get back on the Tour quicker. "Not bad. It's feeling better every day."

Her mother was looking at her with almost clinical detachment, as if she were scrutinizing her swing. "When are you thinking of rejoining the Tour?"

Torrie shrugged as if the answer were obvious. "Three months."

"Isn't that rushing it?"

"Not if I push."

Her mother scanned the horizon made burnt orange by the setting sun and the hazy warmth of the Arizona desert. Her body language gave nothing of her feelings, but when she turned back to face Torrie, her jaw was set and her blue eyes were icy and implacable. The look reminded Torrie of her high school years, when she'd failed to make curfew and her mother would wait up for her, ready to give her hell.

"See, here's the thing."

Torrie mentally braced herself. Ah, yes, her mother's favorite line, the one that always preceded a stern admonishment about something. But for the life of her, Torrie had no idea what she'd done wrong.

"It's time you stopped pushing yourself so much, Torrie."

Torrie's breath stalled somewhere in her chest. Surely she'd misheard. The queen of persistence was suddenly advising her to slow down? *Where was that sort of attitude when I wanted to slack* off my homework? Or dump those hours of practice sessions to *go party with my friends?* "What?"

"Torrie." Her mother paused, her sharp features softening. "I've watched you push yourself for years to get to the top. And I think—"

"Wait. You encouraged me to push myself so hard," Torrie interrupted, her resolve quickly gathering. "And before that, *you* were the one pushing me, remember?" She would not quietly take the blame for whatever her mother was about to blame her for. She certainly wasn't going to feel bad for working so hard all these years. Everything she had learned, including her relentless ambition, had come from her mother, and Torrie had gotten nothing but approval and encouragement along the way. *Why is she doing this? Why is she pulling the rug out from under me?*

Her mother blinked, clearly stung. "I know I did, dear. In

retrospect, I think I expected you to fulfill the dreams I once had for myself."

Her mother was Torrie's first golf coach. She'd given up her own once-promising golf career when she married her high school sweetheart, Jack Cannon, right after college graduation. Torrie's birth had come within the year, then three sons in quick succession. Sarah Cannon had never picked the sport up again, except recreationally. Her primary connection to golf remained through Torrie.

"In some ways," her mother continued slowly, her voice wavering with emotion, "I regret now how hard I pushed you."

Torrie trembled with incredulity. She'd never heard her mother talk like this about golf before. She'd never really heard her talk this way to Torrie about *anything* before. They were a family where a stiff upper lip was the silent rule of the house. Her parents were pull-up-your-bootstraps kind of people, and this was so *not* like her mother. Torrie's career had been the most important thing in both their lives for many years. Their common ambition had driven them, made them practically inseparable at times. It had been all they talked about, all they dreamed about, all they worked toward. "Are you trying to tell me it wasn't worth it?"

"Of course not. You've done far better than I could ever have hoped, honey. Much better than I could ever have done myself." She was looking at her like Torrie had just brought home a report card full of A's. "I'm so proud of you, Torrie."

Torrie's breath hitched. Such emotion was rare from her mother, and it stunned her, sucking some of the fight out of her. "Then what are you saying?"

"You're thirty years old now. You've been on the Tour for seven years. It's time you got some balance in your life, Torrie. It's time you found something besides golf that really means something to you. It's time," she added softly.

Torrie could not believe her mother was counseling her this way. Her *mother*, of all people—the one person who'd wanted this life for her more than anyone else. It was the reward they had worked so hard for, the peak of their long, arduous climb together. Now she was making her career sound like some tired, antiquated stage in her life that she needed to move on from, like having acne or chasing boys. Or in Torrie's case, girls.

"I know what you're thinking." Her mother raised a hand in concession. "You're wondering what's come over me to talk this way." She moved away from the railing and sat down beside Torrie. "The last few years you've pushed yourself so hard. Training, practicing, playing, traveling. That's all you do. You haven't missed a single tournament until now. It's too much, Torrie. I can see that it's too much."

Torrie was confused. Her mother couldn't be more wrong. Getting on the Tour and staying there was dreadfully hard work. Staying at the top was the hardest of all. Any slacking off and she'd tumble. And once she was on the way down, getting back up was practically unheard of. It wasn't that it was too much. It was simply necessary.

"Mom, you know how this works." Torrie was trying to be patient, but it took all her effort. "I can't cut anything back. I want to put in another eight, ten years, and to do that is going to take a lot of work. I mean, you see these young kids on the Tour now. You know how hard they are to beat, when they don't care about anything but winning, and they don't have injuries and they don't have to worry about sponsors, and all the traveling doesn't knock the shit out of them yet. They think they're infallible, and they are."

"You were like that once too."

Torrie ground her teeth against the pain in her throbbing shoulder. "Well, I've certainly discovered that I'm fallible, haven't I?"

"That's exactly what I'm saying, Torrie. You are fallible. You're pushing your body beyond its limit right now. And your mind."

Torrie groaned. "So I'm crazy too?" Was her mother trying to piss her off? Drive her from the family home?

Her mother laughed loudly. "Actually, I am starting to wonder about your sanity. I caught you watching that food channel on

TV the other day."

Torrie laughed too, enjoying the momentary diversion. "All right, I confess. Guilty."

"So you want to be a chef in your next career perhaps?" The question sounded more hopeful than teasing.

"Hell, no. I just watch it sometimes because of the hot women on there."

"Ah. Well, that makes more sense now."

Torrie chuckled bitterly. "Actually, I've been watching because I'm supposed to come up with menu ideas for the tournament I'm hosting in a couple of weeks."

"The Hartford Open, right?" Torrie, as defending champion, was the official host this year, which meant helping coordinate the plans for the championship dinner. "But you don't know anything about planning banquets."

Torrie grimaced. "I don't know anything about food except eating it."

"Well, I'm sure there will be people to help you with it."

Torrie sighed heavily. Her chest tightened as she thought ahead to the tournament and how it would feel, watching helplessly as the others went on with the business of playing and winning. It would be torture. "God, it's going to kill me," she murmured.

Her mother rubbed her arm affectionately. "I know, honey. But it will be good to be among friends again, even if it's only for a week. It's got to be better than sitting around here."

Torrie had never had so much time off from golf. She had no clue how she was going to fill her days and keep her mind and body occupied until she could get back on the Tour. Beer and television weren't cutting it, that was for sure. Her mother had won a small point, at least for now. She needed to find something to do for the summer.

"Mom, look. I know you're concerned, but everything's under control. I love what I do, okay? I don't want to change anything. I'll be fine."

Her mother's face creased with worry. "What are you going

to have when it's over, Torrie? I mean, look how difficult it is for you to take a few months off. You don't even know what to do with yourself."

"Like I said, I'll be fine." Torrie knew she didn't sound particularly convincing. She had rarely given much thought to the future beyond the next tournament or two. Worrying about the present had always been more than enough. But the present sucked right now, and the future loomed like the big monster in the closet ready to burst out. It scared the crap out of her to think of a future without golf, and now her mother was trying to speed her toward it—force her to deal with it before she was ready to. It was like standing on a tee box and taking a blind shot—the kind where you hoped you'd picked the right club and where you had to just trust your instincts and your swing.

"The thing is, Tor, that time might come a lot sooner than you think if you keep on this path."

"I don't get what you're trying to say, mother." Torrie was growing frustrated again.

Her mother's eyes fixed harshly on her as if to drive home the seriousness of her message. "You're getting burned out. Mentally and physically. And if you don't do something to turn it around, your career will be over and you'll be a mess. That's my great fear for you." Her expression grew anguished and the steely eyes watery. It scared Torrie, seeing her like this.

"Oh, Mom." Torrie reached for her mother's hand and held it firmly. "I think you're reaching here. I really do."

"No, Torrie, I'm not." Her voice grew rigid again. "Your shoulder injury is proof that you're pushing your body too hard. And as for the rest of it, you have no other hobbies, no other friends outside of the Tour. You've never even really had a girlfriend."

Torrie flushed with the heat of embarrassment. "I can assure you, mother, I'm not lonely." Hell, she'd had more women by accident than on purpose.

It was her mother's turn to look embarrassed. "I'm sure you're not, dear. But those kinds of relationships aren't *real*. You

29

need someone who loves you for who you are. Maybe someone you can build a life with eventually."

Torrie's exasperation mounted again. "I don't have time for hobbies and girlfriends and stuff like that. Jesus, I might as well just cash in now and go off and play house and have babies…like you did. Is that what you want for me? You want me to be a quitter?"

Torrie knew she'd gone too far when her mother's eyes flared with anger. She'd just scored a lethal hit by calling her mother's biggest choices into question. More than that, by casting judgment on them. *Shit!*

"You might think I regret the way my life has gone because of the way I pushed you into golf. But I don't. And you don't know me very well if that's what you think." Her voice crackled with emotion, like a branch breaking underfoot. "I love your father and you kids. Family is the most important thing to me, and I just want you to find the same. Golf is transient, Torrie. Family isn't. Love isn't."

Torrie let her mother's words dissolve in the dry desert air. It was true, her life was entirely consumed by golf. She hadn't admitted it to anyone, but there'd been fleeting moments when she'd wondered what it would be like to take a vacation, or to be in love. To live a life with someone whose dreams and plans and fears were held in equal priority. Sometimes it felt like her face was pressed up against a store window, looking at the beautiful things she could never have. And her mother was right. There would be a time when she would want those things, after she'd accomplished everything there was to accomplish in golf. It was a natural progression, at least for those who knew how to move on once their time in golf was over.

Torrie was silent for a long moment, gazing off into the distance. When she spoke, her voice was nearly a whisper. "I'm afraid to let anything else in. I'm afraid if I do, I'll lose the only life I've known for the last twelve or thirteen years. I don't know what else to do besides what I'm doing."

Her mother squeezed her hand and smiled her sympathy.

"Take a chance, honey. You've nothing to prove to anyone anymore."

Torrie squeezed her eyes shut. She didn't know the first thing about taking chances, at least not with anything other than her career. "I don't know if I can."

"Try, Torrie. This is the perfect time to see what else is out there. You have to take a few months off anyway. Take the summer."

"And do what?" Torrie felt slightly dizzy. This was all so new to her, and it was like falling off a cliff. The gaping emptiness before her was mortifying.

"You can't stay here all summer drinking beer and watching TV, that's for sure."

Torrie smiled regretfully. "I guess I have been a bit of a lazy slob lately."

"Don't worry about it, dear. But I do have an idea of how you can spend your summer after that tournament you're hosting."

Torrie's eyes narrowed skeptically. "If you say a nunnery, I'll have to torture you."

Her mother laughed deeply. "No, not a nunnery, dear. Though I'm not sure it's exactly teeming with young, single women."

"I see. And just where is this place of idyllic celibacy?"

"Let's see if I can't help you with that menu planning, and then we'll talk about my ideas."

CHAPTER FOUR

Already, Grace could tell there was something profoundly healing about Sheridan Island. Perhaps it was the limitless expanse of water surrounding it, or the simplicity of its narrow dirt roads and the unpretentious shingled or clapboard homes. The place had probably remained the same for the last eighty years or so, with only a few of the faces changing. The family names on mailboxes likely went back generations. It was remarkably untouched by tourism, unlike most other islands off the eastern seaboard, and that alone was refreshing.

The locals seemed friendly and not cynical of a stranger, as Grace had expected. They'd probably know more about her after a week than her longtime condo neighbors back in Boston had learned of her in a decade. It was how things worked in tiny, close-knit communities, and there was something safe and welcoming about the implied intimacy, even though the islanders were giving her space.

Grace did little her first couple of days at Trish's three-bedroom cottage, other than sit on the deck overlooking the ocean and drink too much wine, or take her chocolate Labrador retriever, Remy, on endless walks. Cooking hadn't appealed much, which was unusual, nor did eating. Being in a kitchen had always given her comfort, but she was still listless and in a fog after her hasty decision to leave Aly and take the summer off. In rational terms, she could hardly believe she'd done either. She still wavered over whether she had done the right thing in leaving Aly. Countless times in the last few days she'd fought the urge to pick up the phone, just to hear her voice. She knew if she did that, she would capitulate, and things would be just as they were, with more broken promises, more sneaking around, more empty nights. Grace knew she needed more time away from Aly to sort out her feelings and renew her strength. Giving in after a few days would hardly be fair. Or sensible.

What she doubted just as much was her decision to take a couple of months off work. What had she been thinking? Keeping busy had to be better than moping around, second-guessing herself. How could she possibly have thought that taking the summer off to do nothing was a good idea? How could she find herself, as Trish had counseled her to do, in all this nothingness? It would be like trying to spot a tiny lifeboat in an endless expanse of sea.

Oh, hell. Trish was probably right. She needed to break with all her old patterns for a while if she was going to heal. She needed to allow herself to feel the sting of the finality of the breakup. It had to hurt before it could feel better. She needed to let herself grieve. The self-help clichés ran through her mind in a repeating loop as she sipped her wine. She never thought she'd be one of those people who needed to look for inspiration in dimestore psychology paperbacks or silly talk shows. There were a lot of things she hadn't imagined herself doing.

Grace lifted a socked foot to the deck's railing, momentarily entranced by the sun setting over the ocean, which seemed so voluminous and infinite. The calm surface was turning to a shimmering liquid orange beneath the fading light, shades of red abstractly streaking across the sky. She thought of the old refrain, "Red sky at night, sailor's delight." She smiled. In spite of her misery, tomorrow would be a beautiful day, and that, she decided, was a small victory.

Grace pulled her sweater tighter around her to ward off the chilly spring air and wished it were Aly's arms keeping her warm instead. The thought did not comfort her. She scolded herself, thinking it should be easier than this to cast Aly from her life. Aly was a user, a heartless social and career climber, a liar, a sexual profligate. Grace should hate her, but she couldn't bring herself to. She should be bitter over three wasted years, but she wasn't. She missed Aly, but more for what they didn't have than what they did have.

The problem, Grace decided, was the object of her desire, not the desire itself, and it was time to place that desire in someone much more deserving.

It's okay to want, Grace. Just not her.

Grace knew that slowly she was getting herself on the right track, but the shifting of her life was one of the hardest things she'd ever done. She scanned the horizon without seeing and wondered how long it would take, and whether she could put a time on it, like the careful baking of crème brûlée, or whether it would take the imprecise simmering of a stew.

Still in her pajamas, Grace studied herself in the bathroom mirror, the morning light unforgivable. She was reluctant at first to look, but then she did. And what she saw did not please her.

Her eyes, normally a bright, pastel gray with light green specks, looked dark and gloomy, like a rainy day. There were shadows beneath her eyes. The faint lines in her face were deepening these days. Her hair was badly in need of some sunshine or some bottle highlights—something to punch up the dull blond. Her skin was too pale and needed some sunshine too. Grace made a face at herself. She looked like hell lately, and it scared her. She would turn forty soon.

Maybe my best days are behind me, she thought with a sullen urgency that bordered on panic. *Forty.* The number had such a starkness to it, like some sort of looming juncture, a precipice, a halfway point—halfway between birth and death—and the clock was ticking. Halfway through the journey, she thought, and she was both far enough on that journey to look back at where she'd been, and yet she could still look forward to the future. Whatever that might be.

Grace took a deep breath and dropped her hand to pat Remy. She couldn't undo anything in her past now, but she could still make her own future. Or remake it into something different from the path she was on. She did not want to be in the same place in her life this time next year—busy as hell and trying to juggle it all, with no one to share her life with, no one who really loved her. She had to make changes. She had to take this pile of ingredients she'd been tossed and make something delicious and beautiful out of it. She had done exactly that many times as part of her culinary training. And it had always come easy to her. She'd improvised and been creative and won praise. Now she needed to do the very same thing with her personal life. *Make something out of nothing.*

She smiled down at Remy, who was getting squirmier by the minute. "Trade you lives, Remy. You seem to have everything figured out, huh, buddy?"

The dog grew more excited and as she reached for his leash, he immediately turned into a brown tornado, full of boundless energy.

"Easy, boy," Grace soothed as she headed for the door and bounced down the steps, Remy pulling her along.

The tide was low and the surf calm. It was peaceful and it beckoned to Grace, made her feel nostalgic with a flutter in her stomach. It was so much like the Cape Cod of her youth. The salty, cool spring air washed over her pleasantly and she breathed it in deeply. She walked, secretly wanting to frolic like a kid—make deep footprints in the sand, splash her feet in the cold, frothy water. But her moment of whimsy passed, and instead she simply walked along the dry part of the sand, her sandals kicking up tiny granules, her dog beside her happily tugging on his leash.

The letter. Grace's chest clenched as she recalled the words she'd tearfully written to Aly and mailed on the way to the airport. The warring feelings of resolve, hope and regret burned familiarly in her throat. She'd done what she had to do, she reminded herself. It was time for a fresh start, perhaps for both of them. The letter was short and somber, to the point. And very final. She did not equivocate. She wrote that she did not blame Aly for anything, that she was not bitter, but that she needed to get on with her life, needed to build her happiness around something—someone—more permanent. Their time together was over because it needed to be, and she hoped Aly would understand. She'd signed it: *Affectionately, Grace.*

She blinked away the sting of sudden tears. Writing the words was so unsatisfying, so inadequate. She'd wanted to say so much more, like how much she would miss Aly's smile, her touch, her laughter. Even the excitement of sneaking around, as though the covertness made the relationship more important, more thrilling than it really was. She would miss the sex, the acute need for Aly's body. *There was a time when I hoped you might be the one, Aly. That you were the one…God, why couldn't you have been the one?*

Grace shook her head, determined not to go there. She'd had three years to learn that Aly had no intention of changing anything in her life. Three years of broken commitments and hasty liaisons, aching loneliness and a pervasive hunger that could never quite be sated. Incredible, soaring highs at times and debilitating lows. It was exhausting, distressing and just godawful sad most of the time. It had been both their faults, though blame mattered little now. It was just how it was.

There would always be her work, Grace thought with some consolation. The focused intensity had always propelled her through the rough patches. But now, at least for a couple of months, she would not even have that. *God, what have you done, Grace?*

Remy suddenly bucked and reared, then bolted, nearly sending Grace off her feet. "Dammit!" she yelled, the leash having been yanked from her hand. Remy was off like a rocket, barreling down the beach.

"Remy! Come here, Remy!" Grace yelled and took off after

him, the sand slowing her down. "You little shit," she muttered under her breath.

He was a brown speck far ahead, and she kept after him, puffing like a heavy smoker and wishing she'd been more committed to the gym. *That's it. I'm going to start running regularly, even if it kills me!*

Remy made a sharp turn into shore and disappeared toward a home deep among the pine trees. She visually landmarked his exit spot, still yelling his name, and followed his trail. She came to an ungraceful, breathless halt at the sight of the big lug lying contentedly on a beautiful cedar deck at the feet of a lithe, elderly woman with a big straw hat shadowing her face.

Shy and embarrassed about her dog, Grace approached, her eyes shooting daggers at Remy, but she gave her best TV smile to the stranger.

"Hello there," the tall woman said, getting slowly to her feet. "You must be this fella's master."

Grace pursed her lips and hoped the woman wasn't about to rebuke her. "I am, and I'm sorry about that. I don't know what possessed him. He just gets crazy sometimes, especially when he's outdoors."

The woman's laugh was full of understanding. "I'll bet it was the smell of bacon cooking inside."

"Yep. That'll do it. Remy," she said menacingly to the dog. "Where are your manners?"

"I'm Connie Sparks, by the way." She extended a leathery hand and Grace shook it warmly from the steps of the deck.

"Grace Wellwood."

A mild look of curiosity passed over the woman's face, as though the name should mean something to her. Grace was glad she hadn't been recognized, but she knew that wouldn't last long. Once the islanders realized she was staying at Trish Wilson's place, they would make the connection and her anonymity would evaporate like the morning fog—if it hadn't already.

"It's nice to meet you, Ms. Wellwood."

"Please," Grace said. "Call me Grace."

"Of course." Connie Sparks's blue eyes were penetrating but friendly. "As long as it works both ways. Look, why don't you come and join me on the deck while Remy gets his rest?"

Grace chuckled and threw another glare at Remy. "That spoiled dog does not need rest. He needs punishment, more like."

Connie waved a hand dismissively. "Nonsense. I can tell he's a good boy. He was just looking to make friends, that's all."

Grace wasn't sure she was in the mood to make friends as effortlessly as her dog. She would be poor company for anyone right now who didn't have a tail and four legs. And even then…

"C'mon up," Connie said again, more insistently this time. "I've got coffee brewing."

Remy was stretched out now, nearly asleep in the sun. Nothing was going to pry him from his spot, and really, Grace thought a little morosely, it's not like she had anything better to do. Perhaps the distraction of a quick cup of coffee and small talk with another human being wouldn't be such a bad thing.

She swallowed and summoned another smile. "I'd love to. If it's all right."

Connie warmly beckoned her toward a cedar Adirondack chair. "I'd love the company. What do you take in your coffee?"

"Just a little cream, please. I'm not disturbing your breakfast, am I?"

"Not at all," Connie said from the weathered, wood-framed screen door. "Would you care to join me?"

"No, thank you. I've already eaten," Grace lied, not wanting to impose. Besides, she'd been eating like a bird lately and really didn't feel like breakfast.

"I'll just turn the bacon off for now, that's all."

"If you're sure."

"I am. Just relax."

Grace reached down to pat her stretched out dog, wanting to chastise him, but he was looking up at her innocently with his big hazel eyes. "You big goof," she whispered. "I know I've been lousy company, but really. Running into a stranger's lap. Could you be any more obvious?"

Connie returned and handed Grace a pottery mug full of aromatic, steaming coffee. "Thank you," Grace murmured and gratefully sipped. God, it tasted good. "What's your secret to such fabulous coffee?"

Connie sat down in the facing Adirondack, sipping from a matching mug. "Colombian beans and a twenty-year-old, well-seasoned coffeemaker."

Grace nodded. "Now those were the days when things were made to last."

Connie nodded wistfully, her gaze drifting out to the sea some sixty yards off. "Everything is so disposable now. And not just appliances. Relationships too, if you ask me. If something doesn't work, throw it out and get a new one. That seems to be the way these days."

There was a rush of heat up her neck as she realized Connie was studying her intently. Helplessly transparent, she wondered if it was obvious she'd spent the last three years running around with a married woman, living with some sort of fantasy that she would wake up one day and Aly would suddenly be the woman of her dreams. God, she'd been pathetic—and stupid—if that's what she'd really been doing. Had she really been so out of touch with herself for so long? And was it apparent even to a stranger?

"I'm sorry, dear," Connie said quietly. "Did I say something to upset you?"

Grace pulled her gaze up and shook her head lightly.

Connie chuckled softly. "I don't mean to, but I can be an old fuddy-duddy sometimes. My nieces and nephews like to remind me of that."

Grace smiled and thoughts of Aly fell away, like autumn leaves. "It's okay. You're not being an old fuddy-duddy. But you're right. I guess we do tend to look for the perfect, ready-made thing, and when it's not there, we discard it and keep looking." Like instant meals, Grace thought with disgust. People expected a frozen box to taste like a real roast with mashed potatoes and gravy, but it never did of course. "There's nothing like the real thing," she mumbled, unaware she'd spoken out loud.

"You're right about that," Connie answered her. "Is it really because people don't have the time? Is that why people give up on one another so easily?"

Grace pondered and sipped her coffee, both hands wrapped tightly around the warm, stone mug that was so sturdy and reliable. That was the thing about instant meals from the grocery store. *People think they don't have time to cook, but they make time to commute hours to work each day, or play on their computers or watch TV all evening.* "I think it's more about priorities, Connie."

Connie smiled approvingly, and there was a sudden communion with the stranger, as if they'd met before.

"Where are you staying, Grace? I haven't seen you here before. I'd certainly remember you if I did." Her eyes swept briefly over Grace, and in that instance, Grace knew the woman was a kindred spirit in more ways than one. It made her smile inside. It was refreshing to know that not everyone on the island was straight.

"I'm staying at my friend Trish Wilson's place."

"Ah, okay. Nice woman, but it's too bad she only comes here a week or two a year. If that, sometimes. She's a chef, I understand. Are you a chef too?"

"Actually, I am." Grace was happy for the understating of her career. No celebrity expectations to live up to, no long explanations of what projects she was working on, the people she'd met, the places she'd been.

"Well, good for you," Connie said enthusiastically with a gleam in her eye. "That means you must have quite an artistic streak in you."

Grace's eyebrows arched in surprise. She'd never really thought of herself as an artist, but rather a craftsman, whose skills had been honed by years of hard work and experience. She knew what tasted good, what went together and what worked. And how it could be done over and over with the maximum efficiency and consistency. It was important that her customers knew their favorite dishes would be replicated. "Well, I'm not sure about that."

Connie rose, her eyes ablaze. "C'mon. Let me show you inside."

Grace stood expectantly, then tied Remy's leash to the deck railing. "You stay here and be a good boy."

"Forty years I've been coming here every summer," Connie said, leading the way into the modest house. "When I come here, I become who I really am."

Grace was instantly envious. The place was cozy, peaceful, earthy. The interior was painted with whimsical brushstrokes of lemon, sage green and red pine. The floors were varnished birch, the furniture chunky and worn—inviting. Paintings covered every wall.

"Yours?" Grace indicated the canvasses.

"Yes," Connie answered. "I've been oil painting ever since I can remember."

"Do you still paint?"

"Not so much, no." Connie raised knobby fingers. "The old arthritis. But I try to sketch when I can."

Grace moved closer to study a stormy seascape. It was spectacular in its depth of texture and layering of color. "Wow!" Grace exclaimed. "This is amazing."

"There's something about the island that brings out your inner peace. It inspires."

Grace was tempted to touch the rich, textured brushstrokes. The piece was beautiful and so detailed, right down to the tiny sailboat bobbing precariously in the swollen waves. Her eyes drifted to a nearby watercolor. "You do watercolor too?"

Connie moved beside her, towering over her. Her long, bony fingers gently traced the frame around the pastel painting of a covered bridge. There was a look of reverence on her face. "No, that's the work of my partner of twenty-three years, Helen Crawford."

"It's beautiful," Grace said.

"So was she."

Grace studied Connie's profile. She looked suddenly stooped, weighed down by an invisible cloak of sadness. Her blue eyes were misty when she turned them on Grace. Her smile faltered. "She died eight years ago."

Grace was surprised by the depth of her emotions, even after so many years. Her body spoke the language of her loss. "I'm sorry." It was all Grace could think to say.

"Thank you. We had a wonderful life together. Helen was very special. We meant everything to each other." Her eyes boldly appraised Grace again and her mouth was a serious line. "Do you have anyone special, Grace?"

God, not like that. She shook her head lamely. She didn't know if she would ever have someone like that, who meant everything, and again, there was the fathomless ache of all that her relationship with Aly was not.

There was a flash of pity in Connie's eyes, but it was gone in an instant. "You will. It's the most beautiful, inspiring, terrifying thing in human existence, Grace."

"Terrifying?" Grace quirked a curious eyebrow, and her question was met with a knowing smile as Connie led the way back out to the deck and their sun-warmed chairs, hot coffee and Grace's sleeping dog.

They sat down, Connie expressionless for a long moment. "When you have it, you're terrified of losing it, and when you don't have it anymore, you're terrified you'll never find it again."

Grace gazed at the azure ocean shimmering in the morning sun. She had not known any of that with Aly. She had never been terrified of losing her, only frightened of the prospect of being alone and unloved. Rejected. Of being punished in some way for carrying on with a married woman.

Connie was staring at the ocean too and her voice was far off. "It's kind of like that ocean out there, Grace. Huge and very deep and powerful."

Grace shook her head and wanted to laugh at the absurdity of her own life. "I know nothing but tiny streams and ponds, Connie." *And meandering, shallow rivers that go nowhere except around and around.*

Connie, her face still handsome but craggy, did not look amused. Her features were like chiseled granite, and her eyes narrowed with either displeasure or disappointment, Grace couldn't be sure.

"A nice, beautiful girl like you, Grace? What's wrong with the men…or women…out there?" Her eyes twinkled hopefully at women.

Grace's laughter was a cover for the tears she wanted to shed. She wished it were as simple as attracting the right woman. "The smart women have learned to stay away from me, Connie. I mean, no woman serious about a relationship would want someone as busy and preoccupied as me." It was an uncomplicated answer that fell far short of explaining her relationship failures, but it would have to do for now.

Connie smiled with amusement as though she were watching Grace stumble into a trap. "Ah. You said yourself it's not about time, but rather priorities."

Crafty old devil, Grace thought with surprising affection. "I did say something like that, didn't I?"

"You did, my dear."

"All right." Grace sighed and finished her now lukewarm coffee. In spite of the personal direction the conversation had taken, it seemed surprisingly appropriate. "Maybe that's it. Maybe none of it mattered until…"

Connie leaned in, her head tilted with curiosity. "Until now?"

Grace couldn't speak around the catch in her throat and managed a poor attempt at a smile instead.

Connie patted her knee. "All right, Grace. It's all right. You're here, on Sheridan Island, and I promise you that whatever ails you won't by the time you leave here."

Grace nodded, relieved by the sudden lightness of the moment. "Can I hold you to that promise?"

"I haven't been wrong yet."

Grace silently approved of the bold confidence in Connie's

face and in her deep voice and rigid body. She was a trustworthy soul. "I'll bet you haven't." An idea began germinating in her mind. "Do you cook, Connie?"

"Not much, I'm afraid. My head is so often in the clouds that I rarely think about practical things like cooking."

"Cooking isn't just practical, like a chore, you know." Grace liked the woman too much to be offended, and smiled as Connie held her hand up in apology.

"I didn't mean to insult you, Grace. I'm sure you do wonderful, wonderful things in the kitchen. I guess my creativity just never extended to food."

"Well. If I had your talents with a canvas and a brush, I probably wouldn't have much creative energy left over for cooking, either. Listen, why don't I cook for you tonight?"

Connie's eyebrows arched in surprise and delight. "That would be wonderful. But I don't have much here. I mean, nothing fancy."

"That's okay. I have everything I need back at Trish's. Why don't I prepare something and bring it over?"

Sharing a meal with someone was the quickest way to bridge loneliness. It would be good to not feel lonely for a few hours, and cooking would make her feel normal again. Needed, even.

Connie smiled warmly. "That would be tremendous, my friend. But you must promise to bring Remy as well."

Grace shot a dubious glance at her dog, who looked as if he were the best behaved pet on the planet. "All right. I'll bring Remy."

At the sound of his name again, he sprang up like a coil suddenly let loose.

CHAPTER FIVE

It was only half a mile, but it was a start.

Grace knew she would be able to work up to running a mile soon enough, maybe even two, on the dirt road that circled the island. She used to run more than that earlier in her career, when running was her outlet for stress and exhaustion. She'd stopped around the time she met Aly.

Stepping out of the shower, Grace moved with a newfound energy. Dinner with Connie Sparks the previous night had been a nice change. The conversation had been light and pleasant, which was just what Grace needed. She learned more about the island and its inhabitants from Connie, and this new knowledge made her anxious to do some exploring. Sitting on Trish's deck and drinking her way to the bottom of another bottle of wine had definitely lost its appeal.

Grace was drying herself when the phone rang, the shock of it nearly making her slip on the wet floor. Trish Wilson and James Easton were the only people who had the number for the cottage, and Grace had purposely left her cell phone off. It was hard, cutting herself off so completely from Aly—not knowing if Aly was trying to reach her. She wasn't even sure which would be worse—Aly calling or Aly *not* calling.

She picked up the phone and answered tentatively.

"Hi, Grace."

Grace expelled a tense breath. It was just Trish.

"How are you enjoying things on the island?"

"It's nice. I think I could actually enjoy myself here." She meant it, which she would not have two days ago.

"Good." Trish's tone turned ominous. "Does that mean you're starting to get over her?"

Grace blew out an exasperated breath. She did not want to talk about Aly. "Trish—"

"S'all right. Sorry. I just hope you're doing okay, that's all."

"I'm doing okay, Trish."

There was a long pause before Trish reluctantly said, "I'm not sure how you're going to take this, Grace."

Grace's stomach involuntarily tightened, but she commanded herself to stay calm. "What is it you're afraid to tell me?" God, it could be anything. Had something happened to Aly? Had the restaurant burned to the ground? Had the new architect quit the Manhattan job?

"Something unexpected's come up and I can't do it alone."

"What, Trish? For God's sake, just tell me."

"Look, Grace. You can say no if you want. Really."

"Trish." Grace's impatience was multiplying. Trish treating her like some kind of emotional invalid was new, and she didn't like it one damn bit.

"Okay, okay. We've been asked to cater the championship dinner a week from tomorrow at the LPGA's Hartford Open. I, ah, said yes, even though I don't know how the hell I'm going to do it."

"Hmm. That's not much notice."

Trish sighed impatiently through the phone, and Grace pictured her pacing around her house with her cordless phone to her ear. "I know. The caterers they'd contracted had to back out at the last minute."

Grace easily switched into business mode as she struggled to keep the damp towel wrapped around her. "I'm happy to help, Trish. But do we want the reputation of being available at the last minute to do a job that we weren't chosen for in the first place?" She understood the dilemma but had to pose the question.

"I know. That part sucks. But I said yes because the promotion opportunities for our television show and the new restaurant are too good to pass up. There'll be live television coverage for four days and tons of media. Lots of corporate sponsors hanging about, too, with nothing to do but contemplate where and how to spend their next buck. James is already salivating."

"Well, since you put it like that..." Grace knew a good business opportunity when she heard one. She could hardly say no, not when Trish was already carrying so much of the load.

"You don't mind?" Trish asked anxiously. "I know you're supposed to be on vacation and all. I really wouldn't have asked you if I didn't need you like crazy."

Grace laughed, knowing Trish must have truly been desperate for her help to pull her out of the seclusion she'd pretty much forced on her. "It's fine, really. The distraction of work might actually be good for me."

"It's only a week of your time, Grace. Then I want you back there relaxing."

"Yes, ma'am!"

Trish giggled. "That's more like it. This new, compliant Grace I could get used to."

"Never get used to anything, my dear. Especially *not* that."

"Okay, okay. Look, I've already booked a flight for you Monday afternoon out of Portland. Can you get there yourself?"

"Yes. I have a rental car."

"Good. Someone from the LPGA will pick you up at the Hartford Airport. You'll be staying at the Hilton, which is right next to the golf course. The championship dinner will be at the hotel's ballroom next Sunday, after the last round of play. The dinner will be for about two-fifty."

Grace scribbled a couple of quick notes, her towel falling away. She hoped the welcome wagon didn't pick this moment to

47

appear at one of the many windows with a freshly baked pie or a bouquet of flowers.

"I'll be able to show up the night before the banquet to help you, but I'm afraid you'll have to do the rest of the work leading up to it. James will pop in for a day or so just to kiss some corporate ass for us."

"Do I have kitchen staff?"

"Yes. The hotel will provide us with a sous-chef or two and a half dozen line cooks. Wait staff too, of course."

"What about the menu?"

"Pretty much up to you. Although you have to work on that with the official hostess of the event."

"Huh? What hostess?"

"Last year's tournament winner gets to choose the menu and be the official host of this year's dinner."

Great. Someone who knows absolutely nothing about food in my face the whole time, asking me to do things that are impossible. Or just plain stupid.

Before Grace could complain, Trish was talking again. "Her name is Torrie Cannon. You can meet her when you get there." Grace thought she heard a chuckle in Trish's voice. "She's not playing in it this year because of an injury, so she'll be available to help you the entire time."

Grace cursed into the phone. "I'm going to get you for this, Wilson."

Trish laughed. "See you next weekend, babe."

Torrie Cannon had only a vague idea of who she was looking for at the airport terminal. Grace Wellwood might be well known in some circles, but not in Torrie's. All she really knew of the celebrity chef was that she was one of those cute blondes she'd caught sight of a couple of times on the food channel.

Torrie wouldn't be caught dead holding up a sign with Grace's name on it. It was the kind of degrading thing that reminded her of an auction, so instead, she squinted and lurked in her dark sunglasses, trying not to look conspicuous. She couldn't even remember the last time she'd picked someone up at the airport. It was always the other way around, and then it had never seemed so awkward and confusing. She could easily have delegated the pickup to one of the many tournament volunteers itching for something to do, but she figured—hoped—it might distract her from the pervasive reminders that she would be sitting on her duff all week instead of defending her title.

A sudden tap on her surgically repaired shoulder made her flinch as much in pain as in surprise. She spun around and lowered her gaze to the palest, most luminescent gray eyes she'd ever seen. A small hand thrust out, forcing Torrie to look down, and she shook it after a delay that bordered on rudeness. The strength in the woman's grip surprised her. It surprised her that she had so quickly underestimated her strength because of her small stature. Torrie knew from years of experience on the Tour that often the smaller women were some of the longest hitters and the best golfers. Size had little to do with strength.

"I'm Grace Wellwood. I take it you're Torrie Cannon?" A finely shaped, pale eyebrow rose.

Torrie nodded blankly and drew in a deep breath. Television did not do this woman justice, and it stunned Torrie a little, even though she was often around many beautiful women. Maybe it was because her looks seemed so natural and not covered by layers of makeup, or disguised by pretenses. She did not seem to be going for any particular look or act, nor did she seem to be using her beauty as some sort of card to play—a tool to exert herself or to excuse herself or to be owed something—and Torrie appreciated that. This was a woman who appreciated substance over superficiality, and Torrie liked her honest confidence.

"It's good to meet you," Torrie said evenly as she tried to decide which feature of Grace's many was the most striking. Her blond hair was lush and trimmed neatly to just below her shoulder blades, with a natural wave lifting the tips. Facially, her bone structure was fine, yet her nose was strong and her cheekbones well defined. A dimple on either side accentuated a ready smile, and Torrie was struck by her simple, elegant beauty.

You don't even know how beautiful you are, do you?

Grace adjusted the shoulder strap of her carry bag and said affably, "I didn't expect the tournament champion to be greeting me here. This is quite an honor!"

Torrie smiled back, relaxing instantly, though it took effort not to rake her eyes over Grace Wellwood's body. She didn't think she could handle that just yet. Her hormones were cranked up these days. Her injury, and then the surgery, had pretty much decimated her sex life.

"It was too important a task to leave to just anybody," Torrie answered smoothly, removing her designer sunglasses and slipping them into the front pocket of her short-sleeved guayabera shirt. Her ability to flirt was at least still intact.

Grace smiled again, her eyes crinkling at the edges. "Well, then, I guess I should consider myself rather important."

Torrie knew she was leering a little, that she risked offending a woman she didn't know and would need to work with, but she couldn't quite help herself. Openly flirting was a well-practiced habit, her modus operandi, and one that had always worked so well. Too well. Her voice gamely dropped an octave. "You're an expert at what I consider the second best thing in life. That would make you very important."

Grace crooked an inquisitive eyebrow and met Torrie's challenge. "And what would the first thing be?"

Torrie blushed a little, in spite of her bravado. She was never truly as brazen as she sometimes acted. Perhaps it was the fault of being a professional athlete, where attitude could cover weakness and even propel you to victory. She tried to think of a sassy comeback, even opened her mouth, but nothing would come out. Just as well, because she would probably make a complete ass of herself.

Oh, Torrie, you started this line of flirting and now you're caving in like a child. She scares you.

Grace was still looking at her expectantly. Amusement and unmistakable mischief danced in her eyes, and Torrie knew she had better come up with something good. This woman was not about to let her off the hook.

Torrie gave her best rakish smile—the one that worked flawlessly on the young groupies. "Let's just say it's something equally pleasurable but without the calories."

Grace laughed appreciatively, not the least bit shocked or offended. She even seemed to relax a little more as she pressed a hand to Torrie's forearm and gave a gentle squeeze. "I'm happy I can help you with your *second* favorite thing then, Ms. Cannon." Her tone was friendly but definitive in setting the boundary.

So that's how it's going to be. Torrie tried to ignore the tiny flicker of disappointment. Clearly, Grace Wellwood had no interest in anything but a friendly business arrangement with Torrie. Was the cute little chef straight? *Jesus, that would be such a waste.* There had to be some reason for the subtle rejection, because Torrie rarely, if ever, met with rejection. It never occurred to her that there might not be at least a chance at some fun between the sheets with a gorgeous woman. She found her eyes slipping to Grace's left hand. No ring, so at least that was a good sign.

Baffled and extremely curious, Torrie was torn between letting it drop and rising to this new challenge. They would be working together this week to make the championship dinner a success, and constantly thinking about trying to seduce this woman would be nothing but a time waster. *Chalk one up in the column for keeping the relationship all business.* On the other hand, losing wasn't in Torrie's vocabulary. It'd been awhile, too, since she'd really had to chase a woman. It could be fun. And this woman, she had a feeling, would be so worth the chase.

Torrie checked her watch. It was almost seven. "Can I take you to dinner, Ms. Wellwood?"

Grace's expression was firm. "All right, but under two conditions."

Torrie straightened up like a kid called before the teacher. She liked this stern side of the celebrity chef.

"That you call me Grace and that it's a working dinner. We've got a lot to discuss."

Torrie nodded. *God, she's so damned cute when she's bossy.*

She gave Grace a mock salute and grinned sarcastically. "Deal, Grace."

Torrie's appetite for food—any food—was legendary on the Tour, and she was only vaguely aware of Grace watching her as she joyfully bulldozed her way through a medium sirloin and mashed potatoes with melted cheddar and chives. Weight wasn't a problem for her, thanks to her tall, muscular frame and her strict workout regimen. She loved food. It was comforting. It was the one constant in her life besides golf. Well...sex, too, though not so much these days. She remembered her mother's sage advice just last week, about her transient escapades and how they weren't "real". Of course her mother was right, but it was so goddamned hard to be noble when a sexy woman was sitting across from her. Maybe it was just as well that Grace had made it clear it was to be all business between them. Torrie didn't trust herself to set the parameters, that's for sure. In fact, if she had her way, she would have her *way* with Grace Wellwood tonight.

Turning her attention to another bite, she became more aware of a look from Grace, the same one she'd received countless times over the years from friends and family—the one that said if she didn't slow down, some day she would have to worry about her weight. She had even managed to outpace her brothers in the appetite department.

Torrie set down her fork—a rare thing for her to do while the food was still warm. "I know what you're thinking."

Grace tilted her head speculatively. "And what would that be?"

"That I eat like a construction worker and that some day I'll look like a retired linebacker, if I'm not careful. But really. It's not a problem."

Grace smiled slowly, as though she knew something Torrie didn't. She sipped from her wineglass with deliberation, then studied Torrie for a long moment. Her face was impassive, her voice completely neutral. "You're quite sure of a lot of things, aren't you?"

Torrie shrugged her good shoulder. *God.* She wasn't sure about much of anything these days. Turning thirty and suffering a serious shoulder injury, one coming on the heels of the other, had left her mentally reeling. It was as though she were a boxer stunned by a surprise left hook. But she'd be damned if she'd show it to this beautiful, successful stranger who seemed to have a boatload of cool confidence.

"I'm sure about beauty when I see it," Torrie said, letting her eyes fall slowly and appreciatively over Grace's low-cut, V-necked, tight cashmere sweater that protruded with all the right curves.

Grace's condemning smile and those discerning, narrowed eyes instantly made Torrie want to eat her words. Most women acted flattered when Torrie flirted with them, and the bolder ones returned it in spades. *Not this one, Tor. This one won't be taken in so easily.* It was as if Grace knew Torrie was simply reverting to her tried-and-true old tricks, rather than discussing anything meaningful.

Grace leaned closer, her cleavage that much more tantalizing. "Tell me something, Torrie. Do you always flirt so boldly with women you don't know very well?"

Torrie didn't quite know how to answer. The question didn't sound judgmental, and yet it demanded a serious answer. Torrie did the only thing she could think of—she stalled. She began shoveling food in her mouth again. It was either that or stare at that mouthwatering chest. But Grace wasn't going away. Or changing the subject. She was looking at Torrie, her eyes patient but piercingly insistent.

Torrie washed her food down with a gulp of Cabernet and decided to go for glib. Maybe that would shake Grace off. "Only if they're incredibly sexy. And talented. I'm afraid you qualify on both counts."

Grace shook her head lightly, looking both cynical and amused, a tiny smile curling her full, lightly glossed lips. "I'm not exactly a twenty-year-old groupie, you know."

Christ, isn't that the truth. This one was all woman. And all grown up. Thank God. The truth was, Torrie had begun to have her fill of the twinkies—the young groupies eager to bed a celebrity. She hadn't entirely discarded her skirt-chasing habits yet, but she was increasingly aware that she was ready for a challenge, for a woman who could give her a come-hither look one instant and a kick in the ass the next. *Oh, yeah. This little game could be quite sweet indeed.* In spite of her earlier half-hearted decision to stick to business, Torrie now absently swirled the wine in her glass and figured she had little else to do in her life at the moment but to wipe the smart-ass look off this woman's face with a ferocious kiss. Or at least, the kiss would be a start.

Torrie leaned in and lowered her voice. "So you're saying it takes more than a nice dinner, a few compliments and the undivided attention of a world-class athlete to get you into bed?"

Grace nearly choked on her mouthful of chicken Florentine. *Bull's-eye!* It took another moment for her to mentally regain her foothold. Torrie could see Grace gathering her wits. *Oh, yes. This is going to be fun.*

"What makes you think there's anything you could say or do that would get me into bed?" Grace's eyes had morphed to a battleship gray. It was a dare if ever there was one.

Torrie shrugged lightly, holding her gaze, her own game face firmly in place. "Is that a challenge, Grace? Because I can assure you, I never back down from a challenge. And I always win."

Grace's eyes grew wide and unsure for an instant, as though she was worried she'd strayed too deep into this risky territory. Her fingers tensely stroked the stem of her wineglass. *God. Does she have to be so sexy without even trying?*

"You know what I think, Torrie?"

Torrie shook her head, feeling not nearly as cavalier as she hoped she looked.

"I think you're full of crap."

Torrie's mouth slackened just as their waitress appeared, asking about dessert while fidgeting anxiously. The girl looked like a geyser about to erupt, all nervous energy.

Grace ordered coffee for them both since Torrie had not

recovered enough to put two words together. Ordering a piece of chocolate cake never had a chance.

"I'm sorry," the waitress finally burst out breathlessly, looking at Grace. "I really hate to ask this, but…" She leaned closer. "Are you that famous chef, the one on television?"

Grace smiled politely, as though the intrusion were an everyday occurrence and one that she didn't mind. "I'm afraid that's me, yes."

The young woman squealed excitedly. "God, I love your show." She moved even closer, her bouncy breasts just inches from Grace's face, Torrie realized with sudden annoyance. *Jesus, why doesn't she just climb into her lap, for God's sake!*

"If I, like, brought you a menu later, would you autograph it for me?"

Torrie was wincing, but Grace still smiled accommodatingly. She was cool and smooth and seemingly impervious to the charms of the young, enthusiastic fan. "Ah, sure, I'd love to. Perhaps on my way out."

The girl finally flitted off without so much as even a glance at Torrie.

"You know she's going to give you her number on the way out," Torrie said acidly.

"I don't think so, Torrie."

"Right," Torrie countered. She was jealous, she realized, and for all the wrong reasons.

Grace flashed her a look. "Would you rather she was giving you her number? Is that it?"

Far from it, Torrie wanted to say.

"I could probably arrange that, you know." Grace grinned, obviously enjoying herself.

Torrie had to grudgingly admire Grace's gumption. Her wit was quick and she was so damned good at teasing Torrie. Too good. "I don't need any help, thank you."

Their coffees arrived, the gushing waitress more subdued this time, and Torrie buoyed herself for more verbal sparring. She would not let Grace get the upper hand.

"So, Grace." Torrie smiled sweetly but her tone was hard as nails. "You were saying earlier that I'm full of shit."

Grace set her coffee cup down and sat back to study Torrie with those narrowed eyes that seemed to indicate she knew a hell of a lot more than Torrie could ever guess. She sighed in quiet contemplation before her expression softened. "Look, Torrie. We really don't—"

"No. I want to know." Torrie leaned back too, feigning a cool confidence she didn't really feel. "Please."

"All right." Grace sighed as if to say *you asked for it*. "I think you flirt like that out of habit because you're scared."

"Scared? You think I'm scared of women?" That was a new one.

Grace nonchalantly sipped her coffee as if they were discussing the latest stock market trends. "You're not scared of having sex with women, no. But you're scared of anything deeper. If you keep the emphasis entirely on sex and sexual attraction, it keeps thoughts or conversation about anything else at arm's length."

Torrie harrumphed grumpily, feeling like a specimen on a slide. *God, has she been talking to my mother?* "Look. I find you very attractive, Grace, and I'm not afraid of letting you know that. That's all. I'd take you to bed in the blink of an eye. But you could just say no instead of making me sound like some kind of a head case or something."

Grace actually began to look sorry, as though she'd gone too far and knew it. "You're right, Torrie. I'm sorry. I had no right to do that to you." She rolled her eyes playfully. "Lord knows I'm no expert at relationships."

Torrie smiled on two counts: Grace hadn't entirely rebuffed her advances, and it sounded like she wasn't in a long-term relationship.

Grace yawned, then signaled for the check. "I really should go." She touched her fingertips to her temple.

"You okay?"

"Yeah. Just an exhaustion headache. I've been literally sitting on my butt for the last two weeks. I'd forgotten how tiring it is working for a living again."

Torrie knew something about that. "I know what you mean."

"Ah, crap."

"What?"

"We never did get around to discussing menu ideas." Grace looked flustered. "This was supposed to be a business dinner." She smiled helplessly. "I guess I got a little distracted."

There was satisfaction in having distracted Grace so easily from business, something Torrie guessed didn't happen often. It was almost more gratifying than if Grace had agreed to her proposition. *Well, not quite.*

"Why don't you meet me at the course tomorrow morning? Say about nine. It's only an optional practice day, so it shouldn't be busy. I'll take you on a tour and I promise to only talk about food."

Grace looked relieved, if not entirely convinced. "Deal."

Grace slept fitfully, pissed off for getting so sidetracked with Torrie Cannon over dinner. They'd teased and sparred like they'd known each other for years, playing a little game of one-upmanship that had surprised Grace, and yet she marveled at how easy it'd been. Torrie seemed so familiar in such an intimate way, and while the game had been fun, she was here on business. There was work to be done, and Torrie Cannon was her client, the championship dinner her job.

Time to get to work, Grace.

Dressed in casual khaki Capri pants, a boat neck sleeveless white tee and brown sandals, Grace appeared at the clubhouse dutifully at nine. It was going to be a warm day, and she looked forward to spending the morning outdoors. The next few days would be busy inventorying, organizing and ordering supplies, meeting with staff and getting them battle-ready, mapping out the plan for Sunday's banquet. There'd be a dry run of everything, and while she'd figured out the basic menu during her sleepless moments, she still didn't know what to do about dessert. Maybe

Torrie would actually have something on her mind besides sex.

Her timing impeccable, Torrie appeared and Grace's pulse maddeningly quickened. The golfer exuded sex. And fun and charm, with those dashing good looks and roguish smile. Her short hair was dark and tousled, like she belonged in bed, but her blue eyes were as sharp as the crease in her expensive designer shorts. She was sure Torrie met with little opposition from women, but she was damned if she would be one of them.

I've worked in tight quarters with hot, sweaty, libidinous men most of my life, Torrie Cannon. I can take whatever you want to throw at me.

Torrie shook Grace's hand. There was no sign of the flirtatious seductress this morning, for which Grace was relieved. Or so she told herself. As they rode around in the motorized cart, Torrie patiently explaining the layout of a particular hole and how easy or difficult it played, a shadow of disappointment surprised Grace. There was no mention of their conversation last night, and not once did Torrie try a suggestive line on her. The cockiness had evaporated like the morning dew on the finely manicured grass. In fact, Torrie had hardly even looked at Grace—certainly not in the way she had looked at her last night, all hungry-eyed and cheeky—and Grace reluctantly missed it. As much as Torrie's bold behavior had annoyed her, it had also amused her, even flattered her.

Torrie waved to a couple of golfers in the distance. One shouted something about rain coming and drove off.

Oh, shit, Grace thought with a worried glance at the darkening sky that had seemingly emerged from nowhere, its approach growing more ominous by the second. She hadn't brought a jacket and they were miles away from the clubhouse.

"Hey," Torrie said, clambering out of the cart. "Let me show you this awesome sand bunker, Grace. It's nasty as hell. Eats golfers alive. C'mon already!"

"I think it's going to rain. Shouldn't we get back?"

Hands on her hips, Torrie exuded impatience. "It'll just take a sec." Her grin was a challenge. "Besides, you don't melt in the

58

rain, do you?"

"I might, you know. Like one of those ice sculptures at a fancy martini bar." But Grace was already gamely stepping out of the cart.

"Nah. You're not nearly so fragile."

"Oh yeah?" Grace heard the doubt in her own voice. *For all you know, I might fall apart any minute, Torrie. Unlike you, who's probably never fallen apart or backed away from anything in your life.*

The grin slid from Torrie's face and she stared pensively at Grace, as though she might be trying to read her mind. She'd never looked so serious, and Grace imagined it was how she looked when she stood over a game-winning putt, so focused and intent. Grace wanted the old Torrie back—the one she could quickly put in her place with a smart remark or a castigating look.

"You're far too smart and ambitious to let any weaknesses or fears get in your way for long, Grace. I expect you're one of the strongest women I could ever hope to meet." She held her hand out to help Grace into the deep bunker, then smiled convincingly. "And I do meet a lot of strong women in this business."

Grace took the steadying hand and realized that, for the first time, it was the real Torrie Cannon next to her, welcoming and helpful and sure of herself, but in a subtle and genuine way—like a weightlifter who knows her own strength without having to pick up every heavy object in sight to prove it.

"You know something, Torrie?" They were still holding hands, even after gingerly climbing down into the six-foot deep sand maw.

Torrie looked expectantly at her with a trace of dread in the hardening of her mouth and the narrowing of her eyes. She looked steeled to take whatever Grace might say, whatever challenge or criticism Grace might heap on her, and it rattled Grace a bit, this willingness to just take it. And in that instant, Grace knew she was right when she'd told Torrie that she was afraid of women. Afraid of criticism too. She was really not the cool-headed, warm-blooded slut she pretended to be.

"What?"

"You're far more charming when you're like this than how you were last night."

Torrie laughed. "You mean when I'm being sensitive and thoughtful instead of trying to constantly seduce you?"

Grace laughed. "Insightful too, aren't you?"

"I'm all of those things and more. See what you're missing?"

"Ah. The old Torrie begins to emerge. I'd wondered where she went."

Torrie's hand moved to the soft side of Grace's wrist, stroked it gently once, twice. "Grace, I don't mean to be... I mean... I still think you're incredibly—"

The rain came crashing down all at once, pounding so fast and hard, like tiny needles against Grace's skin. She tried to scramble out of the massive depths of wet sand, but it was both slippery and gummy and she couldn't get any traction. Torrie gave her butt a firm shove from behind. Grace would have reprimanded her for taking liberties, or at least whacked her hand away, but the shove worked well enough for her to tug herself the rest of the way out.

Torrie stood helplessly in the bunker, dripping wet, her hair plastered to her like a second layer of skin. She looked pissed and defenseless. The paradox of this strong woman needing help was not lost on Grace. *It must be killing Torrie.*

"Do you need help?" Grace shouted above the rain.

"My shoulder. I—I don't think I can climb out on my own."

Grace dropped to her hands and knees at the edge of the bunker, oblivious to the muck, and reached her arm out. "Grab on." She dipped lower, reached further, until her body was fully supine on the wet ground.

"Grace, you don't have—"

"Grab on, dammit!" The rain was blurring her vision, but Torrie finally grabbed her hand and Grace pulled with all her strength. Torrie was bigger and heavier, but somehow they managed, and then it was Torrie pulling Grace up from the wet ground with her good arm.

"My God, you're a mess, Grace."

Torrie's eyes flicked briefly over Grace, who felt totally naked in her wet clothing she was sure left nothing to the imagination. She didn't want to look down at herself, at the clinging material that was propelling her cold, wet nipples forward like tree buds eager for spring blossoms. She wanted to run for the cart, cover herself with something, anything. Mercifully, Torrie did not stare at her like a starving animal, and instead took her elbow and led her quickly to the cart.

"I don't happen to have a change of clothes on me, but c'mon. There's a rain shelter at the next tee box."

Shivering, Grace stood under the wooden structure and pulled her arms around herself for warmth. Her teeth chattered with a mind of their own.

"I'm sorry about this, Grace."

"Not...your...fault," she managed between the shivers and the chattering teeth that were on overdrive.

"Jesus, I wish I'd brought an extra shirt or a jacket for you."

"S'okay, Torrie. I know...you want...to be chivalrous."

Torrie winced. "Guess I can't help that butch thing."

"Hey, Tor!" Muffled hollering penetrated the sound of the pounding rain as another golf cart appeared. The figure, swathed from head to foot in bright yellow rain gear, nevertheless sprinted for the rain shelter.

The woman was dark haired and blue-eyed, much like Torrie, only a bit shorter and more angular, as though a wood carver had forgotten to round out and smooth the edges. She was grinning widely.

"Shit, Tor. What are you doing out in this weather? Didn't you see it coming?"

"If I'd seen it coming, do you think I would have let us get caught in it?" But Torrie was grinning back, then both sets of nearly identical eyes landed on Grace.

"Grace, this is my caddie, who also happens to be my cousin, Catie. Catie, this is Grace Wellwood, chef extraordinaire and savior of this weekend's big dinner."

A wet hand shook hers. "Nice to meet you, Grace. By the way, I rarely answer to Catie, at least from the likes of this one." She jerked her head at Torrie. "It's usually Triple C, or sometimes just C. Covers all the bases that way." She winked teasingly, taking a playful punch in the arm from Torrie.

"I see," said Grace. "No pun intended, by the way."

Catie laughed but then her expression turned peculiar. She seemed to study Grace like an object she could pick up and turn round and round. Her eyes stayed a little too long on her chest, then shot back up to her face. "You look awfully familiar."

Grace shrugged, and then it struck her at the same moment Catie suddenly lit up like a Christmas tree. Grace's hand crawled up to her suddenly burning cheek. *Oh, Christ. It can't be.*

Catie grinned stupidly and clapped her hands together in delight. "So you're *that* Grace. Are you still a great kisser?"

Grace was sure the look of mortification on Torrie's face matched her own.

CHAPTER SIX

Torrie wiped the sweat from her forehead with her good hand. She'd remembered to put a sling on her injured side to keep her shoulder immobilized. If she couldn't golf, at least half a workout was better than sitting on her ass, being tempted by the solace of alcohol and the temptation to pine over the elusive, enigmatic Grace Wellwood.

Torrie's mind slid seamlessly to the scene Catie had made in the rain shelter hours ago, and she burned with questions. She remembered so vividly the look of horror on Grace's face, as Catie's stupid question hung in the air, heavy like a rain cloud that had somehow found its way inside the shelter. No one had said anything until Grace very firmly demanded to be taken back to the clubhouse, no matter how hard it was raining. Torrie ordered Catie to hand over her raincoat to Grace as some sort of penance, and she and Grace took off, silent for the entire ride. Grace clearly didn't want to talk about the incident, and it took all of Torrie's self-control not to pry. She was irrationally pissed that Grace and Catie had had some sort of mysterious encounter. She knew it wasn't her business, and yet she couldn't help but feel like she'd just had something stolen from her. How could

Catie possibly have gotten to first base with this smart, talented, sexy, sophisticated woman who seemed to take such pleasure in squashing Torrie's ego? Why on earth would Grace ever have permitted a dalliance with Catie, while treating her like some sort of sexual leper?

Sullenly engrossed in her bicep curl, she barely noticed Catie stroll through the gym's doors and halt in front of her.

"Hey," Catie said cautiously.

Torrie looked up with all the cheerfulness of a bear.

"Are you pissed at me, Tor?"

Torrie set the twenty-pound dumbbell down with a deliberate thud. She couldn't keep the annoyance out of her voice, and her question came out more as an accusation. "Do you have to sleep with every woman you meet?"

"Who said anything about sleeping with her? Jesus! And it's Grace Wellwood I assume we're talking about."

Torrie moved over on the bench to make room. They didn't look at one another.

"Anyway," Catie continued. "Since when do you have a moral issue with sleeping with someone you hardly know?"

Torrie picked up the dumbbell again. "Just forget it." She grunted her way through a few repetitions, then added peevishly, "It'd be a helluva lot more satisfying having this conversation over a drink."

"I'm behaving myself this week, since you decided to loan out my services to Eileen Kearney. Otherwise I'd be happy to get roaring drunk with you over a woman."

Torrie had generously agreed to allow Catie to caddie for another player. It wouldn't be fair to keep her from earning money just because Torrie wasn't fit to play. "The paycheck will keep you in wine and women a little longer. That should make you happy." Torrie knew she sounded judgmental and jealous, but she couldn't help herself. "And I never said I wanted to get drunk over a *woman*."

Catie refused to be baited and bumped shoulders with her affectionately. She'd learned over the years never to take Torrie too seriously when she was blowing off steam. "Look, I wouldn't have opened my big mouth this morning if I'd known you had a thing for her."

"I never said I had a *thing* for her. Jeez. You sound like we're back in high school or something."

Was that what Torrie's feelings for Grace amounted to? A high school crush? A meaningless infatuation meant to distract her from her pitiful life right now? A hollow, self-serving exercise, like all her other relationships had been? Torrie had little experience in matters involving her heart, but she knew Grace was different from the others. Or at least, her feelings for Grace seemed different—less defined and much more boundless than they'd been for anyone else. She hadn't been this excited about pursuing a woman in a very long time, and if she didn't entirely understand the reasons, it was enough to know that she was acting like a jealous teenager.

"Christ, aren't you in a mood."

Torrie reached for a lighter weight and began working her tricep. "Do you think? I've got a bitching, aching shoulder, I can't even swing a golf club for another month at least, and then I find out you had a thing with... All right, with someone I'm interested in. I'm sorry I'm not Miss Fucking Personality today."

Catie howled with laughter. "Well put, cousin."

"Emily Dickinson I'm not."

Catie picked up Torrie's water bottle from the floor and handed it to her. "Sorry. I know this week is tough for you, being here and not playing. And if you can't even get laid, then—"

"Piss off, C."

"All right, all right. Just kidding. So you're interested in her, huh?"

Torrie took a slug of water. "Look, are you going to tell me what happened between you two, or is it some mystery you're taking to the grave?"

"What?"

"This thing you had with Grace."

"I wouldn't exactly call it a *thing*."

"You kissed her, though."

"Yeah, I did. I mean, *we* did." Torrie looked at Catie and wished she hadn't. Catie, *the bitch*, was grinning as though she'd just cleaned out Fort Knox. "Damn, it was good. The kiss. I still remember it. Anyway, I was staying with Aunt Connie on the island. It was six years ago. I think it was a couple of summers after we'd graduated from college. It was your sophomore year on the tour, but you were taking time off to work on your swing, remember?"

"Yeah, I remember." *Torrie sighed. Fuck, I wish I'd gone to Sheridan Island with Catie. Then it might have been me kissing Grace. And maybe Grace would have been game for it back then. Unlike now.*

"I told you about this a long time ago, Tor."

Torrie searched her memory. There were so many sexual adventures on both their parts over the years, she could barely keep track of her own, never mind Catie's. "I don't remember, okay? It's not like I keep a journal of all your little escapades or something. Besides, if I did, I'd have constant writer's cramp."

"Oh, so now you're calling *me* a slut?"

Torrie grimaced. "Relax. Can't you take a joke?" The faint memory of a long ago conversation began to surface. "Was that the summer you had some wild weekend fling with a straight woman or something?"

"Who was about to get married," Catie finished. "Yeah, that was it." She shook her head and smiled again. "You know, Tor, those straight ones are sometimes the most uninhibited in bed."

Torrie clenched her fists at the dawning realization, feeling a little sick inside. *Grace. And Catie. Grace and Catie, getting it on.* "So you did sleep with Grace!" She shuddered at the visions that came unbidden. Anger flared with surprising intensity.

"No, no! Not Grace!"

"What?"

"Grace was just there with her friend, Trish something-or-other. They're both chefs. And older." Her eyes took on a fresh gleam. "I like the cougars, you know? They're so fucking hot, and they always know exactly what they want."

"Christ, would you just get on with it?"

Catie gave a dramatic sigh. "All right, already. This Trish was the one I had the fling with. I guess she was looking for an exotic dish before she settled down for a life of meat and potatoes." Catie giggled. "Yeah, she wanted to try some sushi."

"You're such a pig, C. I can't believe we're related."

"What? Are you the Queen of England now?"

Catie had changed little from their high school and college years of smoking dope, drinking beer and sleeping around. Torrie had managed to tone down her own proclivities, mostly because she'd begun to grow bored with the scene. Especially lately. Somewhere along the line, sex for her had gone from being a prolific hobby to a habit she'd periodically continued more out of boredom than anything. It just didn't hold the same appeal anymore…until now. "Yeah, that's me. Queen Torrie. And you're my lady-in-waiting."

Catie cackled, stood and curtsied.

"Sit down, you clown," Torrie whispered. "Somebody will see you."

"Do you want to know about the kiss or not?"

"Yes, I want to know. Why else would I be putting up with you right now?"

"So. In between all this crazy sex with her friend, I snuck downstairs to grab a beer out of the fridge and Grace was in the kitchen, a little drunk and looking like a frigging goddess in a skimpy tank top and tight little cutoffs. Man, she was a sight."

Yeah, Torrie thought dreamily. *She would look like a goddess.*

"And we just, I don't know, fell into this amazing kiss up against the fridge that went on forever. Well, not forever. Just until Trish went looking for me and found us in a lip-lock." She sighed ruefully. "It was a shame they didn't want to go for a threesome."

"And that was it? The end of it?"

"Yeah, pretty much. Trish thought it was somehow incestuous and kicked me out. Then they were gone the next day. To tell you the truth, I'd pretty much forgotten about the whole thing until

I saw Grace again."

"Huh," was all Torrie could manage. She couldn't quite wrap her mind around the idea of Grace behaving so recklessly. It was something Torrie would do, but surely not Grace. She'd been drunk, however, and it wasn't like Catie and Trish were in a relationship. *And it was just a stupid kiss, after all.* She told herself it was nothing. Except it didn't feel like nothing.

She thought about kissing Grace and wondered how different it would feel, how unlike all the other kisses with women it would be.

Torrie awkwardly cradled the half-dozen, long-stemmed white roses and bottle of expensive brandy in the crook of her bad arm and knocked with her good one. She should have done it the other way around, she scolded herself, juggling the items and feeling abnormally clumsy.

She was such an amateur at this courting stuff, and she knew it showed. She was awkward and probably looked worse. Maybe she could blame it on her injury, on her state of mind at wanting so badly to be able to play and defend her title this week. She was out of sorts, for sure, and not the least bit because she was so intrigued by this woman who clearly had no interest in her sexually.

The door swung open and Grace, slack-jawed with surprise, stood frozen in her cotton pajamas dotted with bright bouquets of balloons, her hair pulled back into a bouncy ponytail. She looked as Torrie imagined she must have looked as a teenager, all cute and cuddly and innocent.

"Nice," Torrie said, her eyes sliding up and down Grace.

Grace flushed before her expression hardened.

"Your pajamas," Torrie quickly clarified. "I…" She glanced down at the flowers and brandy that were beginning to slide out of their tenuous hold. Grace reached out and deftly rescued them. "Thanks, Grace. You just saved me from embarrassment."

"Not to mention a stained rug. Are these for me?"

Torrie leaned lazily against the doorframe and tried to act

cool. "Actually, I thought I'd make a trail of rose petals from your room to mine and see if you'd follow."

"Hmm. I see. And the brandy?"

"To show you what would be waiting for you at the other end." Torrie gave her a sly wink, determined to play out the role of seductress that she'd so firmly cast herself in. She would keep trying and Grace would keep saying no, and they'd go around and around in this little dance until maybe, just maybe, Torrie would finally wear Grace down.

Grace laughed, much to Torrie's relief. "Oh, no, Torrie Cannon. You're not getting me into your room, no matter what's waiting there for me."

"How about a drink with me here, then?" Torrie offered shamelessly.

Grace beckoned her in with a nod and an amused smile. "You don't give up, do you?"

"Do you want me to?" *Please don't say yes.*

"C'mon," said Grace, disappearing for a moment with the flowers and returning with two small glasses. It was not lost on Torrie that she hadn't said no.

She poured them a drink and they sat on the sofa, Grace tucking her legs up under her.

"Actually, Grace," Torrie said, perfectly serious. "I wanted to thank you for saving my life today."

"Saving you from being stranded like a wet dog in that sand bunker hardly qualifies as saving your life."

Torrie sipped the brandy and grinned at Grace. "I could have been there for hours while the hole slowly filled up with water. I could have drowned! Think of the nasty headlines that would have made. *Pro golfer drowns while celebrity chef looks on.*"

"You've got quite the imagination. You didn't set the whole thing up on purpose, did you?" Grace teased.

"Yeah," Torrie answered, deadpan. "Seeing girlie-girls in wet T-shirts doing chivalrous things is always worth risking my life for."

Grace began to blush like a schoolgirl, and Torrie wanted

to giggle and kiss her madly. But she apologized half-heartedly instead, watching Grace contemplatively sip her drink. It began to occur to her that maybe she'd gone too far with the wet T-shirt comment as the silence between them grew. She was always pushing the boundaries with Grace it seemed, always trying to elicit a reaction, see where it got her. She couldn't quite help herself.

"What makes you think I'm a girlie-girl?" Grace muttered quizzically, looking distinctly insulted.

"Would you feel better if I called you a little butch?"

Silence again. A cryptic look from Grace. *God. She could be so hard to figure out sometimes.* Torrie swallowed against sudden panic. "You're not straight, are you?" *Oh, God, no, not that!*

Grace made her sweat it out for an agonizing minute before she broke out into a slow, self-satisfied grin. "I've been with women since I was eighteen."

Relief extended all the way down to Torrie's toes. "Good. I mean, I thought so."

"Why, because I kissed your cousin?"

"Hell, no. Catie would kiss anyone."

Grace shifted uncomfortably. "I wouldn't, you know."

"What?"

"Kiss anyone." She looked embarrassed and totally ingenuous. "I don't know what possessed me to kiss her like that at Trish's cottage. It was stupid. I was just—"

"Grace. You don't need to explain anything to me. Especially something that happened six years ago. I know nothing happened between you and Catie."

"I don't mean to imply that I'm some sort of vestal virgin, you know."

"I know." Torrie smiled. Everyone had a past. But she did not feel threatened by anything Grace might have done. And she was no longer jealous of a silly kiss. Well, maybe a little, but only a little. She was secretly pleased that Grace felt the need to explain.

"So if Connie Sparks is Catie's aunt, I guess she's yours too, by extension?"

"Yeah. Poor Aunt Connie. I'm sure we gave her many conniptions over the years."

Grace shook her head lightly. "I'm sure she loved every minute of it. She seems like a wonderful woman."

"She is," Torrie said reverently. "You've met her?"

"Yes." Grace sipped her drink, casting a quick glance at a stack of books on a nearby table. "Crap. The menu. We keep forgetting."

Ah, yes, that damned menu that Torrie could care less about right now. But anything for an excuse to lengthen their time together.

"Have you any ideas?" Grace prodded.

Now there was an opening for a come-on, maybe even an intentional one on Grace's part, Torrie thought hopefully, but she resisted the bait. "Not really. My mother had a few, but damned if I can remember any of them. How about something with meat and potatoes?" Torrie cringed, remembering Catie comparing a straight marriage to meat and potatoes. "Or fish?" she offered slyly.

Grace strode to the table and picked up a piece of paper. She reached for a pair of half-moon reading glasses that Torrie thought looked incredibly adorable on her. Everything about Grace struck her as adorable, which was new for Torrie. Women were either hot or they were not, and Grace certainly made the temperature needle skyrocket. But adorable? She hadn't thought anything adorable since her childhood teddy bear.

"What do you say to chicken cacciatore, grilled salmon marinated in a creamy lemon dill sauce, rosemary and garlic roast potatoes, a vegetable mélange and a garden salad with vinaigrette?"

Talk about food had never made Torrie want to kiss a woman, but it did now. "That sounds incredible!"

Grace tossed her glasses onto the table. "Ooh, and the best part is dessert." Her eyes flashed with excitement, and it was easy to see that food was her passion.

"Now you're talking." Torrie settled back on the sofa, her legs apart, and tried to expunge the very real fantasy of Grace leaping onto her lap and happily settling there, her arms naturally slipping around Torrie's neck. "Go on," she rasped, her voice deserting her, the vision of Grace as her lover, of Grace capitulating, firmly entrenching itself.

"That fourth hole we nearly drowned on today inspired me." Grace leaned against the table, arms crossed over her chest, and grinned with enthusiasm. She couldn't possibly have a clue what Torrie's mind was fixed on.

Torrie extracted herself from thoughts of Grace lying beneath her, of Grace reaching up to her with her mouth. "What? Mud pie? Some kind of sponge cake drowning in sauce?"

Grace winked. "I'll just have to make it a surprise."

Torrie finished her drink. It was later than she thought, and Grace was yawning now. She wanted to stay and talk, get to know Grace better, to thrust and parry with her some more. But it was only Tuesday night and she had the rest of the week and into the weekend to get Grace into her bed. The chase, she reminded herself, or at least the chase with this woman, was to be savored. She stood and let Grace walk her to the door.

"I guess I'm going to be awfully busy the next few days getting ready for Sunday's dinner." Grace almost sounded like she was apologizing, for which Torrie was ridiculously grateful.

"If there's anything you need…"

"Thanks."

Hand on the doorknob, Torrie turned around, suddenly uncharacteristically contrite. Guilt and shame tugged at her for the way she was treating this highly accomplished woman. "Grace…" She was embarrassed for once, and it was a feeling she never thought would apply to her, at least not where women were concerned. She was a wealthy, professional athlete who was above recrimination…wasn't she? She'd always been excused before. And yet, here she was, in another woman's room, feeling like a spoiled, rude little shit. *You're taking it too far, Torrie, acting like an immature, infatuated asshole.* She just didn't quite know how *not* to act like a jerk around Grace. She liked Grace. A lot. But she was like a bad little kid constantly acting up in front of the teacher, even when she knew it was going to result in a crack across the knuckles.

"Yes, Torrie?"

Torrie mentally stumbled. Grace was a classy woman. She deserved better than what she was getting from Torrie. "I… I'm not normally quite this…" *Fuck, why does this woman make me feel like I can't even form a coherent sentence?*

Grace leaned patiently against the wall, looking slightly amused. "Like what?"

Torrie took a deep breath. "Like such a predatory, rude, selfish, sex-crazed idiot."

Dimples formed around Grace's rather victorious smile, as if she'd been waiting the whole time for Torrie's admission. "You're not?"

Torrie shook her head lamely.

"You have quite a way with words, you know."

"So I've been told."

Grace's smile faded. She paused a few beats, never taking her eyes off Torrie. "Believe it or not, Torrie, I find you very charming. And fun. And your honesty is damn refreshing. Frankly, I've had my fill of pretenses and…" Grace's voice trailed off and her eyes looked unmistakably sad. "Lies."

Torrie swallowed and croaked like a boy whose voice was changing. "Then you don't think I'm a total horse's ass?"

"No. And you needn't have given me this little speech, you know. I already had you pegged as more bark than bite." She raised a teasing eyebrow, and arousal, like a bolt of electricity, shot all the way down Torrie's legs.

"Just be careful not to throw down the gauntlet," Torrie whispered before walking out.

CHAPTER SEVEN

Grace dumped another cup of sugar into the vat of chocolate cake batter and watched it swirl and disappear into the dark folds. She felt much like the batter—at the whim of the mechanical whisk, surrendering to it, folding into itself. There were quiet moments, like this, when she thought of Aly and felt the loss of something that had become so familiar—something she'd come to rely on and to make part of her existence—even if she hadn't been particularly happy or fulfilled. Aly had been habit-forming, and breaking a habit that wasn't good for you didn't necessarily mean it was easy. Grace was like a kite, its string cut—still there, but without direction.

Memories blurred and skidded through her mind, many of them good ones. Peeling onions together in Aly's apartment for an impromptu dinner, their eyes watering like crazy, reading to one another over breakfast from competing newspapers, playing footsies under the table, snuggling together in the soft sheets that would later be wrinkled and damp from lovemaking.

Were those little moments really the sum of their three years together? Because that's all they really were, just moments, Grace thought sadly. It's not like they'd ever shared dreams together, embarked on joint projects, planned vacations together, split the bills, shopped for groceries, opened a joint bank account, accompanied one another to family dinners. Surely those things were the true building blocks of a relationship. What they'd had was pathetic. Like chasing a shadow and never catching it.

"Is this the secret dessert you're working on?"

Grace jumped. She hadn't heard Torrie come up behind her, having long ago tuned out the constant background noise of the large hotel kitchen. Doors swinging open, a dropped utensil, the scraping of bowls, the whirring of appliances, murmured or even boisterous conversations, orders being yelled out. Grace was so used to it all that it hardly registered.

"Sorry, did I startle you?"

Grace, mercifully wrenched from her self-pity, smiled over her shoulder. "No, I'm fine."

Torrie reached around and stuck a finger in the giant bowl. She popped it into her mouth before Grace could swat it away. "Mmmm, yum! I love cake batter. It is a cake you're making, right?"

Grace kept quiet, wanting to keep Torrie guessing, and stuck her own finger in for a quick taste. There was definitely enough sugar, but it needed another splash of vanilla, and a healthy dash of her secret ingredient—rose water. "Could be, Torrie. Or maybe I'm making three hundred mini cupcakes."

"Hmm, you're really not going to tell me, are you?"

Grace switched the machine off. "Nope."

"But I was with you when you got inspired. Doesn't that count for something?"

"Umm, let me think. No."

Torrie gave her a pout, and Grace stepped backward at the rush of sudden desire to kiss those full, down-turned lips. Her eyes fixed on Torrie's mouth and she had to blink to clear her thoughts. She hadn't wanted to kiss a woman other than Aly in years, and it shocked her a little. *Jesus, don't tell me I'm actually starting to fall for her act. Pull-ease!*

"You sure know how to hurt a girl's feelings. Can I bribe you?"

Grace shook her head, crossing her arms over her chest to keep distance between them. For the first time, she was wary of being so close to Torrie. She was both bothered and intrigued by the physical reaction Torrie's presence now stirred in her. It was like all her senses were suddenly becoming keenly sharp around Torrie, like she was stepping from a room that was black and white into one full of vibrant colors. It scared the hell out of her. She didn't even know when it had started. *Was it moments ago? Yesterday on the rainy course? Last night in my hotel room?* But it had started, the way dawn could sneak up when you still thought it was night.

"How about I threaten it out of you?"

"Ahh, so you're going to beat me with your one good arm, is that it?"

Torrie's laugh was devilish. "I never said I was going to threaten you with physical harm." She dipped her finger into the batter again, and her eyes were provocative, challenging Grace. Her tongue swirled slowly and seductively around her finger. Her meaning couldn't be more clear if she'd hit Grace over the head with one of the frying pans hanging overhead.

Grace backed up another step, her breath heavy in her chest. Sweat prickled under her arms. *Oh, God.* This flirting was getting way too intense, affecting her too much, making her hot. Maybe it was because Aly was gradually receding from her every day, like the tide inching out. Or maybe it was just her body's way of rejecting celibacy. Grace just knew that her body was beginning to react powerfully to Torrie, and more than that, she was beginning to feel an affection for her. And she didn't want to. *I can't feel something for her right now, for any woman. Please, no!*

Torrie tensed a little, looking worried. "Is everything okay, Grace?"

"Torrie, I—" *I want you to leave me alone. Except I don't, because I'm lonely as hell, and you're sweet and young and beautiful, and you*

76

make me feel alive and desirable again. "I, I just can't be—"

"Look," Torrie interrupted, looking crestfallen but trying to cover it with a cavalier shrug and a cool smile. "I should probably get back out on the course. See how things are going."

Torrie was halfway across the kitchen before she gave Grace a quick wave good-bye.

It wasn't hard keeping her self-imposed distance from Torrie. Grace didn't see her the rest of that day or the following day. Her duties kept her incredibly busy, for which she was grateful. Two nights now she'd dropped into bed just before midnight, exhausted. Every plan, right down to the place settings, had been mapped out, circulated, discussed and rehearsed with the staff. The massive amount of food had all been purchased, tasks assigned. There'd been some problems too—a freezer on the blink, a chef who'd come down with the flu. It was just two days before Sunday's big event and things were coming together, with James arriving tomorrow morning and Trish right behind him. The three were to meet later Saturday with corporate sponsors and Tour officials. They had even scheduled a local radio show.

For now, there was still work to be done. There was a numbers discrepancy for Sunday's dinner between the hotel and the tournament director. Having just sorted out what felt like her hundredth little problem in the clubhouse, Grace lingered near the eighteenth hole and watched the golfers within chipping distance of the green. They looked so calm, well-groomed, focused and professional. They made their shots with a precision that looked easy. They'd slump a little when they missed and give a quick fist pump when they made it. There was always a cheerful wave to the crowd afterward.

Grace had never been a big fan of golf. She'd played the game enough times to realize how difficult it was, but she had never developed a taste for it. She knew how Torrie must feel about it though, if it was anything like her own passion for food and its preparation. She'd picked up a golf magazine in the clubhouse. There were pictures of Torrie in it, where she alternately looked intense, driven, ecstatic, joyful, disappointed or aggravated. But always passionate. Sexy too. Grace had traced a finger around Torrie's image in one of the photos, admiring her strong physique, her handsome features, her triumphant smile. She'd stuck the magazine in her briefcase, not really sure why she wanted to keep it, just that she did. Maybe it was because, even though she didn't want to think about Torrie Cannon right now, she might one day. Perhaps when her heart thawed. Or maybe when she just needed a flattering memory to lift her spirits, like during her upcoming fortieth birthday. It wasn't such a bad thing that a young, good-looking, independently wealthy young woman found her sexually attractive. It was exhilarating, actually, and Torrie could so easily trip Grace's sexual responders—if she were to let her. *But I won't because I have everything under control.*

Grace drove her power cart along the paved path in the direction of the hotel. At the practice green, she noticed Torrie at the same time Torrie saw her. Her cheeks burned as though Torrie might somehow know she'd been studying pictures of her.

Torrie leapt to the edge of the path, her thumb out, and Grace laughed at the hitchhiking act.

"Care to give a lost golfer a lift back to the hotel so I can meet my agent on time?"

Grace narrowed her eyes playfully. "My mother always told me hitchhikers are dangerous."

"Who, me? Why, I'm as harmless as a little kitten."

"Yeah, right!" Grace laughed, happy that she wasn't as uncomfortable around Torrie as she had been in the kitchen the other day. It's just that Torrie had stood so close to her then, and when she'd licked her finger so seductively, Grace had nearly fainted from shock and unwanted desire. She settled back in her seat. "C'mon aboard. I think I can handle you, even if you are more of a leopard than a kitten."

Torrie slid in next to Grace, the space so small that their shoulders touched. "You're a tough little chef. I don't imagine there's much that scares you."

It was true, there wasn't, but she'd certainly become scared of the person she'd become with Aly, sneaking around, cheating herself out of much more than she deserved. Being untrue to herself. Those were the kinds of things that scared her.

"How's it going, anyway?" Torrie asked.

"Busy." Grace put the cart into gear and drove off.

"Guess that explains why I haven't seen you around. Can I help? I mean, I am supposed to be your official helper or something, aren't I?"

"Can you cook?" Grace asked, not meaning it.

"Probably about as well as you play golf."

"Hey! How do you know I'm not some ace golfer in my spare time?"

"Oh, yeah? What spare time? You look like you don't have much of that."

Grace winced. Did she look that tired and overworked? That intense? "It shows, huh?"

"No, no, not at all." Torrie quickly tried to make up for her gaffe. "It's just, you know, you're everywhere on that food channel and in those magazines in the grocery stores."

Resigned, Grace sighed. "You're right. I don't have a lot of spare time and I'm no golfer." An idea popped into her mind. A sweet, vengeful little idea. "But I do know a way you could help."

Torrie looked innocently hopeful. She could be so eager sometimes. "Sure, anything."

Oh, yeah, this was going to be sweet. "There's a shipment of flowers coming tomorrow. I need someone to arrange them into displays for each table. You look like you'd be perfect for the job!"

Torrie's reaction was predictably hilarious. She paled and began helplessly stuttering. "I—I. Are you...Jesus, Grace. Do these hands look like they were made for flower arranging?"

Grace laughed so hard she had to pull the cart over as the convulsions racked her body. She pictured Torrie fumbling with long-stemmed roses and baby's breath, and the laughter started all over again.

"Jeez, Grace, it's not that funny."

"Oh, yes it is, believe me."

"Sorry, but I'll just have to help another way. Turn around for a minute."

Grace hesitated for only a moment before she did as she was told.

"You don't fool me with your joking around. You're very tight."

Torrie's hands found Grace's neck and shoulders. Strong, capable fingers began to knead her stiff muscles, and Grace slowly began to melt. Every stroke relaxed her another notch and her eyes began to slip shut. *Oh, God.* She needed this. Torrie's touch was magical. Soothing too. She wanted to moan but didn't dare. "Torrie, I'm going to fall asleep right here if you don't stop."

Torrie didn't stop. She spoke softly into Grace's ear. "How about a drink with me later tonight and more of this?"

Grace sat up straighter and turned around, effectively halting Torrie's massage. "Are you crazy? A drink and more of this would leave this tough little chef a quivering, whimpering little fool."

Torrie grinned victoriously.

"Stop it," Grace said. She put the cart into gear again. "You're already imagining what that would look like, aren't you?"

Torrie didn't say anything, just kept grinning while Grace drove. She pulled the cart up to the hotel, and Torrie looked at her with only a trace of the smart-ass attitude this time. "I'm not giving up on you, Grace."

A tickle formed in her stomach at the little thrill Torrie's desire gave her. Nothing would happen, no matter how persistent Torrie remained, and so it was safe to soak up a little of Torrie's hunger for her.

Almost a shame, though. There was something very sweet and enchanting about Torrie Cannon.

"Grace, darling." James Easton strolled up to her, looking impeccable in his pressed slacks, Italian leather loafers and Hugo

Boss shirt. He gave her a quick hug, careful not to wrinkle his clothes.

In the clubhouse, they caught up over a quick lunch of tuna melts, and James, his smile suggestive, whispered to Grace, "Haven't any of these gorgeous women run off with you yet?"

"Please." Grace frowned.

"Or at least propositioned you, I hope."

A moment of panic. Was it that transparent that Torrie had been hitting on her? "James, I'm far too busy for any of that."

He looked around with disappointment. "More gorgeous women around here than men, that's for sure."

"Well, it is a women's tournament, James."

"Pity."

Grace glanced at her watch. "When does Trish arrive?"

"A couple of hours. Oh, did I mention the book signing tonight?"

"What?"

James's mind never strayed from business for long. "After dinner, at a Hartford bookstore. It'll only take an hour, two at the most."

Grace groaned. "Jeez, you're killing me, James."

"Relax," he said, waving a hand like it was no big deal. "It'll be fun. When it's over, the three of us can settle in for a couple of drinks and some girl talk. After all, you've got the rest of the summer to sit on that cute little butt of yours."

Torrie sipped her second martini, wishing for Catie's sake that the alcohol would magically turn her into better company. She could have kept her misery to herself by just hanging out in her room, or she could have gone trolling in a lesbian bar in the city, but both prospects, for different reasons, had appealed to her for all of about twenty seconds. Still, she didn't feel like being alone, so she foisted herself on Catie in the hotel bar and sipped her drink a little too vigorously.

Catie, for all her faults, was trying to cheer her up. She was trying not to talk much about the tournament—the gossip, the hole-by-hole replays. Her player, Eileen Kearney, was in sixth place heading into tomorrow's final round, and Catie was pumped about their prospects, even as she tried to minimize her enthusiasm for Torrie's sake.

Torrie reached across the table and covered Catie's hand briefly in apology. "I know I'm being a drag, C. You really don't have to sit here and babysit me."

"Hey. I know it's tough being here and not being able to play. Hell, you know I'd rather be on your bag right now than anyone else's."

"I know. Thanks." She knew Catie and her friends on the Tour understood how hard this week was for her. But she tried not to say much about it for their sakes, tried to keep her distance. She didn't want to be the downer—the self-absorbed, self-pitying suck—because they had their work to concentrate on. More than that, she knew what it was like to be one of the healthy ones and have a colleague go down. It was almost bad luck to be around the injured too much or to talk about it much, as if the injury could be contagious and you might join them on the heap of the broken.

She went back to her drink, glancing around the half-empty room. Most of the golfers had retired early, the bar patrons mostly strangers. Tomorrow night, after the final round, everyone would party, Torrie knew. But with another day's competition to go, there was still much on the line. The athletes took seriously their rest, their food intake, their routines. Even Catie was behaving herself, nursing the same beer for nearly an hour now. But Torrie had no intention of behaving. Getting a good buzz was the only comfort she could think of right now.

"Hey." Catie nudged her. "Check out the babe at three o'clock."

Torrie gave an obligatory glance, not interested in this little game they'd played many times before. Sometimes they'd rate a woman, debate her physical attributes, guess whether she was gay or straight before finally deciding it didn't matter, that she was hot and deserved a good orgasm—compliments of one of them, of course. They'd try to shock and awe one another with outlandish stories of how they'd seduce their prey and how'd they'd satisfy her. Sometimes they'd even make a contest out of who could get to her first. It was stupid and sick and juvenile, and Torrie knew she would never do it again. Even now, she couldn't believe she'd ever been like that. It was strange, this feeling lately of stepping outside of herself, of seeing herself in a new light. Maybe it was because she had all this time off from golf to think about things, to notice other things. Hell, maybe it was even because of meeting Grace and getting to know the highly successful, talented woman who really didn't give a shit that Torrie was some hotshot pro golfer who could have anyone or anything she wanted.

There was distinct disapproval in Catie's expression. "Jesus, Torrie. If I didn't know you better, I'd say you've got a giant hard-on for Grace Wellwood."

Torrie didn't want to talk about Grace, at least not that way. Her growing feelings and attraction for Grace were incredibly private. They were to be protected from being some sort of fodder for Catie or anyone else to joke about, to minimize as though they weren't important to Torrie. Grace was special and Torrie wanted to keep that knowledge to herself.

"Forget it, C."

"Look, if you're not fucking her, and clearly you're not or you wouldn't be this miserable—"

"C, I mean it. There's nothing to talk about."

"Exactly. Which is why you're so miserable." Catie's tone softened from accusatory to conciliatory. "All right. It's not just the tournament that's got you down, is it?"

Torrie downed the last of her martini and signaled for another. She wanted to get shit-faced. Forget the pain in her shoulder, forget the disappointment of not playing, forget, at least for a couple of hours, that she'd ever met this unattainable woman who'd somehow so quickly made her forget the person she thought she was.

"What is it about her, Tor?" Catie said it so quietly and yet the words nearly crushed Torrie.

She had the bizarre feeling of not being able to breathe for a moment. "God. I don't know. She just..." Torrie strained to find the right word. "Matters." Yes, that was it. *Grace matters to me.* And not in the way Grace first mattered to her, in the strictly sexual wanting of her. Their sporadic togetherness had dulled Torrie's sexual urgency a little, but at the same time enhanced her feelings for Grace. She missed Grace. She missed talking to her, having fun with her, just being around her.

"Huh? What do you mean *matters?* Matters like whether your steak is a little bit overcooked, or matters like winning a tournament?"

Catie clearly had no clue. Torrie shook her head, willing the subject to drop. She'd already said too much. Her third drink arrived and she sipped it gratefully. She could not expect Catie to understand, just as Torrie would not have understood if it weren't happening to her. Whatever *it* was, exactly.

"Do you ever get tired of it?" Torrie suddenly blurted out. She didn't often have meaningful discussions with Catie, even though they were like sisters. But now she had an overwhelming need for Catie to answer her seriously.

Catie looked at Torrie like she'd just sprouted a third eyeball. "What the hell are you talking about now?"

Torrie nodded at the woman across the room Catie had been making eyes at. "That."

"Hell, are you kidding me?"

"No. I'm not."

Catie looked quizzically at her again. "Are you going straight on me or something? Did you fall on your goddamned head?"

Torrie laughed shortly. "No to both, ya moron. I just mean... you know."

"No, I don't, actually."

Torrie sighed. "Never mind." Catie would probably always remain unapologetically promiscuous. She had expected as much of herself at one time, but not anymore. *Christ, maybe I'm just getting old. Or finally growing up.*

Catie stood, probably out of patience for Torrie's melancholy. "I should turn in, Tor. Long day tomorrow." She leaned down and kissed Torrie's cheek affectionately, and then she was gone. It would be just like Catie to run as soon as a conversation about a woman turned serious, Torrie decided.

Maybe what she needed was to talk to Diana Gravatti, her best friend on the Tour. Diana would understand how Torrie's world was rapidly shifting off its axis. How Grace made her feel special, like she was no longer just the stereotypical professional athlete—self-absorbed, one-dimensional and cashing in on every sexual opportunity that came along. With Grace, there was so much more that mattered. Or that should matter. Being around her was like that perfect moment when a wave swells to its highest peak, right before it breaks and collapses into itself.

Shit. What was she thinking? Diana was in contention tomorrow and didn't need the distraction of a soul-searching, heart-to-heart. There was also the fact that Diana, who'd been with her partner for nearly ten years, would probably start sending out engagement announcements upon any talk of Torrie being truly interested in a woman. Diana tended to think everyone should be with someone—that being single was terribly ungratifying.

Torrie sipped her drink, the alcohol beginning to fray the edges of her thoughts, rounding them so that one rolled into another. She didn't normally drink alone, but tonight she would drink, no matter what. And she would feel alone too, no matter whose company she was in, because no one could possibly understand her right now.

When she looked up she instantly sobered. Grace was being shown to a table along with another woman and a very effeminate guy. The three looked like they knew each other very well—their laughter spontaneous, their hands easily resting on one another's arm or shoulder. Joy and friendship was seamless and genuine. Torrie was immediately envious of the intimacy the two strangers had with Grace.

Briefly, Torrie considered sneaking out without saying hello.

Downing her drink, she covertly watched Grace and grew braver. She could no longer deny the acute need to go and talk to her, to share a laugh if she could think of something witty to say, to look into those rainwater eyes and feel helpless for a moment. That was intoxicating, not the vodka.

Torrie stood, feeling a little wobbly. When she arrived at their table, three pairs of intently curious eyes turned to her.

"Hi," Torrie said, looking only at Grace, her thumbs slung loosely through the belt loops of her black jeans.

"Hi," Grace answered, clearly surprised, but she looked pleased.

"I see you're finally enjoying a night off." Torrie gestured at the glass of wine in front of Grace, wishing it were just the two of them, sharing a bottle over the little lace-covered table with the small, flickering candle in the middle of it. "A well-deserved one, I might add."

"Maybe you should wait until tomorrow's dinner before you decide I've deserved the rest." But Grace was smiling.

The woman across from Grace cleared her throat, offered her hand. "Since our friend is being so rude, let me introduce myself. I'm Trish Wilson, Grace's partner."

Torrie shook the proffered hand, gave a little start at the word *partner*, then remembered the two were in business together. She sure hoped Grace didn't have another kind of partner.

"I'm sorry, guys." Grace touched her forehead in a gesture of apology. "This is Torrie Cannon, the tournament's host. And this is James Easton, our manager."

His handshake was as warm and inquisitive as his smile.

"Join us?" Trish said, meaning it as far as Torrie could tell. She was cute with short, curly dark hair and big brown eyes. A face that was pretty in an open, convivial way. Trish Wilson was uncomplicated, Torrie decided. She could see why Catie had gone for her all those years ago.

Torrie's eyes trapped Grace's and there was uncertainty in them. "I don't think so, thanks. Long day tomorrow. For you, anyway."

Trish looked from Torrie to Grace, and Torrie knew instantly that Trish had very quickly added up the emotional math and deduced that there was something between them.

"You're welcome to, Torrie," Grace added, and Torrie nearly agreed. But Grace was with her friends, and Torrie didn't want to intrude. She only wanted to be alone with Grace, and since that wasn't going to happen, she'd rather just be alone. She politely declined again.

"Tomorrow," Trish said. "You'll come by the kitchen and be our taste tester, won't you?"

Torrie beamed. "I'd love to."

They watched Torrie walk away. James and Trish exchanged a look as Grace ominously swirled the red wine in her glass. No one said anything until James broke the silence with a low whistle.

"I thought you said there were no prospects here, girlfriend!"

"I never said any such thing. I said I didn't have time for that kind of stuff." Grace drove home her point with a "drop it" glare, which James promptly ignored.

"I think that woman would give anything if you made a little time for her." He winked and leaned in. "She looks like an all-nighter to me."

Wine sloshed over the rim of Grace's glass. "James! Jesus."

There was a trace of a giggle in Trish's voice. "She did look at you like she wanted to throw you over her shoulder, march you off to her cave and ravish you all night long."

Grace gave them a surly look, even as the titillating fantasy flickered briefly in her mind. Maybe an all-night romp with Torrie was exactly what she needed right now. It would be fleeting, but fleeting had its upside.

"I just... I haven't..." Grace gave up trying to explain. Hot, mindless sex was about the last thing she wanted in her life right now, and yet... If she were going to fall into a transient affair again, Torrie would certainly be a delicious choice. She couldn't deny the appeal of it. *But Jesus. I am not going down that road again.*

Trish's smile was sympathetic. "The only point we're trying to make is that there is life after Aly O'Donnell."

"I know that, Trish. I just don't know that I'm ready. And I certainly don't want to replace Aly with a carbon copy of her."

James sighed woefully. "You girls take sex far too seriously."

"Not always," Grace countered, looking pointedly at Trish, mischief in her voice. "You'll never guess who Torrie's cousin is."

Trish looked bored. "Let me guess, Angelina Jolie?"

Grace chuckled. "As a matter of fact, it's someone you know."

James squirmed excitedly. "In the Biblical sense?"

Grace shrugged coyly and watched Trish grow annoyed. "As a matter of fact—"

"Oh, stop! Just tell me already!"

"Does the name Catie Sparks ring a bell?"

Trish tapped bright red fingernails on the table and shook her head impatiently. "Grace, you know I suck at names."

"Okay, how about this." Grace was enjoying herself. "Sheridan Island. That weekend six years ago, right before you married Scott."

Trish's eyes grew bigger, if that were possible, and her fingers stilled. "No!"

"And the best part is she's here."

"Get out!"

"What am I missing here, girls?"

Grace began to giggle so hard, the table shook. "Let's just say someone from Trish's past has come back to haunt her."

James rubbed his hands together gleefully. "Oh, goodie. I love soap operas."

Trish looked like she wanted to crawl under the table. She downed her drink in one gulp.

CHAPTER EIGHT

"C'mon, Grace, get on out there and enjoy yourself." Trish was half begging, half ordering.

Grace was only too happy to stay in her comfortable world of stainless steel and frenzied cooks who pushed food along as though on an assembly line, dishing up the chicken cacciatore and grilled salmon, the potatoes and vegetables, for the servers to deliver. Voices called out over the din for more of this or that, for something to be warmed up, for more wine. A vegetarian request had been misplaced. Something else was overcooked. It was a frenetic pace and Grace enjoyed it, because as hectic and disorderly as it might seem to an outsider, it actually followed a script, like a stage show. And Grace was the director, the commander who had pulled it all together, starting with her own vision. Now she watched with a critical eye as others carried it out.

Her gaze never left the steady stream of plates being wheeled out, or the bodies that dashed about with purpose. "Keep it going, guys. We're almost there." She called more encouragements, then turned to Trish. "Trish, really, I'd rather make sure—"

"Nonsense. Everything is going perfectly. You've done a ton

of work already. Let me handle the rest."

Grace frowned down at her stained white smock and rumpled checkered pants. "Look at me, Trish. I'm not going out there like—"

"Of course not." Trish brightened, looking smug. "That's why I brought you a gorgeous cocktail dress, exactly your size. It should be in your room by now."

"That was rather presumptuous of you, wasn't it?" Grace couldn't decide if she was annoyed or pleased. She should have figured Trish would have something up her sleeve, and she had a sneaking suspicion it had something to do with Torrie. Undoubtedly, Trish was trying to push Grace into Torrie's arms, as if that would somehow make her forget about Aly quicker—as though there were some formula or recipe for expunging a lover, for softening the loss, like chasing away a spicy aftertaste with a spoonful of sorbet.

"Grace, look. You deserve a little fun, and I know you'll look absolutely irresistible in that dress!"

"I'm not trying to look irresistible."

"Well, it can't hurt."

"Can't hurt what?"

Trish was already shoving her out the swinging stainless steel doors. She was just trying to help, Grace knew, so it was hard to be truly pissed at her. Besides, Grace had little appetite to argue. She was strangely agreeable with Trish these days, and it was because of Aly. It was as though excising Aly from her life had taken all the fight out of her. "All right, all right. I'll be back before it's time for the cake. And don't let Torrie in here to see it while I'm gone."

The Tuleh dress she found waiting for her was simply stunning. It was made of silk, with thin shoulder straps, a squared top cut low, with a dropped waistline and a short, godet skirt. It was a bold floral print in hues of white, black, pink, turquoise and yellow. Perfect for spring, though she would not be able to match its cheerfulness.

The main courses had been served, and by the time Grace

appeared in the ballroom, the post-dinner speeches, thankfully, were over. She plucked a flute of champagne from the tray of a young, bow-tied woman, and drained it quickly. Though Grace was used to the company of celebrities and wealthy people, she never really felt like one of them, even though she qualified on both counts. At heart, she was just a working chef who enjoyed hard work and the results of her labor. She enjoyed the fact that others appreciated the results too, but she knew any adulation was transient. Loyalty could quickly disappear with one bad dish.

She supposed it was much the same for the athletes, as she watched them together laughing, some whispering conspiratorially, others talking loudly, sharing old yarns over a drink, as though they would not be competing against each other again in a few days. There was a common bond among them that looked hard to penetrate, as though their experience could not truly be shared by anyone who did not do what they did for a living. It was true, Grace hardly knew a slice from a draw, but then, how many of them knew what to do with arugula, or how to make perfect puff pastry?

"Hey, I see someone managed to drag you out of the kitchen." It was Catie Sparks, her hand genially on Grace's arm. "Was it Torrie?" Her expression seemed to suggest that it couldn't have been anyone—or anything—else.

Grace scanned the room crowded with women in expensive dresses and suits, but she couldn't spot Torrie. She was mildly disappointed and answered Catie with a nervous smile. "Actually, I'm not sure where our defending champion is. I just got here."

Catie scooped two glasses of champagne from a passing waitress and traded Grace her empty glass. "I'm afraid we can't call her the defending champ anymore. Diana Gravatti is the new champ."

"Of course," Grace said, embarrassed by her oversight. She was glad she hadn't made the gaffe in front of Torrie.

"It's okay." Catie, as though reading her mind, gave her a reassuring smile. "She's not that fragile, you know. She'll get through this, and next year she'll be winning this thing again."

"I know." Torrie would get through her injury and her hurt pride and her doubts, just as Grace would overcome her own issues, too. Eventually. But it would take time. Time that would not pass quickly or easily.

"You know," Catie said quietly. "I feel like I should apologize."

"Oh?"

Catie fidgeted a little. "You know. For what happened between us six years ago."

Grace smiled but really wanted to chortle. Catie wanted to apologize for some stupid kiss all those years ago? *My God, what a sweet, naive girl.* "Oh, Catie. There's no need. Really."

"I didn't, you know, cause problems between you and your friend, did I?"

"Not at all. I'm afraid it would take a lot more than that."

Catie looked relieved and offered Grace a silent toast. "I'm glad."

Amusement quickly gave way to guilt, and the guilt had more to do with Torrie than Catie. Grace felt shame when she saw the hurt in Torrie's face when Catie had blurted out that they'd kissed. "You know, Catie, about that kiss. I think maybe I should apologize to you too." She shrugged. She had no explanation that could justify her behavior. "I was impulsive. It was wrong." *I used you for my own entertainment,* Grace wanted to say, and her thoughts skipped to Aly—the quintessential expert at using people. Grace swore to herself she would never become an Aly O'Donnell. "It was inconsiderate and selfish of me."

"It's okay, Grace." Catie shrugged casually, looking a little mystified. "It was no big deal."

Catie was right. The kiss wasn't such a big deal, but her own behavior had been.

"Your friend," Catie said, interrupting her thoughts.

"Trish?"

"Yeah. I think I should apologize to her." Catie had that aw-shucks look again that was probably irresistible to many women. "I mean, I knew she was going to marry some guy, and still, I...

you know, we—"

"Yeah, I know." Boy, did she ever. She'd heard them through the walls for two nights having endless, raunchy, noisy sex. At the time, it shocked the hell out of Grace that her straight, engaged friend had thrown herself headlong into a wild fling with another woman. But what the hell. It was Trish's business and it hadn't gotten in the way of her relationship with Scott. It certainly wasn't why they'd divorced, and as far as Grace knew, Trish had not been with a woman since.

Grace slid her hand around Catie's forearm and squeezed gently. She knew how Catie felt, sleeping with someone who was spoken for. "It's okay, Catie. Really. But you should probably go say hi to Trish. She's in the kitchen, you know."

"You think that would be all right?"

Grace blinked encouragingly and gave Catie's arm another squeeze of encouragement. "Yes, it would be more than okay." If Catie wanted to make peace with Trish, more power to her.

"All right." Catie shot a wink over her shoulder. "Thanks, Grace. I'll see you later."

Grace secretly relished the idea of Trish being surprised by Catie. She wished she could sneak into the kitchen and watch them—Catie trying to be cool, a little shy and charming at the same time, and Trish trying to hide her discomfort, or maybe thrill, at seeing Catie again. Who knew?

"Good evening, Grace." It was Torrie's voice suddenly behind her, deep and caressing, and it nearly made Grace stumble backward into her, where she was sure Torrie would easily have caught her.

She turned, watched Torrie's eyes rake delicately over her and felt the heat of Torrie's approval on her skin.

"You look incredible, Grace."

Grace knew she looked pretty damned good and was secretly pleased Torrie had noticed, but she wished Torrie would stop looking at her that way, like she was the most beautiful woman in the world. Torrie was good for her ego and nothing more, Grace reminded herself for the hundredth time. Her attention was a pleasant, maybe even needed distraction, but she didn't want the distraction to become a complication. She certainly didn't want to give Torrie false hope.

"Thanks, Torrie." She touched the expensive fabric of Torrie's tuxedoed lapel. "You clean up nicely yourself."

"Thanks. I hope it dispels any myths you might have about jocks not dressing well."

Grace gestured expansively. "Please. These women dress exquisitely. They could put Hollywood to shame. Any one of them."

Torrie smiled rakishly. "Even me?"

Especially you, Grace wanted to say. Torrie was a female Cary Grant or George Clooney in that rich black Armani suit, white linen shirt and lavender bow tie. Grace loved how handsome and strong she looked, with that glint of mischief in her eyes. "I'm sure any leading lady would be happy to walk down the red carpet with you on her arm."

"What about you?" Torrie whispered close to her ear, her voice thick and sweet, like molasses. "Would you be happy to have me on your arm?"

Grace swallowed a quick yes. She'd been to so many events over the last couple of years—awards banquets, guest appearances at lectures, parties, book signings, television appearances. Not once had Aly accompanied her. But Aly, she had to remind herself, was gone now. And so were the years of going about solo, if she chose. She could do whatever she wanted and with whomever she wanted. But in reality, she really didn't know what to do with her sudden freedom, even though she had never actually been tied to Aly. Not in any real way. It was an odd place to be, feeling constrained by shackles that had never really existed.

Grace blinked hard at a faint headache coming on. "Torrie, I—" She didn't want to be having this conversation, not even in jest.

"Are you okay, Grace?"

Grace sipped her remaining champagne. It wouldn't help her headache, but it would help her nerves. "I'm fine, thank you. I just realized we've got to bring out the cake now."

Torrie lit up. "So it is a cake? Can I see it first or do I have to see it with the others?"

Grace laughed at Torrie's childlike enthusiasm. "You can have your own private viewing if you'd like."

Torrie looked pleased. "I would like that."

"So would I," Grace said, knowing she would enjoy the look of surprise on Torrie's face. "C'mon."

Torrie didn't disappoint, and Grace felt like a culinary student again, showing off her prize creation. The cake was nearly five feet long, narrow and curving, its surface alternately smooth and undulating, with rich, grass green icing. It was an exact replica of the fourth hole, where they'd gotten stuck in the rain. Grace had even copied the deep sand bunker, complete with two little figures in it. Flowers and shrubbery were intricately carved in icing, a tiny water hazard was made out of blue sugar water. It had taken Grace and a kitchen staffer almost two full days to make.

"Wow, Grace!" Torrie said, bending close to examine Grace's handiwork. "It's beautiful!" She looked pleased and happy, and it gave Grace a quiet, satisfying thrill.

"What can I say? I was inspired."

Torrie shook her head in awe. "This, Grace, is a work of art."

Grace looked at Torrie as if she should know better. "No. Your Aunt Connie is an artist. I just happen to have an eye for details."

"And an imagination. And the skill to make it all work. No, Grace. You're an artist too. It's just that your kind of work can't be hung in a gallery."

Grace laughed. "Maybe that's why I don't think of food as artistry so much. Don't get me wrong. The presentation can be artful, and how you blend flavors and ingredients takes creativity and imagination. But I guess because it's gone so fast and there's no time to stand around and admire it, or have others admire it, that I don't see it on the same level as a painting or a sculpture.

And then, of course, you have to be able to duplicate it on demand."

"Don't try to deny it, Grace. You're a Picasso of food. Believe me."

Grace narrowed her eyes playfully at Torrie. "Then you're the van Gogh of golf."

"Is this a crash course in art history or something?" Catie yelled across the kitchen. She approached with Trish in tow.

Grace was dying to know what, if anything, was going on between them. She watched them for clues—a secret look, a trace of strain, or maybe even delight, in their body language. But neither was giving anything away. She'd have to talk with Trish later.

"Is this cake awesome or what?" Catie said.

"Almost too good to eat, don't you think?" Trish challenged with a wink.

The two cousins looked at each other and chimed in unison, "Nah!"

"Well then, let's not keep everyone waiting," Grace said.

"Wait," Trish said, pulling a small digital camera from her pocket. "Let's get a picture first." She motioned for one of the other cooks to help her, then gathered Grace, Torrie and Catie around the cake, jumping into position herself at the last second. They posed for a couple of photos, their arms slung loosely around one another, their grins broad and jubilant, as if the cake were the trophy they'd just won.

Grace laughed at the small spectacle they made when the cake was unveiled to the crowd, Torrie supplying an abbreviated version of why Grace chose the fourth hole to sculpt out of batter and icing. The women loved the story and wouldn't stop chanting until first Torrie and then the new champ cut the cake. There were more photos, Grace trying to melt into the background with someone always thrusting her back up to the front. She was enjoying the energy of the room and grew more and more relaxed with another glass of champagne and small talk. Torrie introduced her around, and the women praised her work, many of them already familiar with her television show or one of her cookbooks. A handful had even eaten at her Boston restaurant. Grace was sure there were times on the Tour when there were little mind games, or gossip that was over-the-top, even hurtful. But tonight at least, the women were supportive and welcoming and in a mood to celebrate.

Torrie introduced Grace to her friend Diana, the new champ. She was a big, burly woman, her handshake as warm and welcoming as her smile. She reminded Grace of a big teddy bear.

"I'm dying to dance with the woman responsible for this fabulous dinner tonight." Diana looked at Torrie for permission, which Grace charitably chalked up to nothing more than some kind of butch etiquette.

"I'd love to dance with the champion, thank you."

"Perfect," Diana said, taking Grace's hand. "Since you're responsible for giving me these extra calories tonight, it's your duty to help me burn some of them off."

Grace laughed and let Diana Gravatti twirl her around to Van Morrison's "Moondance," the other couples deftly moving out of their way.

"You've certainly done this before," Grace said.

"What, won a golf tournament?"

Grace could see why Torrie liked Diana. "Well, that, yes. But I was talking about dancing."

"Oh, that. My partner Becky is crazy about dancing. She got me into it about ten years ago, just after we got together."

"Ten years? That's wonderful." Grace was envious of anyone who could keep a relationship going that long, especially someone with a demanding career. "How do you manage it with your career? Or does she travel with you a lot?"

"She has her career too. She's a book publisher." Diana expertly spun Grace out and back to her again, her hand collecting Grace around the waist. "It's better that way. We have so much to talk about when we see each other, and we respect each other's careers so much. We respect each other so much."

Grace pondered this, happy that it was possible that two very driven people could remain together in a solid relationship. "Thank you, Diana."

"For what?" She looked surprised, though pleased.

"For giving me hope."

"There's no secret formula. Just a lot of love and commitment."

"It's surprising how few people are capable of those two things."

Diana gave her an appraising look. "If given the chance, you might be surprised at how many people are." She glanced quickly in Torrie's direction. "Looks can be so deceiving, don't you think?"

"Sure. Of course," Grace said benignly, following Diana's gaze.

"Take my friend Torrie, for example." She gave a little laugh. "She'd kill me if I told you this."

She certainly had Grace's attention now. What deep, dark secret might Torrie be holding? Her imagination began to run wild. Maybe Torrie had been married at one time and had a couple of young kids somewhere. That she couldn't quite picture, though it did give her a moment of amusement.

"Every winter when we're down in Florida getting ready for the new season, she sneaks off to a hospital in Miami almost every day. She's religious about it."

"Is she sick?" Grace asked, alarmed. She looked into Diana's eyes for the truth.

"No, not at all." Diana smiled, a trace of mischief playing on her lips. "She spends a couple of hours holding the newborn babies. You know, the ones that are sick or in incubators. The unwanted ones too."

The shock of Diana's revelation made Grace miss a step. "Whoa, I've got you," Diana said, clasping her a little tighter. "Are you okay?"

"Yes," Grace replied, feeling a little dizzy. Torrie holding babies, rocking them, comforting them… It seemed so incongruous, and yet the thought of it pleased Grace to no end. She'd suspected Torrie was a softie, but not to that extent. Now Grace realized she'd made a lot of hasty assumptions about Torrie that didn't come close to a true picture of her. The mystery of who the real Torrie was would probably never be known to her, she realized, and she regretted this.

"Now remember, don't you dare tell her I told you," Diana said, flashing a look at Torrie. "Speaking of our friend, I think she's getting a little anxious."

Torrie did look a little fidgety, like she couldn't decide whether to cut in or not.

Diana sighed loudly. "You'd be amazed at how many times I have to save that woman from herself." She glided them over to Torrie. "Thank you, Grace. I enjoyed meeting you. And I will meet you again, I'm sure."

"I hope so," Grace replied. "Thank you, Diana."

"Having a good time?" Torrie asked, leading Grace back out to the dance floor.

Grace smiled up at Torrie, glad to be dancing with her. She had that funny, slightly nervous feeling in the pit of her stomach that they were on a date. It felt alarmingly good. "I am, actually. They're a great bunch of women, especially your friend Diana. I can see why you enjoy spending time with her."

"Yeah, she is terrific. They all are, in their own way. We're like a big family. We have our spats sometimes, but they always blow over."

"You must like big families then."

"I do. I have three brothers and loads of cousins. A two-year-old niece too. What about you, Grace?"

Grace shook her head. There was really only herself. "No siblings. My father died when I was a teenager and my mother lives in Europe now. We're not close."

Torrie looked at her with sympathy but not pity. "I bet you would love a big family, Grace."

"Trish and James and I are like a family."

Torrie held her a little tighter. "No. I mean a real family, with siblings you can fight with and play with, and parents who push you and protect you at the same time. And little nieces or nephews to keep you humble. Grandparents too, or in my case, my Aunt Connie to fill my head with good sense every now and then and to just let me be who I am."

Grace gave Torrie a spontaneous kiss on her cheek. She both envied Torrie and was happy for her. "You're a very lucky woman, Torrie Cannon."

Torrie was blushing a little, and the contradiction made her more alluring than ever—suave in the fine tuxedo, yet vulnerable and chastened from a simple kiss. *Yes, it would be easy to get swept away by someone like Torrie. Too easy. And then she would be gone and I'd be picking up more pieces.*

"Something wrong, Grace?"

Grace shook her head and was grateful the song was ending. She pulled away, though Torrie still lightly held her hand. "I'm fine. It's been a long day, though. I think I'll call it a night."

Regret flashed briefly in Torrie's eyes. "I probably won't see you in the morning. I have to fly out really early for a doctor's appointment. How about a last drink for the road, just you and me? To say good-bye?"

Grace wasn't sure if it was another come-on line or if Torrie was serious about just wanting a few quiet minutes alone to say good-bye. She shook her head lightly, deciding not to chance that it might be the former. "I think I'll go up to my room, Torrie."

There was no mistaking Torrie's disappointment, but Grace knew it was for the best. As much as her ego might enjoy another come-on from Torrie, the truth was, Torrie was getting harder and harder to resist. And Grace refused to be the kind of person who quickly replaced one lover with another, to pave over her hurt with a brief sexual fling—to use Torrie in order to forget about Aly. Having a long affair with a married woman had been a huge lapse in judgment, and she would not compound it with another.

"I'll be in my room in a few minutes if you change your mind," Torrie said hopefully. "We can forget the drink. You could just stop around and say good-bye."

Grace smiled regretfully. She gave Torrie another kiss on the cheek then tenderly brushed away the faint lipstick smudge. "Good-bye, Torrie. I'll always remember this week." *I'll always remember you.*

Torrie looked deeply disheartened, and it surprised Grace. She thought Torrie was more of a heartless seductress than that. Where was that callous, carefree Torrie of a few days ago, the one that knew she could have any woman she wanted? That a rejection from Grace could only be temporary insanity on Grace's part?

Up in her room, Grace kicked off her heels, closed her eyes and contemplated a hot bubble bath. It would be just the tonic after such a long day...a long week, actually. Her feet ached, her back was a little sore. She'd barely sat down all day. Then she pictured Torrie and her indisputable disappointment just moments ago. Torrie's request hadn't been outrageous, had it? It's not like she couldn't share a few moments with Torrie in her room, to talk about the week and its successes, to wish each other well, to part friends. They'd spent time alone before and nothing had happened. What was she afraid of, after all? That Torrie would force her into something? That she would have to fight her off? That she wouldn't be able to say no? *You're being ridiculous, Grace. Cowardly and foolish and rude.*

Grace hastily put her shoes back on, arriving at Torrie's room a few minutes later. Torrie looked astonished to see her. Shocked more like, and it was almost laughable, seeing her mouth drop and her eyes widen, as though Grace were some ghostly apparition. Yes, I'm actually here, Grace wanted to say, but she only smiled and held her hands up as if to ask for forgiveness.

"Come in," Torrie said in a rush. She poured them a brandy without asking, her hands trembling a little when she handed Grace her glass.

"Thanks," Grace murmured, taking a sip. The liquid was fiery in her throat before settling warmly in her belly. It calmed her instantly.

"I'm glad you came by, Grace."

"You didn't think I would, did you?"

Torrie laughed. "There wasn't much there to misread. You were pretty clear."

"I was. But you didn't expect me to change my mind."

"No. Why did you?"

Grace swallowed more brandy and wished she hadn't directed the conversation this way. Torrie was sitting back on the sofa patiently, her good arm lazily slung over the back, the other cradling her drink. Her bow tie was gone, along with her jacket, and the top two buttons of her dress shirt were undone. Grace thought she looked even more dashing this way, if that were possible—all casual butch sexiness. The woman exuded sex appeal without even trying. But then, Torrie probably knew that. In fact, she'd probably perfected the look over the years, so that it now came off as effortless.

Grace swallowed the dry lump in her throat and decided to be honest. "I'm not sure."

Torrie sat up straighter, as though her senses had suddenly sharpened. "You're not?"

Grace shook her head once. "Not really. I guess maybe I thought I owed it to you."

Torrie looked puzzled, then perturbed. "Owed it to me? As in being polite? Or paying off a debt? What?"

"No. I…" Grace faltered. Things weren't coming out the way she meant them to. The room was warm, closing in on her, and Torrie, dammit, looked so goddamned provocatively enticing. Maybe she'd really just wanted to test herself by coming here. See if she could resist the charms of Torrie Cannon one last time. See if she was immune to the growing attraction between them, as though she could toss it off as easily as she was tossing off her brandy.

"What do you want, Grace?" Torrie asked pointedly.

Grace set her empty glass down. Confusion and misgivings gave way to indignation. "Why do you think everything is so easy, Torrie? So black and white?"

Torrie shrugged indifferently. "It can be if you let it."

102

Grace stood. "Not everything is a game, you know. Not everything in life has a list of rules and a winner and a loser at the end of the day."

Torrie stood too, her lips pursed. "I'm sorry, Grace. I'm not trying to offend you. I'm really not, but I seem to a lot, don't I?"

Grace strode toward the door. She was no longer angry with Torrie, no more than she was with herself. But she needed to leave, needed to end this growing attraction between them. She didn't need more complications in her life right now. Her back against the door, she turned to face Torrie, who too easily seemed to be able to push her emotional buttons. "Look, Torrie, you don't offend me. And I'm not pissed off, okay? It's just this isn't a very good time for me in my life right now. Endings seem to be where I'm at, not beginnings."

Torrie looked confused for a moment, started to say something, then stopped. She stepped closer to Grace. She took a deep breath, then let it out heavily as if she were expelling a great disappointment. "Then I guess it's good-bye."

"Yes," Grace croaked, feeling less sure the closer Torrie got. Her legs trembled, and then Torrie's arms suddenly snapped around her waist, supporting her with firm gentleness. Grace melted into Torrie's strength, her hands clutching her biceps, then her shoulders and back, as their bodies fused into a slow embrace. Torrie was both soft and solid, her hand drawing tiny, tender circles over Grace's exposed back. Torrie was much more tender than Grace had expected, her touch far more electrifying than Grace had imagined. Goose bumps broke out on her arms and chest as her pulse quickened. *Oh God, this could be dangerous.*

Torrie's warm cheek was brushing hers, Torrie's hot breath tickling her ear, and more pleasurable shivers raced through Grace. She needed to say or do something to stop this. She was trying to form the words of rejection in her mind, but it was like cream that kept separating from the sauce. Her thoughts refused to coalesce.

Torrie's lips were against her ear, nuzzling, almost kissing her. "You're driving me crazy, Grace." Her voice was husky with desire and urgency. "I can't stop thinking about you. About our conversations, about your eyes when you're annoyed with me, about your mouth when you laugh at something I say. The way you move—so sexy, so confident. The way you smell." The velvety lips brushed just beneath Grace's jaw, and Grace tilted her head back to accommodate the soft kisses. "Oh, God, and the way you feel, Grace."

Grace gasped in pleasure and shock. She knew Torrie had the hots for her, but not like this—so tender and romantic, reverent almost. Torrie's touch, and the feel of her arms around her and her body against her, was so much more powerful and sensual than Grace was prepared for. In quiet moments before sleep the last couple of nights, Grace had lain in bed and imagined sex with Torrie as rough and hurried, animal-like in intensity, Torrie's hands and mouth impatiently eliciting and demanding things from Grace. She'd dreamed it would be a hot, hasty and fevered seduction, not soft and sensitive and slow like this. *Oh, God!* Grace grew achingly wet as fingertips fluttered against her thigh, inching her dress up just a little. No, this was far worse than a quick, fevered roll in the sack. This was far harder to jettison from her conscience. This near torture would be impossible to forget.

"Torrie," Grace mumbled, wanting it and not wanting it to end. "I can't." She knew she didn't sound very convincing, her heart pounding its consent while her mind cried out a shrill warning.

Torrie's breathing was ragged against her exposed throat. A well-muscled thigh moved between Grace's legs, and Grace leaned back hard against the door for support, moaning softly. She thought she'd stopped breathing, she was so turned on, and then she surprised herself by raising a trembling hand and guiding Torrie's mouth to her own. More than anything right now, she needed to kiss Torrie, and Torrie enthusiastically welcomed the invitation. Her lips, soft and skilled, kissed Grace back with a tenderness that quickly turned spirited. They were both breathing hard, their bodies moving against one another, their mouths fused in undeniable desire. The kiss went on, along with the pressure from Torrie's thigh and the fluttering caresses on Grace's leg. Fingers teasingly inched higher, so close to her drenched panties now, maybe an inch away. An inch away from a feathery touch, a slow, agonizing stroke. Grace knew she was close to exploding, and the thought of coming right there against the door, against Torrie's thigh, both repulsed and excited her beyond reason. She did and didn't want it this way, with a woman she hardly knew and was on the verge of never seeing again.

"Wait," Grace said, pulling back forcefully. It took all her willpower to do it. "Please, Torrie. I can't."

Torrie stilled herself, hitching her breath one last time. "Why not, Grace? I like you so much. I want you so much."

"I just…I can't…do this. I'm sorry."

Blue eyes, inky with hurt and disappointment, probed Grace. "Are you with someone?"

"No. I just can't get involved." Grace wanted to explain, but she was ashamed of her affair with Aly. Ashamed to be carrying around this private pain for a woman who didn't love her enough to want to be with her. Torrie would never understand.

Torrie grinned wickedly. "I don't even know how to get involved, Grace. I want to make love to you, not marry you."

The words slammed into Grace like a hurled stone crashing into a pond, shocking at first, slowly reverberating outward. It was Aly all over again. *Good enough to fuck but not to be with.* Well, she'd had it with loveless sex, with getting off treated like some sort of necessary bodily function. All self-gratification and no substance—as fulfilling as a money transaction or remittance. No. She would wait for someone who mattered, for someone who wanted to be with her. She would not repeat her past mistakes.

With her hand on Torrie's chest, Grace firmly pushed her away.

Over breakfast the next morning, Grace tried to ignore the shadow of a hangover. She rubbed her temples between bites of scrambled egg.

105

"Rough night?" Trish teased.

"I could ask you the same," Grace shot back.

Trish shrugged cryptically. "I'm only asking because I noticed you and a certain tall, dark and handsome golfer disappear last night at about the same time."

Grace ground her molars briefly against the dull ache in her temples, wishing last night had never happened. She was glad she'd left Torrie's room when she had, before things had gotten completely out of hand. She had taken control of the situation the way she had to, though the look of hurt and confusion on Torrie's face when she'd pushed her away still tugged faintly at her, like fragments of a dream that kept resurfacing. She should never have kissed Torrie, given her all the wrong messages, letting her think casual sex was a possibility.

"Regrets…I've had a few?" Trish sang, grinning.

Grace gave her a withering look. "What? There's nothing to talk about."

Trish stuck out her tongue. "You never want to talk about the good stuff anymore."

Grace groaned. "Can't we just go back to the days where we barely talked and just did nothing but work our asses off?"

"No way. This is more fun." Trish sipped her coffee, regarding Grace seriously over the ceramic rim. "Are you okay, Gracie? Did something happen with Torrie last night?"

Grace stalled, knowing it was impossible to explain her conflicting emotions last night—how she could go from being so incredibly turned on to so easily putting the brakes on her desire. How she could just walk away from one of the hottest make-out sessions she'd ever had. She squeezed her thighs together under the table, the memory undeniably making her throb all over again. "No. Not really. Same story all week. Girl keeps trying to seduce girl, but girl not interested."

Trish had to know there was plenty Grace wasn't saying. "Whatever you say, Grace. But there's something more between the two of you than that."

Grace swallowed another forkful. "Actually, there's really

106

not." She just couldn't fathom the possibility of exploring more with Torrie right now. It was over between them, whatever it was.

"Get outta here. I saw the way you looked at her when she wasn't looking at you, Grace. Which, by the way, was almost never. I could practically hear your heart hammering right out of your chest whenever she was around." Grace held up a hand, but Trish ignored the stop sign. "Torrie Cannon's a nice woman. She's young, good looking and hotter than hell for you. A little horizontal dance with her might be just what you need right now."

"Trish!" Grace was aghast. "You're disgusting sometimes."

Trish grinned back. "Yeah, but I'm right."

It was always simple with Trish, always an easy solution to a problem. "Look, I'm sick of talking about my sad-sack, sorry love life, okay?" Grace leaned closer, narrowing her eyes. "I'd much rather talk about yours!"

"Mine?" Trish squeaked.

"Yeah, and don't feign innocence with me. What's up with you and Catie? Doing a little more horizontal dancing with her?"

"No!"

Grace laughed, enjoying turning the tables on her friend for a change. "But you'd like to, wouldn't you?"

Trish looked comical, so uncharacteristically uncomfortable.

"C'mon, spill it. You owe me, you know, after me putting up with all your questions lately."

Trish set her cup down loudly. "Okay, fine. Now I get to do the avoidance act."

"Oh, come on, I'm not that bad."

Trish laughed. "No, you're not, in your own way."

"So? Back to Catie."

Trish rolled her eyes good-naturedly. "Just like you, there's nothing to tell."

"You didn't sleep with her last night?"

"No."

"Did Catie want to?"

"Yes."

"Why didn't you?"

Trish shrugged and looked away contemplatively. "I don't know, really."

"Not willing to come over to the dark side again?" Grace smiled.

"No, it's not that. Though I guess that whole thing is good for at least a dozen sessions with my therapist. Maybe I'm like you. Maybe I'm losing my appetite for meaningless sex." Trish grinned widely. "Do you think it means we've finally grown up?"

"Well, I don't know about you, but I've definitely aged a few years over the last three weeks!"

"Well, don't age too much, old girl. At least not until after your fortieth birthday."

Grace groaned loudly. "Did you have to mention that?"

CHAPTER NINE

Grace was glad to be back on Sheridan Island, not only for the pastoral setting she'd come to appreciate, but to gain some much needed space and perspective from her week in Connecticut. Too much had happened. Too many feelings had surfaced that she wished hadn't. But now it was all behind her, and she could just breathe. Just be.

She stirred the risotto in the saucepan, added more broth, stirred again, listened to the faint rustling noises of Connie Sparks in the next room playing with Remy. Grace was cooking dinner for her to thank her for dog sitting Remy while she'd been away. Connie had asked her questions about the golf tournament and they'd chatted a little about it, but Grace couldn't bring herself to admit how much time she'd spent with Torrie, or how unexpectedly fond she'd grown of her. And certainly not how attracted they'd been to one another. It was almost as though they'd done something shameful and forbidden—something no one else would understand. Hell, Grace didn't even understand it and she certainly didn't want to talk about it.

Grace stirred some more and added another half cup of broth. She couldn't quite believe she would not see Torrie Cannon again, not after the intense heat between them. When she first came back to the island and collected Remy from Connie's, she kept stealing furtive glances at Connie, looking for facial similarities between aunt and niece. She was curious about Torrie's childhood, about what she'd been like as a kid, as a teenager, what the rest of her family was like. *But there's no point, Grace, because you won't be seeing her again. And just as well, because you were about to make a damn fool of yourself with her.*

"Shall I fetch the chicken off the barbecue, Grace?"

Preoccupied, Grace gave a little start at the sound of Connie's voice. "Yes, that'd be great. The risotto is almost done."

Thickening nicely now, Grace gave it a final few stirs, then spooned it into a bowl. She carried it and a cold bottle of Chardonnay to the table, then helped Connie with the chicken, which she'd marinated in garlic and olive oil and paprika before grilling it.

"Smells wonderful," Connie said, breathing in the garlic aroma. She poured their wine and offered a toast. "To you, Grace. Thank you for being my friend."

Grace clinked glasses. "No, thank you. And thank you for looking after Remy. He may never want to come back to me."

Connie laughed, cutting a piece of her chicken and popping it into her mouth. "That would be fine with me. You've already done the hard part, getting him through puppyhood."

"That's an understatement!"

"Oh, Grace, this is wonderful."

Connie had begun eating ravenously, and Grace flashed back to Torrie and her rapacious appetite. She smiled at the memory, then sampled the Lebanese chicken and the risotto, satisfied with both. Torrie would like her selections as much as her aunt, she supposed.

"I'm sorry, Grace. I eat like I haven't eaten in days. But it doesn't mean I don't appreciate your food. It's quite the opposite, actually."

"It's okay. Tor—" Grace tried to stop herself, but it was too late. Something had sparked in Connie's eyes at the mention of

Torrie. *Dammit, I don't want to talk about Torrie.*

"Yes. We both eat like it's our last meal," Connie said.

Grace tried to imagine Connie as a young woman. She'd probably looked a lot like Torrie, with her blue eyes and handsome, chiseled features, her strong frame. But she couldn't quite picture Connie as a young Casanova, chasing after women, seducing them recklessly the way Torrie did. Connie seemed so much more grounded and wise than all that, but then, age had a way of moderating behavior. Maybe Torrie actually would grow up in another twenty years. Or not.

"My niece Torrie and I are a lot alike, you know. More than she knows." Connie became lost in private memories, and Grace prayed the conversation would move on. "Did you get to know Torrie very well at the tournament? You said you met her, but…"

Shit. "Um, not real well, no." *Liar. You got to know her well enough to nearly sleep with her.*

"That's too bad, dear. She's a fine young woman. Smart as a whip. Full of life." Connie frowned a little and studied Grace. "Maybe a little too much of a handful. I get the feeling you're a lot more serious than she is. You probably wouldn't have enough in common to be good friends."

"Well, I don't think I'd—"

"Please. That's a good thing. Torrie could stand to be a little more serious sometimes." Connie waved her hand dismissively and tried to cover her concern with a laugh. "She's young, yet."

Grace knew exactly what Connie wasn't saying—that Torrie was promiscuous and acted like she hadn't a care in the world. It was true, and yet Grace couldn't deny she had seen glimpses of something much deeper in Torrie—a sensitivity and vulnerability, an unnamed need. Things she didn't show other people, or maybe didn't even know herself were there. But they were there—in Torrie's eyes, in the timber of her voice, in her touch, and certainly in her kiss. *Oh, God, that kiss. So tender and passionate, the kiss of a caring lover, not a soulless seductress.*

"The garlic too much for you?" Connie asked with concern.

"You look overheated."

"Oh," Grace exclaimed, taking a cooling sip of wine. "No, I'm fine."

"You did like Torrie okay, didn't you?"

Grace tried to smile reassuringly. "Yes, Connie. I did."

Relief immediately softened Connie's face. "Thank goodness. Because she's coming here for an extended visit starting the day after tomorrow."

Grace dropped her fork on the plate with a clang.

Grace was more than annoyed. She was downright pissed off, and nothing Trish was saying over the phone was reassuring her.

"She must be following me here, Trish."

"Why the hell would she do that?"

"Maybe to try to finish what we started. I don't know." Was Torrie really that bad at handling rejection, that she wouldn't give up until she got what she wanted?

Trish's sigh was one of frustration. "Look, Gracie. I know you're a hot little piece, but really, she could have any woman she wanted."

"Thanks for the vote of confidence."

Trish chuckled. "Okay, I guess that came out wrong. But you know what I mean. Unless…"

"Unless what?"

Trish grew excited. "Unless she's madly in love with you and can't possibly live without you."

Grace wasn't sure if Trish was kidding. She hoped she was. "Trish, are you on drugs?"

"I wish. Why?"

"Because you've either lost your mind or you're bullshitting me. Torrie Cannon is not in love with me." No. Torrie had made it clear what she wanted with Grace, and it wasn't to ride off into the sunset together, which suited Grace just fine. Aly had certainly taught her that sunsets and happy endings were just a load of crap anyway.

"All right, all right. Torrie's probably not the falling-in-love type."

"Probably not?" I want to make love to you, not marry you.

Trish giggled through the phone, clearly loving this conversation far too much. "Maybe if you just give her what she wants, she'll leave you alone."

Grace's cheeks were burning and she was glad Trish couldn't see her. "Heard from Catie since you left?"

A long silence ensued, but Grace waited her out. "Maybe," Trish finally conceded.

"What exactly does that mean?"

"We've e-mailed a couple of times, that's all."

Grace smiled to herself. "Hmmm, I see. Any plans to get together, or are you just going to type sweet nothings to each other?"

"Nothing's going to happen between Catie and me, Grace. What happened years ago is ancient history between us."

"How can you be so sure?"

"Because she's not my type, that's why."

Grace wanted to pursue the topic with Trish some more. She was dying to ask her if she would consider another lesbian affair, only this time, maybe something a little more serious. But Grace knew it was better left for when they could talk in person, particularly after a glass of wine or three. She was sure deep down that Trish wasn't as stubborn about Catie as she seemed, that it was probably just a defense mechanism until she sorted out her feelings. On the other hand, Grace knew she could ill afford to point fingers. Was she too being stubborn about Torrie as a way of avoiding her deeper feelings? *What am I so afraid of with her?*

"Aw, shit, Trish." Grace dreaded the moment she would see Torrie next, because she had no clear idea of how she would feel or what she would say. "It just complicates things to have Torrie here, that's all. I just want to be left alone."

"It'd be a lot easier that way, wouldn't it?"

"Yeah, it would."

"Grace, why don't you admit you have feelings for her? Why

don't you give her a chance? See where it goes?"

"No," Grace replied emphatically, trying hard to separate the wheat from the chaff in her mind. She knew exactly where things would go. They'd have a raucous good time in bed, and then Torrie would breezily wander off to greener pastures while Grace would be right back where she started—alone and searching for something meaningful. Worse yet, she might get too close to Torrie, which would make Torrie's leaving that much more painful.

"All right, all right," Trish said. "You've already made it plain you don't want to pursue anything with her. She'll respect that, Grace."

"I hope so."

"She will." Trish chuckled. "And if she doesn't, just get her aunt to put her over her knee."

Grace chuckled at the vision. "I'll bet Connie could just do it too."

"Torrie, honey, are you okay? You're as white as a ghost."

Torrie wiped the sweat from her face with the back of her hand.

"I'm fine, Aunt Connie. Just not used to running lately." Torrie was still catching her breath, and not from her run. *Goddamn.* Surely it couldn't have been Grace, the figure walking a big brown dog up ahead of her on the beach just moments ago. That blond hair and sweet little ass looked stunningly familiar, and the vision—or maybe it was desire—had slammed hard into her, nearly making her double over. She wanted it to be Grace, and yet the idea horrified her, and so, like a coward, Torrie had promptly turned and sprinted back to her aunt's. She'd run off, the way she had when she was seven years old and her best friend dumped her for the new girl on the block.

Torrie had purposely chosen not to mention Grace to her aunt. After all, what was there to say? *Oh, by the way, Aunt Connie, I met a woman you might recall from a few years ago on Sheridan Island...you know, the delicious-looking blond chef? Well, she rocked my world last week, and now I can't get her out of my mind. Except she doesn't want me, or at least she says she doesn't.*

In the shower, Torrie convinced herself that her eyes were just playing tricks on her. She thought so often of Grace—wanted her so much still—that it came as no surprise that she would imagine her around every corner. Surely that's what this was too, her imagination.

"Torrie, dear, I have a favor to ask," Aunt Connie said once Torrie emerged.

"Sure. What is it?" Torrie had nothing to do and welcomed any chores her aunt could suggest.

"I'd like to ask a new friend of mine to join us for dinner. I want you to meet her."

Torrie nearly burst out laughing. "You mean we're supposed to cook?" Jesus. Had her aunt lost her mind? Aunt Connie was never one to cook and Torrie could barely scramble eggs and fry bacon.

Aunt Connie looked only faintly concerned. She plucked another wet dish from the rack and dried it. "Well, yes, I thought we would. Surely we could throw together something, my dear girl."

Torrie shrugged. Impressing Aunt Connie's friend with their questionable culinary abilities was the least of her concerns. She just didn't want to kill anyone with food poisoning. "I'm game if you are, but it might be the end of a very promising friendship for you."

"I don't think so. She's very easy to please. We should at least be able to give her some nice conversation."

"That part I think I can handle."

"Good. Now, why don't you go invite her here for tomorrow night?"

"Can't you just phone her?"

"She's only three houses away. At the Wilson cottage." Aunt Connie shot her a look of disapproval. "You young people are too quick to pick up the phone or do that…that, whatever they call it, that typing with your phone."

Torrie rolled her eyes. "It's called text messaging, Aunt Connie."

"Whatever. It's no substitute for personal contact."

"All right, all right. I'll go ask. What did you say her name was?"

Connie smiled with satisfaction. "Why, you've already met her, Torrie."

"I have? I haven't seen anyone since I got in yesterday."

"You met her in Hartford last week."

Dread came over her sharp and quick, the way it did when she knew she'd hit a bad golf shot as soon as the ball left her club. *Oh, no. Not Grace. It couldn't be. Grace cannot be here. And she cannot possibly be friends with Aunt Connie. No way. This is not happening. I'm not going to go crawling to—*

"Torrie, dear. You look like I've just told you there's no Santa Claus or something."

"Grace Wellwood is here on the island?" Torrie barely recognized her own voice.

"You didn't know she was spending the summer here?"

Torrie shook her head, feeling foolish. Feeling fooled, more like. Why hadn't Grace mentioned it? Then again, neither of them had talked about their immediate plans. It had never come up. What mattered now was that her aunt was looking expectantly at her, a little worriedly even.

Torrie grasped the edge of the counter for support. Christ. Did her aunt really think she and Grace could sit across the table all evening as though nothing had happened between them? That they could carry on some kind of innocuous conversation like polite strangers suddenly thrown together? That they could so easily forget the searing attraction between them that had almost landed them in bed—or at least, in a compromising position on the floor of Torrie's hotel suite? Torrie, to be sure, could not forget those things, nor the way desire had flared in Grace's eyes in direct contrast to her uncompromising words as she blew her off. "I, ah…" Shit. How the hell could she get out of this?

Aunt Connie was clearly growing impatient, snapping her

hands to her hips, her arms stiff as tree branches. "What is the matter with you two?"

"Huh?" Torrie was instantly reduced to a chagrined third-grader, capable of only one-word answers.

"Where are your manners? Grace is a very pleasant woman. Surely you saw enough of her at the golf tournament to know that much!"

"I…well, we didn't really get to—"

"You don't dislike her, do you?" Her aunt's tone implied there was only one reasonable answer.

"Of course I don't dislike her."

"Good. Then please go ask her to join us for dinner. I haven't seen her for a couple of days, and I thought it might be nice for the two of you to renew your acquaintanceship."

Oh, so that's what it is…an acquaintanceship. Yeah, right.

"All right, go on then. When you get back we'll sit down and figure out what we're going to cook."

Oh, God. Torrie put her hand to her forehead, which suddenly hurt like hell. It was going to be a disaster, but Aunt Connie was hell-bent, and any more stubborn opposition on Torrie's part would just lead to having to give a long and objectionable explanation. She sighed in resignation. "Okay. I'll be back in a few minutes."

Torrie took her time, still not believing her bad luck. First, that Grace was on the same island, and second, that her aunt had befriended the woman who made her heart leap into her throat every time she thought of her. It would all have been incredibly great luck if only the feelings had been mutual. But Torrie had blown her chances in Hartford, practically forcing herself on Grace, her body boldly suggesting things—wonderful, pleasurable things, but things nevertheless that Grace ultimately did not want. Or at least not with her. Grace had been skittish from the start, and Torrie had stupidly, selfishly ignored all the warning signs.

She knocked lightly on the door, hoping Grace wouldn't answer, and that if she did, she wouldn't at least heartlessly slam the door in her face. Her heart thudded wildly in her chest, her ears rang, and it was all she could do to stay and not run off again. God. This was far worse than a sudden-death championship playoff, where she could decide her own fate with one masterful swing of her club.

The wood-framed screen door opened with a creak and Grace stood, looking up at her, her expression one of expectation, not surprise. Clearly, she'd known Torrie was on the island and would show up on her doorstep eventually.

"Torrie, if you're here to—"

"I'm not." Torrie tried to edge a little closer, but there was no invitation forthcoming. "Aunt Connie sent me."

Grace smiled scornfully. "Your aunt made you come to the island? And then sent you to my door?"

"No. I mean…yes." Torrie shook her head helplessly. Grace made her so confused sometimes. Made her forget herself.

"I suppose it's her fault too that you tried to seduce me last week?"

Torrie swallowed her insolence, unprepared for Grace's abrasiveness. She wanted to match Grace blow for verbal blow. Remind her that it was she who'd come to Torrie's room that last night. That Grace had thoroughly kissed her back. But she knew that would only make things worse between them. "I'm not here about us."

Grace leaned against the paint-flaked, weathered doorframe. "It seems a little odd to me that you're here at all, Torrie. Did you follow me here?"

"No, I did not follow you." Torrie nearly spat out the words, her temper flaring. "I do not need to follow women around the globe."

"Oh, how silly of me to forget that women usually swoon and fall at your feet with a mere glance in their direction."

Okay, now she's just being mean. "I'm surprised you would even recognize such a reaction, Grace."

That got what Torrie wanted. Grace stiffened visibly, her jaw quivered a little, and the vein in her neck throbbed. "Is that the way it's going to be between us?" she asked quietly, her earlier attitude gone. There was no challenge in her question this time.

Torrie stepped closer and tentatively touched a fingertip to Grace's bare forearm, then another, until her hand closed loosely around Grace's wrist. "No." Her voice was thick with emotion. "No, it's not how it's going to be."

"Then how?"

Torrie stepped into the doorway and Grace wordlessly let her pass. A quick glance around told Torrie that Grace was alone. A dozen questions popped up in her mind like whitecaps on a raging sea, so many that she didn't know where or how to begin. "I don't know, Grace. I had no idea you were here for the summer. If I had, I—"

"Wouldn't have come?" Grace supplied.

Torrie shrugged helplessly. Would she have stayed away had she known? Did it really matter now? "Did Aunt Connie tell you I was here?"

"She told me two days ago that you were coming."

"Why didn't you tell me last week that you knew my aunt, that you were staying here?"

"I'm sorry about that, Torrie. I didn't think it mattered because I didn't expect to ever see you again."

"Are you still angry with me?" Torrie asked. She still didn't understand why Grace was upset with her, just that she clearly was. Grace had stormed out of the hotel room that night, and she was still pissed and acting like Torrie had insulted her in the worst possible way by merely hitting on her.

Yes, I wanted to take you to bed that night, Grace. But not in the way you think. It wouldn't have been like the other one-night stands. You wouldn't have been like the others.

Grace turned toward a worn and comfortable-looking leather couch and fell into it. Torrie followed and sat down opposite her, knowing she could not bring herself to say the words she wanted to say.

"I'm not angry, Torrie. I just want you to understand that I meant what I told you last week about not wanting to get involved."

With difficulty, Torrie tried not to let her exasperation show. She really didn't need Grace treating her like a little kid who had to be taught the same lesson over and over. "Look, I know you don't want anything to do with me, okay? You've made that very clear."

"No, that's not fair, Torrie. I never said I didn't want anything to do with you."

"Could have fooled me. You didn't exactly leave me your card when you left." Torrie's voice had risen along with her anger. She wasn't used to women blowing her off, especially someone who had actually mattered for a change. "I don't think Aunt Connie would appreciate us acting like we hate each other in her presence."

Grace looked at her sharply. "Is that what you think? That I hate you?"

"I don't know what to think," Torrie answered, calmer now. "I thought we were getting along really well. That we connected, you know? That we liked each other."

Grace looked fresh-faced and youthful—her skin tanned, her golden hair pulled casually back into a ponytail, a baggy T-shirt and cargo shorts giving her a decidedly adolescent look. But she looked anxious, unsure, her body taut beneath the clothing, and the contradiction struck Torrie as so typical of Grace. Always the mixed signals, with the real Grace Wellwood as elusive as ever.

"There's more to it than that, don't you think?" Grace asked quietly.

Grace was looking at her so disarmingly, with such raw honesty, that Torrie leaned closer. She wanted to put her arms around Grace, beg for another chance. Tell her how she hadn't been able to stop thinking about her, how she'd come to the island not just to recover from her injury, but to try to purge Grace from her every waking moment. She had to look away, her eyes fixing on the distant sea through the large floor-to-ceiling windows at the rear of the house.

"Of course there was more to it than that," Torrie admitted

grudgingly, unwilling to risk anything more. She'd been rejected by Grace for the last time.

"Torrie… I couldn't… It wouldn't have been right for me to sleep with you. I—"

"You don't have to explain," Torrie said more harshly than she'd intended. "You already made it clear you want nothing to do with me sexually, or—"

"Torrie—"

"No, it's okay, Grace. You're not attracted to me. You don't want any sort of relationship with me. I'm cool with it, okay?" She'd be damned if she'd show she wasn't cool with it, nor would she let Grace see how much she still wanted her. Torrie stood abruptly. "I won't bother you here, Grace. You have my word. My Aunt Connie, on the other hand… She asked me to come over here and invite you to have dinner with us tomorrow night."

"That's very sweet of her."

"I'll make sure I'm not there."

"Torrie, look. That's not necessary."

Torrie was at the door in five long strides. "Connie likes you, Grace. I don't want to get in the way of your friendship with her. I'll tell her—"

"No, you won't tell her anything." Grace leaped after her and grabbed Torrie's hand, her touch sending a jolt that shot straight up Torrie's arm and into her chest. "She would be offended and upset, Torrie. There's no need to do that to her. We can…you know, just…"

"I'm not sure that I can, Grace." Torrie pulled her hand free.

Grace looked startled, as though Torrie's words were a slap. "You mean… Torrie, please—"

"Look, I'll try. Okay?"

"All right." Grace nodded her relief. "I'll see you tomorrow night."

The painstaking effort Connie and Torrie had gone to was evident, and Grace was pleased. Their meatloaf was more than passable and the scalloped potatoes even had a sprinkle of fresh parsley on them. She thanked them again, pushing her empty plate aside and raising her glass of Chardonnay in a meaningful toast. Connie looked thrilled. Torrie, on the other hand, had been perfunctorily polite through dinner, but little more.

Torrie served coffee on the screened-in veranda at the front of the house, dashing in and out to fetch first the sugar, then the cream. It was obvious she was looking for any excuse to escape. A ringing phone took her away again. Connie rolled her eyes, clearly sensing something was amiss, but she kept silent. Grace chattered on more than usual, trying to cover the tension, but she knew Connie wasn't fooled.

When Torrie finally returned and edged her way onto the swinging loveseat next to Connie, her aunt fondly tapped her on the knee.

"You know, I was hoping the two of you might get to know each other better."

Torrie and Grace shared a fleeting look in the dim light.

"I'm going over to the mainland for a couple of weeks."

"Is everything okay?" Torrie asked worriedly.

"Of course, dear." Connie patted her knee again. "I'm going to spend some time visiting with my friends Hilary and Jane. You remember them, don't you?"

"Sure. But I thought they usually spend time here with you every summer? It usually takes a winch and a dozen big lumberjacks to get you off this island in the summer."

Connie laughed. "Who says an old dog can't learn new tricks? Besides, they've promised me all kinds of fun, with day trips here and there and evenings of card games. Maybe even a little poker."

"Ooh," Grace teased, wagging her finger. "Just don't let them talk you into strip poker, Connie."

"Ahh, now that sounds like the voice of experience talking." Connie winked slyly.

Grace knew Torrie was looking at her, and she blushed a little, again remembering their searing kiss and how her legs had trembled beneath Torrie's touch. She cleared her throat hard and forced a smile. "A woman doesn't strip and tell. Just remember that."

They laughed, Torrie included.

"I promise I won't reveal anything about my time away," Connie said.

"You're not hooking up with someone, are you?" Torrie's tone was playful. "You got some little chicky on the side you haven't told us about?"

Connie swatted Torrie's leg. "I think one playgirl in the family is enough, my dear girl."

Torrie looked a little sheepish, and Grace couldn't resist taking her own poke at Torrie. "You wouldn't just have one chicky on the side. You'd have a whole flock, wouldn't you, Torrie?" She raised an eyebrow in challenge.

That familiar gleam appeared in Torrie's eyes, and it was the old Torrie again—the playful, teasing Torrie that Grace found so irresistible.

"Mother Goose seems to know a lot about the topic." Torrie waggled her eyebrows at Grace then narrowed her eyes accusingly. "Maybe you're the one with the hot babe on the side."

Grace unconsciously sucked in her breath. Torrie had just unknowingly landed a lethal shot and it hurt like hell. Shame and guilt flooded over her, and she shrank further into her wicker chair. Yes, I was the other woman. *Yes, I was selfish and stupid. And yes, I was an idiot.* She wanted to disappear, forget about the worst mistake she'd ever made in her life. What would Torrie and Connie really think of her if they knew?

Torrie was leaning forward in her seat as though she wanted to spring to Grace's side. She looked mortified, not judgmental at all, and her concern touched Grace.

"I actually wish you did have a hot little number on the side, Aunt Connie." Torrie rescued her by reverting her attention back to Connie.

"Well, just maybe I'll meet someone. You never know." Connie smiled eagerly, instantly lifted by the kind of youthful hope that only the thought of romance can bring. "Anyway,"

Connie continued. "It would be nice if the two of you could chum around together while I'm away. You're probably the only two young single women on the entire island."

Grace certainly couldn't disagree. The women on the island were either much older or married with an armful of kids. "You're right. It's not exactly a haven for young, nubile lesbians, is it? It's a good thing I'm not in the market for one."

Connie laughed and looked dreamily at Grace. "If only you were in the market for a crusty old dyke. That I could help you with!"

Grace and Torrie both erupted in laughter, Grace finally reaching out and grasping Connie's hands in hers. "Connie, if I were in the market at all, you'd be the first one I'd approach."

Connie shook her head, clearly not buying it. "I should be so lucky, young lady, and you're far too kind to this cynical old woman. But…" Her eyes were kind, but there was a sadness in them too. "I'm sorry to hear that you're not in the market, Grace. And not just for my sake, believe me. You're far too good a catch to spend your time alone." Connie turned to Torrie and her voice held an edge. "Don't you agree, Torrie?"

"I…sure. But how come you don't say nice things like that about me?" Torrie tried to look offended, which only made her aunt frown deeper.

"I would if you actually spent any time alone."

"Hey, I'm alone right now," Torrie protested. "I'll have you know that I've been an angel the last couple of months."

"Ooh," Connie teased, pointing her finger. "That must be a new record for you."

Grace was enjoying the interaction between them, their roles honed to perfection over the years. Aunt and niece were so much alike, she decided. *They must have had some wonderful spats when Torrie was a teenager.*

"You know records don't mean a thing to me, Aunt Connie."

Connie guffawed in delight. "Sure you don't. How many golf records do you own?"

Torrie shrugged. "I don't know. Two or three maybe."

"Hmm, let's see. There's the lowest score by a woman ever on the Tour for both an eighteen-hole round and a tournament. There's the most number of wins in one year. There's that streak of how many tournament cuts you've made. What else…most money earned in one year by a woman golfer—"

"All right, all right." Torrie broke into a silly grin and kissed Connie on the cheek. "You never forget a thing, do you?"

"That's right, and don't you forget it. Someone's got to keep you on your toes." Connie winked at Grace. "And in my absence, I'm counting on you to do it, Grace."

"Me?" Grace was thrown by Connie's curveball.

"Don't worry. You're up to the task."

Torrie looked resigned and gave her a tiny shrug. Grace stared back in disbelief. Connie was far more astute and prescient than either could have predicted.

Connie yawned, pulled herself up slowly from her seat and stretched gingerly. "I know it's early, but this crusty old woman is going to bed. Torrie, will you walk Grace home?"

"Really, I'm fine to walk home," Grace said.

"No, I insist. Or rather, Torrie insists, don't you, Torrie?"

"Yeah, sure. C'mon, Grace, I'll walk you home."

They were silent on the short walk to Trish's cottage, Grace still in awe of Connie's crafty ways. She had to hand it to her. She knew how to get her point across, how to get what she wanted. As they approached the stone walkway to the cottage, Grace stole a glance at Torrie. "Torrie? Do you think your aunt knows about us?"

"What's to know?"

"Well, you know…" *Okay, so you want to play that game, do you? You want me to remind you of how you had me up against that door, grinding into me, making me wetter than that beautiful big ocean out there while you kissed me silly and made me forget about everything else in those few delicious moments? How I practically came right there against you and screamed for more because there was nowhere else I wanted to be but in your arms, having you do what you were doing to me?* Grace swallowed hard, the unseasonably warm June air suffocatingly close. Torrie was looking at her, waiting. *Well, I won't play that remember-when game, Torrie. I'm not going to tell you what I really felt that night. How much I wanted you.* She calmly slid her key into the lock. "I get the feeling she's trying to throw us together, that's all."

"Connie's just being concerned, that's all. And a bit of a troublemaker, I suspect."

Grace turned the key, unlocking the door, but she didn't open it. "Concerned?"

"About you. About me. She just wants everyone to be happy, that's all. Wants everything in its place, I guess."

So Connie was really an optimist. A romantic at heart and not the curmudgeon she sometimes pretended to be. "Your aunt is very sweet, Torrie. I think the world of her."

"Yeah, me too."

"Would you like to come in for a drink?"

"No, thank you."

Grace gave a mild start. She didn't expect Torrie to turn her down.

"Torrie." Grace turned to face her, their bodies only inches apart. She could smell the sun and outdoors on Torrie's skin. Her shampoo, the lavender laundry scent of her clothes too. As much as the seeds of friendship were beginning to blossom between them again, there were still hurt feelings that needed to be addressed. She took a deep breath before she spoke. "I really need to apologize to you."

"Grace, you don't have—"

"No, I do. I'm sorry I hurt you." Grace knew she'd been unfair to Torrie, dumping her and then dumping on her for their near indiscretion. She'd been to blame too. She hadn't meant to be a bitch, a tease, and then to drop her without an explanation. She just didn't know how to explain in a way that Torrie would understand.

"Grace, you didn't—"

"I did. I did hurt you, Torrie. And I wish I could take it back." Grace took a deep, ragged breath, and then Torrie's arms were suddenly around her, holding her firmly. Torrie's face nestled down into her shoulder, and Grace let her body sag into the embrace. It felt so good to be held, to be cherished this way. Protected, almost. It took her breath away.

The hug lingered, Torrie gently extricating herself after several minutes. There was no awkwardness, no sexual tension, no looming kiss or roaming hands, thankfully. Torrie gave her a final smile that was more humility than hubris. "I'll see you around, Grace."

Grace leaned heavily against the door, watching Torrie disappear down the path and into the darkness. Just when she thought she had Torrie figured out, the woman did something that totally threw her. Turned her inside out. Restored her respect and renewed the intense feelings of fondness for her.

Torrie Cannon was a special young woman. Of that, she was sure.

CHAPTER TEN

Her reputation for being organized intact, Connie had her bags packed and lined up neatly in the hallway, even though she wasn't leaving for the mainland for several hours.

Torrie spotted her on the back deck, sketching with charcoal. The image of Connie reaching toward a canvas—a pencil, charcoal or brush in her long, gnarly fingers—would always be with Torrie, and she stood admiring the sight, remembering the countless times over the years she'd watched her aunt in the same pose.

"Hey," she finally called out, the slam of the screen door behind her startling her aunt. "Sorry."

Aunt Connie smiled fleetingly, pulling her gaze back to the large sketchpad on the easel in front of her, and Torrie's eyes followed. With bold black strokes, Connie was sketching a woman walking on the beach, a stick in one hand, a large dog beside her intently watching its master. Torrie stepped closer, peering over Connie's shoulder, and was immediately struck by the sketch. It was Grace on the canvas, her hair loose around her shoulders, a look of pure delight on her face, the cuffs of her jeans pulled up to her knees. The figure walked bare-toed in wet sand, the surf lapping just inches away. The attention to detail was magnificent, and Torrie sucked in her breath. "It's beautiful, Aunt Connie."

"She's a beautiful subject to work with. She makes it easy."

Torrie couldn't take her eyes off the sketch. Grace looked so youthful, carefree, happy—the way Torrie imagined she would look if she were in love. "You like her a lot, don't you?" she asked, her gaze still pinned to the sketch.

"Yes, I do. Why don't you, Torrie?"

Torrie couldn't look at her aunt for a moment, afraid the shame of her unrequited feelings would be revealed. But Aunt Connie had set down her charcoal and was leaning back in her wicker chair, looking at her insistently.

Torrie sat down heavily in the adjacent chair. "I like her just fine, Aunt Connie." She really wanted to tell her aunt to leave it alone, to quit bugging her about Grace. To quit trying to force them together. Grace had certainly been right about Aunt Connie's matchmaking intentions, but the pointlessness of it was getting tiresome.

"You don't really act like you do. Both of you act more like you're just tolerating each other."

"That's not true."

"I certainly hope not, because I've arranged for you to have dinner with Grace at her place tomorrow night. I don't want you to starve while I'm away. Or be lonely."

Oh, Christ. It was hard enough being just a few houses away from Grace. Being forced to spend time with her was far more than she could handle. It was downright painful. The hug last night had been frighteningly fantastic. Their bodies fit together perfectly, and Grace was so supple and warm against her that Torrie had had to remind herself that it was merely a friendly hug, that nothing more would ever happen between them. "Please tell me you didn't do that."

"Of course I did. Grace was very gracious about it. More than you're being."

Oh, God. When is this nightmare going to end? Aunt Connie couldn't know her feelings of emptiness and worthlessness since she'd left Hartford, and not because Grace didn't want her. The sexual rejection was only a part of it. Mostly, it was because since meeting Grace, she saw what her life was really worth, hopping between one-night stands, never really letting anyone in, never caring about anything but her career, never even letting herself question what she wanted for her future. Somewhere, she had allowed her soul to become barren, and it was for that reason that a woman like Grace would never want to be with her. It was the worst kind of rejection.

"Torrie, dear, you look upset!" Connie looked at her worriedly. "Did I say something?"

"No, no." Torrie tried to dismiss her concerns, but it was no use. What she really wanted to do was crawl into her aunt's lap the way she had when she was a child. "I'm sorry, I—" Torrie's voice faltered. She wished Grace didn't make her feel so weak, so vulnerable. So goddamned scared for the first time in her life.

Aunt Connie reached over and squeezed Torrie's hand affectionately. Her scrutiny was piercing, her voice that of an adult commanding a child. "Look at me, Torrie."

Slowly, Torrie brought her gaze level with her aunt's. A tiny quiver had formed uncontrollably in her bottom lip. *Goddammit!*

"Oh, honey." Aunt Connie was on her knees in front of her, her arms flung tightly around Torrie's shoulders, and Torrie, reluctant for only a moment, let herself be held. "I had no idea. Why didn't you tell me you're in love with her?"

Torrie could only shake her head, knowing that if she spoke, she'd cry. She was so close to tears, she could taste them in the back of her throat.

Aunt Connie delicately rubbed the back of her neck and muttered softly to her. Torrie let herself be soothed, the way she had when she would awaken from a nightmare as a small child, or after she'd scraped her knees from chasing her mischievous brothers around the island. She loved her aunt for her ability to comfort and console her, even though she had been a firm, sometimes overbearing presence in her youth. Aunt Connie had had high expectations of the youngsters. She was not easy to please, did not allow the easy road to be taken, but she had always showered rewards and love on her nieces and nephews when they deserved it. They strove to please her, their respect for her immense.

"Why is it so hard loving her, Torrie?"

Torrie, still nestled into her aunt, had no single answer. "Lots of reasons," she said hoarsely.

"Tell me the biggest one, then."

"She doesn't want me," Torrie rasped, realizing it was the first time she'd spoken the truth about Grace to anyone.

"Ah, I see." Aunt Connie pulled herself free, gently cupping Torrie's face in her calloused hands. "And why do you think that is?"

Torrie was no expert at deciphering the complexities of love, but she had a pretty good idea why Grace couldn't fathom a relationship with her. Torrie's youth and bold promiscuity were the two biggest factors, she was sure, but she would keep it simple with her aunt. "I think I came on too strong at the start. I guess I scared her."

Aunt Connie eased herself back into her chair. "You thought she was just another girl."

"Yes. I was attracted to her. So much." Torrie still remembered the shocking little sensations in her stomach when she'd met Grace for the first time, how she'd begun to crave Grace's smile, how right Grace had felt in her arms when they danced. Her desire for Grace had grown exponentially. Even now, when she knew there was no hope, her need for Grace was like a wall of fire that scorched her skin and sucked the air from her lungs.

"But she wasn't like the others," Aunt Connie answered for her.

"Not even close."

"Have you told her how you feel?"

"No," Torrie said emphatically. "And I'm not going to."

"What?" Aunt Connie looked dumbstruck. "Why not?"

"I told you, she doesn't want me."

"Maybe if she knew how you really felt…"

"No. It's no use, Aunt Connie."

"Oh, Torrie." Aunt Connie reached over and clutched her hand sympathetically. "You've never been in love before, have you?"

Torrie had never discussed her love life with her aunt before, but she knew Aunt Connie was aware, at least vaguely, of her wild ways and her reputation with women. Although Aunt Connie had never been judgmental about her personal life, for the first time, it occurred to Torrie that she was a failure for never having had a serious relationship before. God. What could possibly have made her think Grace would even consider her? Winners like Grace didn't want anything to do with losers, and that's exactly what Torrie was, no matter how many golf trophies lined her shelf. She was a loser who had no idea how to love someone, how to treat a woman beyond the seduction and conquest.

"Grace would never go for someone like me," Torrie said bleakly, the truth of the statement reverberating through the landscape of her soul like tiny shockwaves.

"Oh, nonsense." Aunt Connie squeezed her hand for emphasis. "You're a good woman, Torrie. You're strong, you're smart, and you have a wonderful heart. Remember that little boy who used to live down the road here?" She smiled at the memory. "He was a couple of years younger than you. What was his name again?"

Torrie thought back to the chubby, shy little boy, and wondered where her aunt was going with this. "Robbie something-or-other."

"Oh, yes, Robbie Sommerset. He used to get picked on all the time. One day you threatened to beat up the other kids if they didn't leave him alone, and then you brought him here and told your brothers that if they didn't become friends with him, you'd kick their butts too."

Torrie laughed, remembering her brothers' protestations quickly dying on their lips while she loomed over them, full of unpredictable fury. They'd done exactly as she'd ordered, and the rest of the summer was an enjoyable one for little Robbie Sommerset.

"Grace just needs more time to get to know you, Torrie. Don't throw this chance away. Don't you let that woman go without a fight. And you do know how to fight for things."

Torrie gazed out at the sea, or what she could see of it through the pines. She was not afraid of a good fight, but she wasn't stupid about it. She never saw the point of exerting the physical and emotional energy if success were not at least a reasonable outcome. And in this case, the odds were far from in her favor.

"I don't know if I want to," she answered quietly, her words carried off by the breeze.

Torrie was nearly overrun at the door by Grace's huge chocolate Lab, whose tongue was the most aggressive thing about him. He was a big baby, ravenous for Torrie's attention, and she was happy to give it to him. It gave her a few moments to gather her composure in Grace's presence. She was still unable to shake the futile feeling that she'd lost something significant—that her best chance with Grace was behind her, and that the most she could hope for now was a friendly truce.

"That's Remy, by the way," Grace said, and Torrie gave the squirming beast the affection he craved, patting him roughly, then tickling him under his chin. "I hope you're hungry," Grace called over her shoulder as she padded into the open concept kitchen, her feet bare on the oak planks.

"Are you kidding?" Torrie said, following.

"Right. What was I thinking?"

Torrie was always hungry. And not just for food, as Grace's tight little ass in those navy Capri pants quickly reminded her. There was still the undeniable pull of desire whenever she was near her, like now. Her libido did not understand reason.

Grace poured them each a glass of Cabernet Merlot, and Torrie was anxious for the alcohol to calm her. She wasn't sure how things would be between them. They'd need to feel their way, define this new relationship. Torrie couldn't help but feel like she was stepping up to the first tee box of a very crucial match, where the first drive would set the tone and determine whether the round was going to be easy or a struggle.

Torrie sipped her wine contemplatively. In spite of her concealed anxiety, she was determined to remain in a good mood tonight. She just wanted them to get used to each other again in a pleasant way and forget there were little walls between them—things they hadn't really talked about. *Like why Grace won't give me a chance.* She looked at Grace and produced a smile. She could have a pleasant time as long as she didn't expect too much.

"You know, Grace. Contrary to whatever my aunt has told you, I really won't starve in her absence."

Grace, her hip against the five-burner, stainless steel gas range, smiled at Torrie. It was a cordial smile, nothing more, but it still sent tiny shivers racing up and down Torrie's spine. She only wished the smile were an invitation, so they could forget about dinner and—

"I know you won't starve. But don't you find eating dinner alone is just, I don't know, so lonely?"

"I hadn't really thought about it, to tell you the truth. I mean, isn't, you know, eating the whole point?" To Torrie, it certainly was.

Grace frowned in her direction. "Tell you what. Let's not make food the focal point of this dinner tonight."

"Umm." Torrie took a bolstering sip of her wine. "What else would you like to do, then?" A thousand ideas raced through her mind, none of which would appeal to Grace, unfortunately.

Grace laughed, turned her back and lifted the lid to the cast iron pot simmering on the stovetop. Torrie nearly dropped to her knees at the divine smells that seemed to be shooting straight past her taste buds and into her stomach. Beef, onions and mushrooms simmered in some sort of thick broth. Grace stirred the wonderful concoction and Torrie stepped closer, inhaling deeper. She was in heaven.

"My God, what's in that pot, Grace?"

"Beef bourguignon." She added a little red wine and stirred

some more.

"Jesus, I want to climb in there. What's in it?"

"Beef, red wine, some button mushrooms, pearled onions, garlic. I'll serve it over noodles, garnish it with some fresh parsley, and I've got some nice crusty French bread to go with it."

Torrie inhaled again, dizzy from the aroma, the wine she was drinking and the fact that this sexy woman was cooking such wonderful, exquisite food for her. This was more of a turn-on than she'd bargained for. "Sorry. What did you say earlier about the food? That we're not supposed to eat it or something?" If that were true, she'd surely pass out on the spot, the way her mouth was watering and her stomach gurgling. It would be agonizing. And such a waste.

Grace set the wooden spoon down on the granite counter and grinned at Torrie, managing to look both mirthful and flirtatious.

"Don't worry, I wouldn't torture you like that, Torrie."

Torrie swirled the wine in her glass and gave in to the temptation to tease Grace. She gave her a knowing look. "What? Get me so stoked that I'm just about ready to explode, then pull the plug on me?"

Grace didn't say anything for a long moment, just sipped her wine and innocently studied Torrie. Then her mouth curled into a slow, tantalizing smile. "I guess I am guilty of that. I probably even deserve a bit of my own medicine."

Torrie leaned back against the counter next to Grace. She didn't want to stray too far from the delicious smelling pot. "So, I just have to find something you really, really want and then snatch it away from you at the last second?"

She knew she was walking a fine line, but it felt surprisingly good to be making light of that night in her hotel room. She knew she was being a little evil now, twisting the knife a bit too much, but then, Grace did deserve it.

Thankfully, Grace laughed. "All right, you could get me tickets to that Diana Krall-Herbie Hancock concert at the Boston Symphony Hall at the end of September, and then make up some outlandish story about it being cancelled."

Torrie made a mental note. She'd see if there really was such a concert and whether she could get tickets. "Wouldn't happen. Lucky for you, I don't like to disappoint women."

Grace gave her a dubious look, and a surge of desire streaked through Torrie's veins until her body was humming with it like a taut, electrical line at full power. It was definitely time to change the subject. She didn't trust herself not to grab Grace, hoist her up on the counter and kiss her into the next century.

"So," Torrie said with effort. "Back to the food not being the focal point of the dinner. What did you mean by that?"

Grace turned the elements off and began draining the noodles. The bread was already sliced and in a basket, and she asked Torrie to take it to the table. "There's a lighter on the table too, if you wouldn't mind lighting the candles."

Torrie was impressed. The table was set for two, with fresh cut flowers and two tall candles. Piano music was playing softly—Herbie Hancock she presumed. It was incredibly romantic, and she wondered if that was Grace's intention, or if it was just her stylish way of preparing an intimate, friendly dinner. Torrie couldn't be sure, and while part of her—a big part of her—hoped it was the former, she really didn't want any more head games from Grace. She didn't think she could handle getting her hopes up again, only to have them crushed by rejection.

In the kitchen, Torrie topped up their wineglasses as Grace deftly spooned the beef bourguignon over the egg noodles, then with a flourish, sprinkled it with fresh chopped parsley.

"This food," Grace said, setting their plates down on the table, "we will enjoy." She sat down and Torrie did the same, spreading the linen napkin across her lap. "But it's the company, the conversation, the wine..." Grace gestured demonstratively around them. "The music, the candles, the view of that sunset out those windows. We're going to enjoy all of those things just as much as the food, if not more."

"Sounds good to me." Torrie took a piece of bread and began buttering it. "But I thought, with you being a chef, that it's the food that matters most."

"Food always matters." Grace smiled, took a discerning bite and seemed pleased. "But it's the whole dining experience that makes me love the business I'm in. It's not just food you're creating for people, it's memories. And the ambience and the atmosphere is all part of what people take away from the experience. They remember that as much as the food."

Torrie took a bite of the beef bourguignon and nearly had an orgasm on the spot. The meat was so tender, it melted in her mouth. "My God, this is incredible! If you're going to make food this good, I think you just lost the argument, because nothing beats this." Torrie took another huge bite, then reminded herself to slow down.

"You really do love food, don't you?"

"You're just figuring that out now?"

Grace laughed. "Not really, no."

Torrie looked around, pleased with the trouble Grace had gone to. The table and the room did look nice, and the music was perfect. Everything was perfect, even the woman across from her, except for the tiny fact that this perfect woman didn't want to date her. She forced herself to smile. "I do like the other stuff you talked about too." Torrie wanted to stay in a good mood. She knew she needed to stay in the moment, to take this evening for what it was—a nice dinner between friends. It was not the time to feel sad or hurt, to lament what might have been.

"How's the shoulder, by the way?"

"Coming along. I can start exercising it now, and I can probably even try swinging a club in a couple of weeks."

"Really? That soon?"

"It'll still be months before I can play on the Tour again. I'm aiming for September."

"I'm sorry you're losing so much of your season."

Torrie concentrated on her food and tried to pick out the individual flavors. She knew she would enjoy food even more if she slowed down when she ate. She could enjoy a lot more things about life if she just slowed down and smelled the roses, as her mother seemed intent on reminding her these days. It just wasn't that easy, not when her whole life had been about conquering a different golf course every week, about owning that little white ball and making it do whatever she wanted, as if it and the club were an extension of her. She knew she had transferred those same powers of focus and control to other parts of her life, and that it was not healthy for her. It had certainly hurt her ability to forge any real relationship with another woman.

"You know, I didn't mean to remind you about your injury and make you feel bad," Grace said softly.

"Don't worry about it. It's not like I'm not thinking about it all the time anyway."

"You're right. So let's talk about something more fun, shall we?" Grace's eyes were gleaming. "Tell me about the first really important golf win you ever had."

There were so many, but the first...that was easy. "It was the national junior golf championship. All the best high school aged kids in the country. I was one of the youngest invited at fourteen. I was so nervous on the first tee box that I flubbed my drive, big time. It hit somebody standing about forty yards away. Jesus, it was so embarrassing."

"Did you steamroll the competition?"

Torrie chased another mouthful of food with a sip of wine, which seemed to blend perfectly with the flavors of the beef. She hadn't thought much before about how food and wine were paired, but Grace obviously had, and she'd managed it perfectly. Torrie had been wined and dined at many expensive restaurants over the years, but this...this was special. Grace had created an exquisite dinner and a warm, charming atmosphere that made her so easily forget there was a world outside this room. For once, there was no rush to get through the meal and on to the next event on her itinerary, no wait staff hovering or autograph-seeking fans lurking. No cell phone chirping. It was just the two of them—no pressures, no expectations, no demands. It was beautiful, like the perfect arc of a ball cutting singly through the air.

"What?" Grace was smiling over the rim of her nearly empty

glass. "You're staring."

How could I not stare, Torrie wondered incredulously. She loved the way the candle's flickering flame rose and fell in Grace's pale eyes, the way those little dimples made her smile look both innocent and playful, how her hands looked so graceful as they expertly maneuvered knife and fork. She looked ethereal taking delicate mouthfuls and modest sips, and it made Torrie crave to see the other side—the wild, careless, demanding, greedy, sexually charged side of Grace. She'd seen glimpses, like when she'd kissed Grace and pushed up against her—Grace so close to losing control. She wanted that Grace, the one without the emotional chains. The one who wasn't afraid to let go.

"Sorry," Torrie said weakly, carnal thoughts still consuming her and undeniably turning her on. "I just couldn't help but think how beautiful you look tonight."

"Torrie—"

"I know, I know," she said. She did not need to be rejected again, nor did she want to challenge Grace. Not tonight. She reached for the bottle and refilled their glasses. "So. The golf thing. Anyway, I got my act together over the next three rounds and became the tournament's youngest champion ever."

"Wow." Grace held up her glass in salute. "That's awesome, Torrie."

"That's when it all really changed, though. I had to get an agent after that. Colleges came calling. Tournaments wanted me to make an appearance. TV and magazine interview requests. Suddenly there was a lot of pressure."

"And I'll bet you hardly batted an eye."

"Well, I wouldn't say that. But it worked out."

"Did it ever. You've done so well, Torrie. You must be very proud."

Torrie fought back a blush. She heard these compliments all the time from people—so often that the words had long ago lost their intended impact. But from Grace, highly successful in her own right, it meant so much more. "What about you? Queen of the culinary world, isn't that what they call you on TV? Now that's something for the old scrapbook."

Grace laughed and took another bite, her plate nearly finished. "It's not so bad. But I doubt it attracts the rabid fans the way sports does."

"Are you kidding me? Women love food, and cooking, and celebrity chefs and all that. Your whole world is women. You've probably got fifty fans for every one of mine!"

"Hardly." Grace downed half her glass in one gulp, her face coloring instantly.

"Oh, come on, Grace. You've probably had more women than there are peppercorns in that pepper mill right there."

"I have not!" Grace looked shocked, offended, then broke into a provocative grin. "I might have had a few meaningless romantic liaisons in my time, but at least I grew out of them."

Ouch! It was Torrie's turn to look flabbergasted before she mopped up the remainder of the beef bourguignon with a hunk of bread and popped it into her mouth. "Maybe I've grown out of them too."

"So you're telling me the young, predatory leopard is changing its spots?" Grace finished the rest of her wine.

"Maybe." Torrie drained her own glass. "People can change, you know."

Grace considered her seriously. "Some people can, yes."

On a different day, Torrie would have pressed her to elaborate. But she stood instead, stretching her good arm over her head. "Any more wine in this joint?"

"As a matter of fact, there's another bottle waiting for us on the counter."

"Ah, another bottle ready to sacrifice its life for us. I love it."

They brought their plates to the sink and Torrie opened the fresh bottle.

"Shall we murder these fermented grapes in the living room?" Grace asked.

Too bad she didn't suggest the bedroom. "I thought you'd never ask."

They poured the wine and sat on the well-worn leather couch, more candles having been lit, the ocean black and indiscernible behind the glass. It was the same easy connection she'd felt with Grace the first time she'd dined with her back in Hartford. She yielded to the familiar allure of mischief. "My turn for a question. Tell me, my little culinary cheesecake. When did you first kiss a girl?"

"Oh, God." Grace laughed at the memory and shook her hair from her shoulders. "You really want to hear about that?"

"Yes," Torrie said eagerly. She wanted to know all sorts of things about Grace.

Grace tried to suppress a giggle and failed. "I was eighteen and on my first summer job at a restaurant."

"Some customer looking for a little lovin' on the side? A little extra something for dessert?"

"No!"

"Come on. Don't tell me you've never had some slutty restaurant patron want to give you a special tip. And I don't mean money!"

Grace screwed up her face adorably. "I can see where your mind is tonight!"

"Well, we are talking about sex, aren't we?"

"I thought we were talking about a kiss?"

"All right, all right. The kiss. But did it lead to your first time with a woman?" Torrie leaned closer, wanting to know every last detail of Grace's romantic past. She hung in suspense, trying not to look too eager, but it mattered to her. Like crazy. At the same time, this curiosity about Grace's past was so incredibly foreign to her. She'd never wanted to know about her lovers' past girlfriends before. Didn't care about their history, what they'd done before or whom they'd done it with, what they hoped to accomplish in the future. Too much information just cluttered a relationship, killed the fun faster than a double bogey sullied a scorecard.

Grace waited, took another sip, then took the bait. "It did, actually."

"Well?"

"Well what?"

"The details! Was it your boss? A customer? An older woman? Who?"

Grace rolled her eyes. "Are you taking notes or something?"

"Nope. Just committing it to my steel trap-like memory."

Grace's eyebrows shot up teasingly. "So you can sell it to the tabloids later?"

"Hell, no. But I might use it to get another meal like this one out of you." She wasn't kidding, either.

"Okay. I can handle that, even without the blackmail."

It was a simple agreement, like acknowledging it was a nice day, but Torrie was stupidly happy about the prospect of Grace cooking for her again. "You haven't finished your story yet."

"My, aren't you curious."

"Aren't you going to tell me?"

Grace laughed and affectionately poked Torrie in the thigh. She looked a little doubtful, like she hadn't discussed her first romantic interlude—or even thought about it—in ages. "She was three years older than me. We were working together at a restaurant in Provincetown. I was on salad station. She was the grill cook, which was, like, a huge step up from me."

"Ah, so you were like the ball girl in a tennis match, looking up to the big girls with envy and adulation. You wanted to be just like her some day." It was getting harder not to slur, but Torrie took another drink of wine, enjoying the thickening alcoholic haze.

Grace looked a little dreamy-eyed, and it produced an unexpected twinge of jealousy in Torrie. "Yeah, I did wanna be her. I also wanted to do her."

Torrie howled with laughter. "Woo-hoo! I didn't know you had it in you!"

"Gimme a break. I was eighteen and just learning that I liked girls."

"So what'd you do, bend her over the counter one night after closing and have your way with her?" That gave Torrie a whole new fantasy to think about. Her heart was like a battering ram in her chest.

Grace gave her a don't-be-ridiculous look. "Give me some credit! It was a lot more romantic than that, I'll have you know. Jeez, Torrie."

"Hey, I can be romantic too!"

"I seriously doubt that." Grace was looking haughty and imperious, and it made Torrie want to kiss her into submission.

"It's true, as a matter of fact." Torrie was pretty much bullshitting, not having discovered her romantic side yet, if she even had one.

Grace shot her a wink. "Then tell me your most romantic moment."

"Not until you finish your big story that I'm sure will be very hard to top."

Grace stuck out her tongue, and Torrie laughed. Grace looked so damned cute, teasing her like this, and Torrie had the sudden fantasy of pushing Grace fully onto the couch, pinning her from above, showing her who was boss with ravenous kisses and relentless tickles. She had to practically sit on her hands to keep herself from doing it.

Grace took a long drink of her wine, growing coy. "Promise me you won't laugh."

"I wouldn't dare," Torrie lied.

Grace undoubtedly knew full well Torrie couldn't be trusted, but she gamely went on. "We actually had a day off together at one point. So I borrowed my cousin's motorcycle and went and picked her up and took her for a picnic dinner on a private beach. It was right around sunset, and we had a bottle of Chardonnay and corned beef sandwiches and these really spicy pickles I'd made from scratch. Oh, and candied apples for dessert."

"And what else did you do for dessert?" Torrie waggled her eyebrows.

Grace gave her a smack on her good arm. "Do you want to tell the story, or do you want me to?"

Torrie put on a pout. "Sorry. Go ahead."

"Well, after I filled her with wine and food, I finally worked up the nerve to tell her I had a crush on her."

Torrie grinned wickedly. "And then you made mad passionate love on the beach?"

"No! She sat there kind of stunned, and I didn't know what to do. I panicked and peeled off my clothes and ran into the water for a skinny dip. I was hoping the water would swallow me up right then and there, figuring I'd just made a horrible mistake. But the next thing I knew, she was running naked into the water too."

"And then you made mad passionate love on the beach?" Torrie's heart was thumping like a runaway train. She couldn't imagine any woman in her right mind turning down a naked, propositioning Grace Wellwood. She certainly wouldn't.

Grace smiled slyly. "Actually, yes."

Torrie expelled a long, fluttering breath. "So that was your first time, huh?"

"Yup."

"And how was it?"

"It was pretty cool, actually. I mean it reaffirmed my choice to be with women. But…"

"What?" Torrie asked anxiously. She loved the way Grace pushed and pulled her, coaxed and teased, lifted her up or dropped her with a look or a few words, or even the curve of her smile. She was like a book that never ended, each page yielding new surprises, each chapter veering off into a new direction.

Grace shrugged. "In retrospect, it wasn't the best sex I ever had. But that's okay. At the time I didn't know any better." She laughed cynically. "I thought she was the best lover in the world."

"And did she break your heart?"

"Nah. Not really. We both had college to go back to in the fall. We promised to keep in touch and all that, but it never happened."

Torrie reached for the bottle and emptied it into their glasses. "Well, I'm glad you weren't hurt."

"What about you, Casanova of the golf world? Tell me about your most romantic experience."

Torrie groaned. Most of her flimsy relationships had been the antithesis of romantic. More like a race to get into bed and see who could come first. She was embarrassed by it, but she owed Grace an answer. "All right. I was seventeen. My golf coach at the time announced one day that she had plane tickets to Paris for the two of us for a weekend. We had dinner in the Eiffel Tower, lots of wine, an evening stroll along the Left Bank."

"Wow. That's romantic."

"Then she took me back to her room and…" Torrie batted her eyes playfully. "Made a woman out of me."

Grace shook her head in admiration. "Okay, jetting off to Paris definitely trumps my first time. How much older was this woman, anyway?"

"Oh, twelve or thirteen years I guess."

Grace gave her a look of shock. "Isn't that kind of icky? I mean, unethical at least, since she was your coach?"

Torrie shrugged. "Yeah, I guess. I mean, now that I'm older, sure. But at the time, I thought we were madly in love."

"And did she break your heart?"

Torrie thought back to the time when she thought she was a woman, but really she was just a kid still, and love and sex were interchangeable in her mind. "Yes, she did. Five months later, she took up with another protégé. A girl who was a year younger and only half the player I was."

Grace looked aghast. "I guess she liked them young, didn't she?"

"Yeah. She was pretty much a predator, I realized later. I was pissed off for a while at how she'd used me. Unfortunately, I kind of decided to take a page out of her book as some sort of revenge and began screwing any woman who would have me." Torrie had picked up some bad habits with women over the years. She'd just never traced them back to her first love affair and the crushing of her tender heart.

Grace reached over and traced her fingers over the back of Torrie's hand. Her touch was tender and sympathetic. It sucked the breath out of Torrie, and she knew she wanted more of Grace's touches, even if it was under the guise of friendship.

"Sorry," Torrie squeaked, her voice reedy. "I don't really have any romantic stories beyond that. And that was pretty sick, as far as those things go."

"Maybe you just need to meet the right woman to bring out that creative, romantic streak in you."

Torrie stilled the gentle ministrations of Grace's fingers and held her hand tightly. She wanted to kiss each of those soft, capable fingers, but didn't. Grace was more right than she could possibly know, because Torrie wanted to do romantic things with Grace. She wanted to ply her with expensive champagne and chocolate-covered strawberries, dance with her under the moonlight to Ella Fitzgerald, jet her off to Paris or Rome for their own romantic interlude. It's you, Grace, Torrie wanted to say. *You're the woman I want to do romantic things with. Only you.* But the prospect of getting rejected again was too much to bear.

"Torrie?" Grace looked at her a little uncertainly. "Maybe we should talk about…you know, what happened back in Hartford."

Torrie stood abruptly, setting her empty glass down on the coffee table. "No, Grace. It's been a perfect evening and I don't want to spoil it."

Grace looked confused, a little hurt. "I'm sorry, I—"

"No, it's fine." It hurt to smile. "I had a great time. And you're right."

Grace stood too. "About what?"

"That the food isn't the only thing enjoyable about dinner, because I enjoyed everything about our dinner tonight."

Grace looked relieved. "I'm glad. I enjoyed it too."

Torrie kissed her quickly on the cheek and strode to the door, turning around just before she opened it. "Are you free tomorrow, by the way? Early afternoon?"

"Um, let me check my busy agenda." Grace laughed. "No, I'm not busy."

"Good. I'll swing by and pick you up around one."

Torrie expertly maneuvered the boat out of the marina. It was a fourteen-foot Zodiac with a thirty-horsepower engine. Grace knew something about boats, her father having been a fisherman off the Cape, and this one skimmed over the tiny waves as if it were pond water.

She'd had no idea what Torrie was up to when she pulled up to the cottage in her rented convertible sports car. Still didn't. Torrie looked tanned and fit in her shorts, sandals and T-shirt, her eyes a cool contrast to the tropical air mass that had wended its way up the coast from the Gulf of Mexico. It was sweltering for June.

"Where are you taking me, anyway?" Grace yelled over the noise of the boat and the wind.

"You'll find out soon enough." Torrie winked reassuringly at her, and Grace was unexpectedly excited by the anticipation. It reminded her of the one time Aly had surprised her by taking her to P-town for an overnighter. Her shock quickly gave way to delight and they'd had a wonderful time, feeling like they'd really gotten away with something delicious and naughty. She decided not to press Torrie and ruin the surprise.

They arrived at a small island a few minutes later. It was much smaller than Sheridan Island—about the size of a square city block, and it was completely uninhabited. Torrie cut the engine and let the Zodiac drift into a small cove, where the water was not more than a foot deep.

"Almost nobody comes here," Torrie said. "It's so shallow, you need to have a boat like this or a canoe or kayak."

"Do you come here a lot?"

Torrie jumped out and offered her hand to Grace. The water was chilly on their toes and ankles as they pulled the boat ashore.

"All the time when I'm visiting. Especially when I was a teenager. It was the only place to get away from my brothers and my cousins when I wanted time alone."

"It's wonderful here," Grace said, admiring the rocky outcrops and the silhouette of Sheridan Island a mile or so in the distance. It was perfectly quiet, save for the quiet lapping of the waves and a pesky gull overhead. "It's so incredibly peaceful. Is it called anything?"

"I don't think it has an official name, but Catie and I call it Smoke Island."

"Smoke Island? Why's that?"

Torrie grinned as though the answer should be obvious. "'Cause of all the dope we smoked here."

"Ah. Very creative of you."

Torrie had gone back to the boat and was pulling back a tarp. She handed Grace a smaller cooler while she grabbed a picnic basket and carried it up the rocky slope to the shady sanctuary of a tree. She began spreading out a blanket on a patch of tall grass, tromping it down until it was smooth.

Grace smiled at the way Torrie was trying to make everything perfect for them. She could see it was not something Torrie did every day—whisking a woman off to a private island for a quiet picnic. It touched her that Torrie would do this for her, take her to this place that was so much a part of Torrie's history.

"Come and sit," Torrie said, retrieving two plastic glasses from the basket, then a bottle of Chablis from the cooler. "I won't bite, you know."

"I don't know about that. I know how hungry you get."

Torrie flashed her a look that was a little too lusty and spoke of the kind of things that could easily ignite Grace's desires. She sat down, keeping a polite distance, and took the glass of wine Torrie offered her.

"This is very nice, Torrie. Thank you for bringing me here."

"It was the least I could do after that fabulous dinner last night. I'm afraid it's not anywhere near as fancy as that."

"Fancy is overrated, you know."

Torrie gave her a grateful smile, and Grace realized how ingenuous Torrie was. She was a woman with simple, honest needs and a sometimes brutally frank demeanor. There were no hidden agendas, no ulterior motives. She said what she wanted and she meant it. She was a beautiful, talented young woman full of life and energy and an ability to love that Grace sensed went

148

much deeper than even Torrie realized. And while she did come on a bit strong at times with the seduction act, she was a joy to be around. The restaurant and entertainment business was insanely competitive and full of snakes. Snakes without consciences. And then there were people like Aly—one of the beautiful, successful people—always striving for more of whatever it was that drove them, whether it was more money, more recognition, more power, more sex.

What bothered Grace most was the way Aly and those like her went about accomplishing their ambitions, with a take-no-prisoners attitude. Lying, ruthlessly climbing over others, manipulating. Doing whatever it took. Not Torrie though. As a professional athlete, Torrie's accomplishments spoke for themselves. She earned her score on her own, whether it was a good score or a bad score, and it struck Grace how much Torrie's profession mirrored her own. She couldn't fool a discerning palate, no matter how great the dish looked.

Torrie was cutting hunks of aged cheddar with her jackknife, and she handed one to Grace, who eagerly took it. Its sharpness went wonderfully with the smooth wine, and Grace thought she'd never tasted anything better.

"You must have gotten inspired by our little stories last night," Grace said.

On the blanket between them, Torrie was busy setting out hunks of Italian bread, thin slices of salami and prosciutto and seedless grapes. "Just taking your advice and creating memories with a little food, a little atmosphere. Am I doing okay so far?"

"You're doing wonderfully." Grace reached for a slice of meat and another piece of cheese.

Torrie looked pleased. "It's a far cry from the beer and pot Catie and I used to bring over here when we were kids. I like this a lot better."

Grace had visions of Torrie as a youngster, unrestrained and full of hell. "I bet you were a real handful for your Aunt Connie."

"How'd you guess?" Torrie stretched out on the blanket,

propping herself up on her good side. She looked so mouth-wateringly strong and muscular, in spite of her injury.

"Just a stab in the dark."

Torrie popped a grape into her mouth. "I'm surprised we didn't give Aunt Connie a heart attack many times over. Jesus, we were bad sometimes."

"Tell me some stories," Grace urged. She'd had an unremarkable childhood as an only child and always wondered about the kids from big families.

"I remember one time when Aunt Connie was so mad at us kids. My younger brothers one day set off some firecrackers under Old Man Robertson's porch, with me and Catie as the lookouts. Trouble was, we didn't realize a neighbor was watching us from an upstairs window down the road. Aunt Connie made us all apologize to both Old Man Robertson and the neighbor, and then she tried to ground us."

"Tried to ground you?"

Torrie laughed. "We drove her so nuts around the house after a day that she shooed us out again."

Grace took another sip of wine. It cooled her, but not enough. Her ribbed tank top was damp and sticking to her from the heat. "Was that the worse trouble you got into?"

"Hell, no. Another time, when Catie and I were teenagers, we went to a dance at the community hall in town one night." Torrie drank her wine, then poured them both some more. "We got a little friendly with a couple of girls. Started making out with them in Aunt Connie's old Ford. Problem was, their boyfriends went looking for them and found us."

"Oh-oh."

"Yeah, it wasn't pretty. I ended up with a black eye and Catie with a split lip. Aunt Connie was so mad at those boys, we had to physically stop her from taking out her shotgun and going after them."

Grace smiled at the vision of Connie as a shotgun-wielding vigilante, out to avenge her beloved nieces.

"But it was okay. Catie and I gave those boys more than we

got."

"And your aunt still loves you after all that."

"Yeah. She loves us like crazy." Torrie was silent for a long moment, her forehead a roadmap of concentration. She stared unblinking at the plastic cup in her hands, turning it around and around. She was very still otherwise, but Grace sensed she was churning inside. When she finally looked up, it was with heavy, moist eyes that contained none of her youthful joviality. Her voice was low and grave when she said, quietly, "How come you don't want me, Grace?"

Grace was stunned more by the finality of the tone than the words. It nearly broke her heart. "I... Last night you said you didn't want to—"

"I do want to now. I want to know what it is about me you find so..." Torrie shrugged lightly. "Unappealing. So horrible."

"Oh, Torrie." The words came out on a long sigh and Grace reached over and stroked Torrie's hand, needing to reassure her that it wasn't her fault. "It's not you."

"But it is. It's me you don't want, Grace, when I find you the most—"

"Sshh. Please, don't." Grace did not want to hear the words she was not capable of reciprocating.

"That night in my room," Torrie went on, "when I said I only wanted to make love to you, not marry you, I thought that's what you wanted to hear."

Grace was sure Torrie had spoken those words many times to other conquests. How could she have known Grace was different? That she needed so much more than just a good fuck? "I'm sorry. It wasn't what I wanted to hear." Grace thought of Aly again and all the words Aly had never been able to say, all the dates Aly had broken, Aly's lapses in commitment.

"What's going on, Grace? Are you with someone?"

"It's a long story."

"We have all afternoon."

Grace didn't want to go through the whole sordid story of Aly. She knew Torrie would think she was a fool, or worse. But Torrie was demanding the truth, and Grace had to grudgingly admit she deserved it. Torrie'd been honest with Grace right from the start, which was more than Grace could say about herself. She'd hurt Torrie, and she didn't want to hurt or deceive her anymore. "There was someone until very recently."

"Is that why you've been hanging out on Sheridan Island?"

Grace laughed bitterly. "More like hiding out and licking my wounds."

"I'm sorry."

The simple acknowledgment of her pain made Grace wince. "I don't know where to begin, Torrie."

Torrie sat up and began stroking the hand that just moments before had been caressing hers. "I don't care where you begin, Grace. I just want to make sense out of what—or who—has hurt you so badly that you can't even give me a chance."

"You'll think less of me."

"Why don't you let me worry about that?"

"Torrie—"

Torrie gave Grace's hand a squeeze then brought it to her lips and kissed the back of it tenderly once, twice. "It's all right, Grace. You're safe with me."

Safe. Grace needed to feel safe. To trust. "You're very sweet, Torrie. And I thank you for that."

"Fuck sweet." Torrie's eyes had solidified to an icy blue. "First I want to kill the bitch and then I want to make it all better for you."

Grace smiled through an unexpected tear. She closed her eyes for a moment and let Torrie brush it from her cheek. It was such a simple but comforting gesture. This protective, nurturing side of Torrie shocked her a little, but it felt right and it was just what she needed. She took a deep breath. "Her name is Aly. She's a well-known criminal lawyer in Boston. Her husband's a politician."

Torrie's eyebrows shot up. "Her husband?"

Grace nodded severely. "We met three years ago at an event I was catering." It seemed like yesterday in some ways, and in other ways, like years. "She was so beautiful and smart and sexy. Extremely charismatic. And she knew exactly what she wanted."

"Which was you, right?"

"Yes. I was easy prey. I was a walking cliché. Lonely, working myself like a dog. I'd pretty much forgotten the whole concept that anyone might find me attractive."

Torrie's frown was one of disbelief, but she didn't say anything.

"So we started an affair. We'd get together every couple of weeks, sometimes more, sometimes less."

"For three years?"

The shame of her past burned hot in Grace's cheeks. "Yes. For three years. It went by so quickly. I was working so hard, and so was she. And then one day last month, I woke up beside her and I knew I just couldn't do it anymore."

"Were you in love with her?"

Grace didn't need long to think of her answer. She'd turned the question over in her mind many times before. "I thought I was at one time. I certainly was with the whole idea of us. We were so good together for a while. We looked good together, we were good in bed together. We understood what it was that we needed from each other. I mistook that for love."

"What was it you needed from each other?"

"Sometimes just coming together after a long, exhausting week at work and not having to talk about anything important. Or when we just needed sex without the complications. You know, not having to answer to one another."

Torrie looked boldly at her. "That doesn't seem like enough for a woman like you."

Grace smiled at Torrie's astuteness. She was no fool. "Sometimes it was, sometimes it wasn't. I pressured her for more occasionally, but it just wasn't in her. It never was, I think. And I finally just decided that I wanted more. That I deserved more. That'd I'd been giving everything of myself to my work over the last few years and that it was time to put some of that into me. That if I was going to share my life with someone, I was really going to share it."

"But not with her."

"No. Not with her. I don't think the idea of a relationship is enough to actually build one on. And certainly not all the lies and sneaking around and all that forbidden stuff that was as exciting as hell, but..."

"Yes?" Torrie was hanging on every word, trying so hard to understand.

Grace took a long, cooling drink of wine, already feeling so much better. Talking about Aly with Torrie gave her new permission to cast off the invisible restraints of the last three years. It was much more cleansing than talking to Trish, with whom she felt the need to defend herself and make excuses because they'd known each other so long and had so much respect for one another. "It wasn't real. And it took me that long to figure it out. I can't blame her, though. It wasn't her fault."

"That she doesn't want to be with you?" Torrie looked flabbergasted. Her naiveté was charming. "Whose fault was it then, the mailman's?"

"It was just as much my fault as hers," Grace said. It was the truth, no matter how hard it was to admit it. "I mean you don't choose to get into a relationship with a married woman expecting a storybook ending. Especially with someone who has so much invested in everything else in her life."

"So why did you get involved with a married woman?"

The question was spoken out of concern, not criticism, and it gave Grace renewed strength. And hope. It was a question she needed to answer—mostly for herself. "I've been asking myself that every night for the last month. Longer, even."

"Sorry."

"Don't be." Grace knew now that Torrie wouldn't hold this new information against her, that she wouldn't be disgusted by her poor judgment with Aly or her moral compromises, and for that she was absurdly grateful. She leaned over and kissed Torrie's cheek, touched by the pleasurable twitch Torrie gave in response.

"What's that for?" Torrie asked sheepishly.

"No reason." Grace had gained a new level of admiration for Torrie. "Anyway, I wish I would have asked myself that question much earlier, but I didn't."

"At least you did eventually."

"Yes, I did. I can only think that on some level I purposely chose someone so unavailable. Maybe…I don't know, so that if it failed, it wouldn't be my fault. So that I didn't really have to work at it, to make sure I was being a good partner. I had a built-in excuse if it didn't work out."

"You're a perfectionist?"

"Of course. All chefs are to some degree."

"But she still hurt you."

"I don't know about that, Torrie. I think I hurt myself more than anything."

Torrie looked perplexed. "But you're, like, a world-class chef. You have staff and you run businesses. I've seen you, Grace. You don't take any crap from anyone. I just can't picture you being some big-shot, married woman's booty call."

Grace laughed at the words. "It is rather funny, isn't it?"

Torrie was deadly serious. "No, it's not. Not with you."

Grace looked at Torrie for a long time, enjoying the aqua tones of the water reflected in her eyes, and tried not to see what was so obvious. Torrie cared for her. A lot. And it couldn't be more obvious than if she'd spoken the words out loud. "You're right, it's not funny. I give out orders all day long. Try to keep everything running smoothly, make sure everything is just right, whether it's with the restaurant or the TV show. Sometimes…" Grace absently fingered a tall strand of grass. "Sometimes it's just nice to not have to be the one in charge. To not have to plan everything to perfection, to think about every single thing I'm doing and worry about everything I'm not doing, and about everything in between. I guess there were times I wanted to just be. And with Aly, I thought I could do that, because there were no responsibilities or expectations. We didn't owe each other anything. But it was just so one-dimensional, Torrie. She was an escape, when what I really wanted was someone to go home to."

Torrie nodded, realization burgeoning in the heaviness of her brow, the tightness of her mouth. "That's why it hurt you when I said I only wanted to sleep with you."

"Yes. I didn't want another Aly again."

Torrie moved a little closer, raking her eyes over Grace as she did so, and it was like a warm caress. She knew Torrie still desired her, had probably never stopped, and Grace undeniably wanted Torrie too. Really wanted her, and not, this time, because Torrie was grinding up against her and igniting all her physical desires. She had underestimated Torrie—had given her short shrift because she'd come on like a dog in heat and had expected Grace to give in so easily. But it was an act—a brazen, arrogant, reckless one that was merely a cover for her fears and insecurities. Grace understood that so well now, just as she understood there were so many more layers to Torrie.

"Please forgive me for treating you like that," Torrie said with feeling, her gaze poised on Grace's lips. "I would never want to be the fool that Aly was."

"You're not," Grace said firmly.

"What if she changes her mind?"

Grace chuckled bitterly. "She won't." She froze, a little entranced, as Torrie's mouth moved closer. Propelled by pure instinct, she closed the remaining distance and captured Torrie's mouth with her own. They kissed tentatively at first, as though afraid they'd both have second thoughts—of the kiss being all wrong. But it was sweet and tender and thrilling, and Grace wanted more, not less. She closed her eyes and let herself melt into Torrie's embrace and into her warm, welcoming mouth. Torrie's lips were so soft, so pliant. Patient too, and it was Grace who began to push back harder. She knew that Torrie would be kind and tender with her, but she didn't want the careful, delicate treatment of a china figurine. She wanted Torrie to touch her with that feverish passion that her eyes and smile had promised so many times—to plunder her body with her mouth and hands the way Grace knew she could, to hold nothing back. Thoughts of what Torrie could do to her made Grace moan a little and press her body harder into Torrie's. She was ready to give Torrie what she'd wanted all this time. She was ready to make love. Ready to please and be pleased. Ready to give her body up to Torrie, because she was cleansed, finally, of the poison that was Aly.

She'd almost verbalized her desire when Torrie's hand slowly crept under her tank top. She squeezed her eyes shut and nearly screamed out in pleasure when Torrie's quest finally ended in the cupping of her breast. Grace began to nip and suck the soft skin of Torrie's neck near her collarbone even as her own body began to undulate against Torrie—rocking gently against her, quietly insisting on more.

The hand on her breast suddenly froze. Torrie's body had stiffened. Something was wrong.

"I can't do this, Grace," Torrie said shakily.

Grace reeled, mentally struggling to understand why things were crashing to a halt. "I want this, Torrie. I want you. Please."

"No." Torrie began forcefully pulling away from Grace, avoiding her eyes. "I—I want to be sure."

"You mean you're not?" The moment was like a balloon that had just lost all its air. How could Torrie not be sure anymore? How could she have changed her mind so suddenly?

Torrie was shaking her head like Grace would never understand. She started packing up the food, and Grace had to firmly grab her arm to make her stop. "Look," Torrie finally said. "I need time with this, Grace."

"I thought you wanted me?" Grace was confused. Was Torrie trying to repay her for the way Grace had rejected her at the golf tournament? Did she just not find Grace attractive anymore?

Torrie looked almost ashamed, and her voice cracked with regret. "You're not just someone I want to fuck anymore, Grace."

"I'm not?" Grace didn't know whether to laugh or be offended.

Torrie turned a hot shade of crimson. "I mean...you are, but... Oh, shit, Grace. I... I want us to go slow. To be sure of

157

what's happening between us."

Grace's sigh came out deeper than she'd intended. She was stunned and disappointed, incredibly so, but after a quick moment, her heart lurched pleasurably. This was definitely not the woman who'd told her in Hartford that she'd go to bed with her in the blink of an eye. "You've changed, Torrie."

Torrie shrugged but looked pleased. She returned to gathering their things.

CHAPTER ELEVEN

Torrie had just downed another shot of Jack Daniels when the door to her aunt's cottage was flung noisily open.

She jumped up from the rattan couch she'd been getting slowly drunk on and tried to pull herself together. It was only Catie, typically jocular and full of energy, bursting in like she'd been expected. She stood in front of Torrie with a wide grin on her face.

"What the hell are you doing here?" Torrie demanded, unsteady on her feet.

"Fine greeting that is, cousin." Catie dropped her large duffel bag on the floor and disappeared into the kitchen. She returned with a glass and poured generously from Torrie's bottle. "Heard you were alone and thought you could use some company."

Torrie groaned and fell back on the couch. "Alone, yes. Wanting company? Not so much."

"Shut up," Catie teased, taking a noisy slurp of bourbon. She dropped onto the couch beside Torrie, hoisted her booted feet onto the coffee table. "What's up with you anyway, sitting here getting drunk all by yourself?"

Torrie filled her glass again, her eyelids beginning to droop a little. What she could use right now was a nap.

Catie reached for the stereo's remote control and turned down the James Blunt CD. "Christ, Torrie, you're all lovesick over Grace Wellwood, aren't you?" She sounded grumpy about the prospect.

"Shut up." Torrie couldn't think of anything more profound to say.

Catie looked at her like she was out of her mind. "I've never seen you like this, Tor. Maybe I should take you to the hospital. Or at least a good psychiatrist. Christ, you're scaring me."

"Fuck off."

They really were like sisters and could be rude to one another the way no else could. Catie just laughed and patted Torrie's knee. "Oh, my little Torrie is growing up to be a woman right before my eyes."

Torrie scowled at Catie. "Just you wait."

"Oh, no. Don't give me some speech about how when the right woman comes along, I'll suddenly become a walking romance novel like you." Catie shook her head. "I never would have thought you'd be such a sucker."

"Well, maybe that's you're problem. Not thinking."

"Hey, don't take your troubles out on me. Jeez. At least tell me you've gotten Grace into bed by now. I mean, if you're going to be this miserable, you'd better at least be getting a good piece of ass out of it."

Catie was right about Torrie feeling miserable. She'd blown it with Grace—again. First she'd pushed too hard, and now, just when Grace was finally ready to sleep with her, she'd turned her down. She just couldn't seem to get it right with her, no matter what she did. She looked at Catie and didn't bother to hide her feelings.

Catie's eyes widened a little with instant recognition. "Christ, Torrie. You really are serious, aren't you?"

Torrie took a deep, painful breath and twirled the glass in her hand, watching the amber liquid helplessly swirl and give in to gravity. She was a little disoriented, detached, spinning like the whiskey, because she no longer knew how to define her relationship with Grace. It had gone so quickly from raw attraction to something so much more ambiguous, so much deeper.

"I think I'm in love with her," she said plainly. She took another burning sip, wishing it would make things better, or at least make her forget how complicated they were. Things were so much simpler when she just wanted to bed a woman and move on.

"So what's wrong? She doesn't want you?"

Torrie shook her head. "She didn't, but now she does. I think."

"So what's the problem?"

"She wanted to make love yesterday and I said no."

Catie nearly fell off the couch. "You what?"

That got a smile out of Torrie. "I know, I know. But I'm serious, C. About her."

Catie took a long, musing sip of her drink. "So you can't be serious and have sex? Jesus, if that's the case, I'm never getting serious about anyone!"

If nothing else, Catie was at least good for a laugh or two. "It's not about the sex, Catie. But I feel like, if I do sleep with her right now, then it will become all about the sex. And I don't want that. It's too soon."

Catie concentrated on her glass for a long time, her dark brows furrowed in rare contemplation. It'd been a long time since they'd bared their souls to each other about anything, or even had a serious discussion about anything other than golf. Torrie had tried to talk to her about Grace back at the golf tournament, but Catie just hadn't wanted to go there. She knew Catie was thoughtful, sensitive and very bright under all that butch sex appeal and turbo-charged libido. She knew it because they were so much alike.

"So what do you want, Tor?"

Torrie set her untouched glass down on the coffee table. She didn't want any more alcohol. It wouldn't help her clarify things with Grace anyway. "I want to be with her. I mean, really spend time with her, talk to her, go places with her, share things with her. I want to be important to her. I want her to look at me like… Christ, I don't know." Torrie sighed heavily, unable to conjure up the right words. "I've realized a lot of things lately, C."

Catie looked apprehensive, as though whatever affliction had come over Torrie might be contagious. Torrie couldn't help but chuckle. "Relax, would ya?"

"I'm trying," Catie said. "This whole new you is a little bit of a shock, that's all."

"You mean you didn't see this coming after I met Grace in Hartford?"

Catie shrugged. "Yeah, I guess I did. But I thought it was a passing thing. That you weren't yourself because of your injury and stuff."

"I'm not myself at all. And it's because of both the injury and Grace."

"Huh?"

Torrie began massaging her temples, knowing she was going to feel like crap in a few hours—maybe even sooner. "See, if it hadn't been for my injury, I wouldn't have taken the time to get to know Grace last week. I would have written her off the first time she turned me down. But I've got all this time to think, Catie. To see things differently."

"And?"

"And my mother was right."

"About what?"

"She told me there was more to life than my career."

"There is?"

Torrie smacked Catie on the thigh, knowing Catie was just pulling her chain. "Yeah, stupid, there is. I just never realized it til now."

"Just like that? And from a woman you've never even slept with?"

Torrie stared absently at one of her aunt's paintings on the far wall, one that she'd looked at so many times, she didn't even see it anymore. "Meeting Grace made me realize I had so little to offer a woman. I've been living my life like some shallow, self-absorbed idiot. Like life is my own personal smorgasbord of fun, just waiting for me to pick and choose what I want. It's pathetic, Catie, and I don't want to be like that anymore. I'm fucking tired of it."

Catie took a long sip of her drink. When she looked at Torrie again, her face had that doubtful expression that reminded Torrie of the time when they were kids and Torrie, being a year older, explained the birds and the bees to her. "Okay, let me get this straight. You're tired of slutting around and you want to settle down. Fine, but you're not quitting the Tour, are you?"

"No, I'm not quitting the Tour. And yes, I want to settle down." Torrie could hardly believe the words herself. She wouldn't have even thought them weeks ago, let alone speak them. But so much had changed. She had changed. She wanted so many things now she never thought she would.

Catie looked relieved. "Okay. Thank God I still have a job. So how does your little chef fit into all this?"

Grace. Who'd opened so many doors in Torrie's life and who'd probably closed just as many. "I don't know. I love her. I want to be with her, but..." Torrie fumbled with her hands and fumbled with her thoughts.

"What? You said she was begging for it yesterday. She obviously wants you. What's the problem?"

Torrie frowned at Catie's choice of words. She could be so crass sometimes. "I'm not sure how she feels about me. And like I told you, I don't want it to just be sex with her."

"Well, duh. Talk to her about it."

Torrie drummed her fingers on her thigh. She did need to talk to Grace, tell her how much she meant to her, see what they both wanted. It scared Torrie far more than anything else in her life had. What if Grace wasn't ready to jump into another relationship? What if she was scared off by Torrie's track record with women, the demands of her career, or... There were so many obstacles, it seemed.

"Aw, Christ, Catie. This relationship stuff is harder than the worse bunker shot you could ever imagine. Worse than those damn pot bunkers at Carnoustie in Scotland."

"So I'm beginning to see."

"Hey, what about you?" Torrie grinned and tried to lighten the mood. "You cooking anything up with Trish Wilson?"

Catie shrugged and did her best to look coy, but Torrie knew it was a poor act. "I wish I was. I mean, I'd like to."

"Be nice to her. She's a chef, which means she's probably very good with knives!"

Catie laughed. "I might just find out. She's coming in tonight."

"She is? Grace never said anything yesterday."

"Grace doesn't know. Trish is surprising her for her fortieth birthday tomorrow."

So it was Grace's birthday. She hadn't mentioned it. "Damn, I've got to get her a present."

"I don't think that's a good idea. Trish says Grace will kill her if any of us make a big deal out of it. She's not big on birthdays."

Somehow, that didn't surprise Torrie. Grace was pretty low-key and down-to-earth, though she could certainly picture Grace making a big splash out of someone else's birthday. Making it perfect with all her special touches.

"Anyway," Catie continued, "Trish invited us to come over for dinner tomorrow. Just the four of us."

"Ah, so that's really why you're here, because Trish invited you."

Catie didn't look the least bit guilty. "Well, she did send me an e-mail saying that if I happened to be on the island, to come by for Grace's birthday. And to make sure I brought you."

Torrie winced. "I'm not sure Grace is going to be all that excited to see me."

"Bullshit. She's not going to go from throwing herself at you one day to not wanting anything to do with you the next. Trust me."

Torrie wasn't so sure.

§

Torrie took her time playing with Grace's dog, avoiding Grace's eyes, though she felt them on her. She was afraid to look at Grace and discover that Grace might have emotionally banished her, the way Grace had woken up one day not long ago and decided she no longer wanted to be with her lover. Had she already done that with Torrie? Decided she didn't want her, after all? She couldn't really blame her if she had. Grace had opened herself up to Torrie, took a chance with her on that blanket on Smoke Island, and Torrie had turned her down.

God! Was I stupid or what?

A drink was finally pressed into her hand. It was an ice-cold beer, and she smiled her thanks to Trish.

"Why don't you two enjoy your beer on the deck and we'll be out in a minute?" she said to Torrie and Catie.

"It'd be much nicer if you two came out with us," Catie said hopefully. She hadn't stopped grinning since they'd arrived, nor could she keep her eyes off Trish.

Trish laughed, and her eyes lingered on Catie. Their mutual attraction was obvious, and Torrie was happy for Catie. Maybe it would give her cousin a sliver of understanding of what she felt for Grace.

"We have a few things to do in the kitchen first," Trish replied. "Then we'll be happy to join you."

Torrie wrinkled her nose and inhaled deeply. "Is that corn bread I'm smelling?"

"You have a keen sense of smell, Torrie."

"I do where food's concerned."

Trish left them to join Grace in the kitchen, Catie's eyes following her the entire way.

"C'mon," Torrie said, leading the way outside, ushering Remy out as well.

"Are you going to talk to her, Tor?" Catie plopped down on a wooden chaise lounge, but Torrie decided to stand by the railing, unable to relax until she knew whether Grace had forgiven her for her impetuous decision. She couldn't help but think she'd blown the one real chance she'd ever get with Grace, and now she'd need to brace herself for the unknown. It was like walking blind into a tournament without having scouted the course and taken careful notes, or without knowing her opponents. She hated feeling so out of control.

"I don't know, Catie. I suppose it's hopeless, anyway."

Catie lowered her voice to a whisper. "It is not. I saw the way she looked at you when we came in."

Torrie shrugged. What the hell did Catie know? Grace had probably given up trying to figure her out. Hell, she couldn't even figure herself out anymore, how she could go from being such a womanizer to the lovesick pile of mush she'd become. And to throw up her hands and say she needed more time. *Christ!* Of course Grace was going to think she had no clue what she wanted, that she was fickle and emotionally immature.

Torrie turned toward the fading sun over the ocean. The waves were short and made rhythmic lapping noises against the shore. It was hypnotic and soothing. She sipped her beer, wishing desperately to make things right with Grace because she could not walk away. She did not want to give up, not without exploring what lay between them. In a dream just last night, they were making a life together, even talking about having a family together. Torrie had laughed to herself about it when she woke up, especially the part about having a family together, but maybe, she thought now, the concept wasn't so far-fetched. Perhaps it had been there as a simmering need all along, that had somehow shifted and risen to the top since meeting Grace.

Grace as my wife. Grace as a mother to our children. She gasped loudly, her chest painfully clenching with a yearning so great and so sudden, she couldn't breathe.

"You okay, Tor?"

"Yeah," Torrie croaked and suddenly bolted for the door. She needed a splash of cool water on her face.

When she emerged from the bathroom, Catie and Trish were on the deck together, drinking their beers, laughing, touching each other as though by accident. Grace was in the kitchen, her back to Torrie, in front of the oven. Torrie waited only a beat or two before she strode purposefully to Grace. It might be her only chance to get her alone tonight, and she would not wait any longer to find out her fate. Their fate.

She halted at the sight of Grace bent over the open oven door, stirring some hashed brown potatoes that were browning crisply. Her long, form-fitting khaki shorts made her ass look spectacular—so round and tight that Torrie wanted to shove herself against it, feel its firmness tight up against her thighs and crotch.

Stop it, Torrie, just stop it!

Grace spun around and made a little noise of surprise, letting go of the oven door. It slammed back into place with a loud rattle.

"Hi," Torrie managed.

Grace smiled tentatively, her eyes probing Torrie, her head quirked in silent question. There was no sign of hostility, only curiosity.

"Grace. I'm sorry about the other day. About—"

"It's okay, Torrie," Grace said gently. If she was surprised Torrie had brought it up so quickly, she didn't show it.

Was it really okay? Torrie didn't think so. She wanted Grace to understand, to forgive her and say they could start again. "No, it's not. I let you down."

Grace seemed to be gathering her thoughts in her stillness. Or maybe she was just trying to come up with a way to let Torrie down gently. "You didn't let me down, Torrie," she finally said. "I respect you. You were scrupulous and sensitive and you did the right thing. It was right that we didn't..."

Say it, say it.

"...make love."

"I wanted to." I still want to, Torrie failed to add. *More than ever.* The thought of Grace's body and what she wanted to do with it burned hot in her mind, the way bright sun remains imprinted even behind closed eyelids.

"So did I." A gentle heat was glowing from Grace, and Torrie hoped it wasn't from the oven.

"I care for you, Grace. I don't want you to ever think I'm using you."

"Oh, Torrie." Grace reached up and softly traced a finger along Torrie's jawline, and the touch made Torrie's legs quiver. She'd never known a woman's touch to do that to her, to make her feel so alive and scared and so full of hope, all at the same time.

"Hearing you say that means everything to me," Grace continued in a quavering voice.

Torrie's mouth met Grace's in a simple, sweet union of soft, yielding lips that spoke of so much more, of holding hands on a lonely beach, of softly touching during sleep, of shared smiles and stolen looks. There were a thousand memories of things yet to happen in that kiss, and yet there was something incendiary lurking there too. Torrie knew that if she parted her lips just a little, pressed her tongue against Grace's mouth a tiny bit, moved her hands up just a notch, they'd have a hard time stopping. Even now, her heart raced like she'd just sprinted a mile. This is what it's like to be in love, she told herself, deepening the kiss even more, and the revelation thrilled her.

"Okay, you two," Trish said with a lilt in her voice. "Break it up or I'll have to get the fire extinguisher out." She swatted Grace affectionately. "You know how I feel about fires in the kitchen."

Torrie, laughing, pulled away from Grace. She leaned in and gave her one last, quick kiss. "Happy birthday, by the way."

Grace flushed a shade deeper and gave a little gasp. She beamed at Torrie, her pleasure evident. "Thanks."

"Why don't you keep that cousin of yours busy on the deck while we finish up here?" Trish said.

"Sure, if it means it'll make dinner faster." Torrie smiled at them both, but it was Grace her eyes tried to devour. "I'm starving."

"I'm so glad," Grace said, her voice low and sexy, and Torrie wanted to press herself against her again.

"Run along, now," Trish said, turning to Grace with a

conspiratorial giggle.

Torrie, feeling so light she had no idea how her feet were staying on the ground, rejoined her cousin and took a long, satisfying gulp of beer.

"Taking a celebratory drink?"

Torrie regarded Catie, knowing she couldn't possibly wipe the smile off her face right now. "Maybe."

"Maybe my ass." Catie laughed. "I take it you've kissed and made up?"

"Something like that."

The food followed, and it was a veritable orgy of Southern cuisine—fried chicken, corn bread, hashed brown potatoes and a salad Torrie couldn't quite decipher.

"What's in this?" Torrie asked.

"It's Grace's creation," Trish said. "Arugula with watermelon and feta."

"Wow," Torrie said, happy for another excuse to keep her attention on Grace. "It's incredible." *You're incredible.*

"With the feta and the watermelon, I wanted something sweet and salty at the same time." Grace spoke over the rim of her beer glass, looking suggestively at Torrie. The desire there was unmistakable beneath the mischief.

A flash of heat surged through Torrie so intense it forced her back into her chair for support. She was suddenly wet and aching, her breath coming in little bursts, and she knew that if she didn't get hold of herself, she would unapologetically drag Grace off to the nearest bedroom and ravage her within earshot of their friends. Screw the fact that she wanted to be sure their feelings for one another were mutual before they made love. The future was the furthest thing from her racing thoughts and pounding heart right now. Waiting was purely an academic term, and one she wanted no part of at the moment.

Speechless, Torrie knew her mouth was open. She just hoped she wasn't drooling.

"Sweet and salty's good," Catie chimed in, giving her own little look to Trish.

"Woo-eee! I think it's getting a little hot out here," Grace said, laughing. "I think it's time for some mint juleps. Which of you southern belles would like to help me make them?"

Catie jumped up first, beating Torrie to it. "I will."

They all cleared the table, Torrie sneaking a few scraps to Remy. Catie and Grace stayed inside to mix the drinks, and Torrie idly wondered what they were talking about.

Trish cleared her throat noisily. "Grace told me you know about Aly."

Torrie contained her surprise that she was about to get the friendly don't-hurt-my-friend speech, and it gave her new respect for Trish. She was happy Grace had someone watching her back. "She did."

"She's a little vulnerable right now, Torrie. I don't think she's ready to—"

"It's okay, Trish. I have no intention of hurting Grace. Ever."

"Ever?" Trish seemed to grasp the longevity of Torrie's intentions, and while she looked a little surprised at first, she seemed pleased.

"Ever," Torrie repeated. "And I want her to take all the time she needs. I can't wait, but at the same time, I can. I don't want to wreck this, Trish."

Trish nodded crisply. "I understand." The silence between them lengthened as they sipped what was left of their beers. Finally, Trish said quietly, "Aly was just wrong for Grace on so many levels. I just want her to be—"

Catie and Grace began clattering their way onto the deck with a tray of drinks, and Torrie shared a final look of acknowledgment with Trish. They understood each other, their silent pact being Grace's happiness. Torrie knew she'd made an ally of Trish.

The four of them watched the last of the setting sun over their mint juleps, and then Trish slipped away to retrieve a birthday cake she'd hidden somewhere inside. She'd made it at Connie's house so Grace wouldn't suspect.

Grace shook her head as they sang "Happy Birthday," shooting invisible daggers at Trish, but she threw her head back and laughed like a kid after she missed extinguishing almost half of the forty candles.

Torrie came to her rescue, blowing out the rest. "Did you make a wish, Grace?"

Grace gave her a secret little smile that ignited Torrie's imagination. "I did."

It was getting late, and Torrie began gathering her things after they caught Catie and Trish necking over the kitchen sink, their task of drying dishes long forgotten.

Torrie turned to Grace with a wink. "I think these two need some time alone before we witness something I really don't want to see."

Grace nodded her agreement.

"Walk me home?" Torrie whispered.

"I'd love to." She yelled at Trish across the room. "Don't wait up for me. And keep an eye on Remy."

Trish waved her off without breaking from Catie, and Torrie and Grace headed for the door without a glance back.

The air had cooled and Torrie, who must have noticed Grace shivering, dutifully slipped her arm around her shoulders, instantly warming her.

"Looks like Catie and Trish are picking up from where they left off a few years ago," Torrie said.

"They're both big girls. I just hope the house is still in one piece when I get back."

At Connie's, Torrie invited Grace in and offered her a drink. Neither was ready for the evening to end yet, though Grace was keenly aware of the danger and delight of being alone with Torrie. Her skin prickled.

"Actually, I think I've had enough to drink for one night. Those mint juleps were potent!"

"How does Perrier sound?"

Grace settled into the couch, feeling instantly at home surrounded by Connie's art and the worn, comfortable furniture. "Perrier sounds perfect."

When Torrie returned with their drinks, it was as if she couldn't decide whether to sit beside Grace or keep some distance between them. She hesitated, then started for an armchair until Grace patted the couch beside her.

"I'm not sure I can get used to you like this."

"Like what?" Torrie asked innocently.

Grace enjoyed seeing Torrie a little rattled, knowing it was so unlike her. The fact that Grace had the power to do that reassured her that Torrie's feelings for her ran deep. Torrie finally relented and sat beside Grace, their thighs just inches away.

"Kind of shy," Grace said.

"Well, don't get too used to it. I'm still a tiger underneath." She gave a playful growl and Grace laughed long and deep, yearning to kiss Torrie the way they'd kissed in the kitchen hours earlier.

They sat in silence for several minutes, sipping their water, and Grace unsure of what should happen next. She knew she wanted to make love with Torrie—her body certainly reminded her often enough of that. But Torrie had been right the other day, that it was too soon for them. She didn't want to lead Torrie on, nor did she want to try to her push herself to give more than she was capable of right now. Perhaps, she considered, she should say goodnight and leave. She was sure she could find earplugs somewhere at Trish's.

"Hey." Torrie broke into her thoughts, her smile bursting with a secret. "I found out your middle name."

"I'm sure that took you about ten seconds to Google."

"No, not that middle name. Your second middle name."

Grace gasped. She never used that name, the one her parents gave her in honor of her older sister who'd died of SIDS at the age of two months. Even Aly had never bothered to find out the name she'd managed to keep so private.

"How did you find out?"

"Catie got it from Trish for me. So. Grace Margaret Kristen Wellwood. How come you never use Kristen? It's a nice name."

Grace didn't want to talk about the sister she'd never known, her lonely childhood. Not tonight. "I guess I wanted to keep something about myself private."

"Yeah. I can understand that. My official bio has my birthday off by one day. That way, I can have the day to myself if I choose to. I don't get inundated with the two hundred e-mails and phone calls until the day after."

"That's rather clever of you." Grace's smile faded quickly.

"Is everything okay, Grace?" Torrie asked. "Is something bothering you?"

Grace gave a tiny, inadequate smile. "I'm fine." She wasn't really, but she would be. Life had a way of sorting itself out, especially now that she had the conviction to live her life more honestly. "I guess we should talk, shouldn't we?"

"All right." Torrie fidgeted a little, the bob in her throat betraying her nervousness.

"Torrie." Grace took a calming breath. It was important to lay out her feelings. It was what Torrie wanted, after all, for them to explore how they felt, what they wanted. "There are so many things I want to give you right now."

"There are?"

Grace suppressed a smile. "Yes, there are." *Oh, yes. And it would be so easy to.* She cast her gaze over Torrie, enjoying the mix of worry and excitement in her eyes, the slight tension in her muscular frame, as if she were poised for some sort of battle. Her strong hands clenched and unclenched in her lap, and Grace loved how Torrie wore her emotions. She did not want to hurt her, or even disappoint her, but there were things right now that Grace needed to give to herself. Mostly, permission to love herself, but also permission to identify and accept what she needed in her life. Permission too to be selfish in an entirely different way than she'd been with Aly, where selfishness meant shirking responsibility.

"What kind of things?" Torrie pressed.

Grace did smile this time. "Oh, Torrie. You are so wonderful." She swallowed and tried to speak around her burgeoning emotions. If there was anyone she would like to fall in love with right now, it was Torrie. "I want to give you everything, but I can't right now. I can't give you my heart." *It's too soon. But I would like to. Some day.*

"It's okay. You don't have to."

"But you deserve so much more, Torrie. You deserve someone who can give you everything you want. And I'm not ready to do that."

Torrie placed her hand on Grace's thigh. Her fingers were warm and solid, but also soft and tender on her cotton shorts. "Grace, I want you so much. I know you're still hurting, and that's okay. I won't push you. I won't try to make you say things you're not ready to say, or do things you're not ready to do."

Torrie's fingers were lightly circling Grace's thigh, and it was like throwing white gas on burning embers. Her desire was so close to igniting, and she knew it was dangerous. She would not be able to say no if Torrie kept it up.

"You were right to say we should wait," Grace said, her body fighting her words. Dammit. Why did the words have to be so incongruous with what her aching body needed right now?

"Grace." Torrie's mouth was suddenly near her throat, her breath delicately tickling Grace's sensitive flesh. "Let me love you. Please. I don't want to wait for that."

Grace's breath left her in a rush. Her heart was pounding in her ears, and without permission, her head tilted back, exposing more of her flesh to Torrie. Soft lips brushed her throat, her collarbone, and Grace silently screamed for Torrie to touch her.

"Stay with me tonight," Torrie whispered in her ear.

Grace swallowed hard and tried to find her voice. "But I thought…"

"I can't go slow, Grace. I want you now. However much of you I can have."

Her hand had crept up Grace's inner thigh, leaving a blazing trail of sweet, prickling desire in its wake. "But…" Oh, hell. What was she thinking, protesting, hesitating? Perhaps love was overrated after all, because she could think of nothing but Torrie's hands on her, Torrie's mouth devouring her. Being lost in Torrie's body. Merging their hot, furious, slick desire. She'd warned Torrie she couldn't give her all of her, and yet Torrie still wanted her. Maybe that was enough.

Her voice strangled with lust, Grace said the only words that mattered right now: "Yes, Torrie."

Their mouths found each other with a hard urgency that awed Grace, their lips pressing like they might bruise each other, as though it were a kiss they'd waited their whole life for. Grace moaned as Torrie's hand slid higher up her thigh, her fingers brushing fleetingly where the seams of Grace's shorts met. Grace sucked in her breath, feeling dizzy under the weight of her own crushing desire. Torrie's hand gently cupped her, then stroked her through the thick cotton, dancing an invisible pattern over her throbbing center. She pushed back into Torrie's hand, tentatively at first, then much more demandingly. Torrie palmed her roughly, stroked her lightly, hinted with her flicking tongue on her throat what might happen next.

"Oh, God, Torrie," Grace whimpered urgently. "If you don't slow down a little—"

Torrie chuckled against Grace's throat, her lips vibrating against her skin. "Don't worry. I don't want you coming yet."

"You don't?" Grace teased, her breath still coming in short bursts as Torrie's hand stilled against her. She wanted Torrie so badly, it hurt.

Torrie smiled cockily at her. "When you do come, it won't be by accident."

Grace was feverish with desire. She didn't want to be teased and toyed with all night. "Torrie, I don't think I can stand much more."

Torrie laughed, then studied Grace with growing seriousness. "Oh, Grace." Her voice was low and husky and thick with desire. "I want to make sweet love to you all night long. I want to love every inch of you over and over again. The way you deserve to be made love to. I want to feel you and taste you everywhere."

Grace's answer died on a moan as she kissed Torrie impatiently, even as tears pooled in her eyes.

"Come upstairs with me," Torrie said between kisses.

"Yes."

Up in Torrie's room, she let Torrie peel her cotton shirt over her head, and she thrilled at how Torrie's eyes eagerly and approvingly roamed over her naked chest, hesitating on her breasts like she was either memorizing them or planning everything she would do to them. It was the way she imagined Torrie surveyed a golf course—looking for the most direct, successful line, imagining the setup, the approach.

Torrie licked her lips. "Are you sure, Grace?"

Grace nodded, never taking her eyes off Torrie's face. She was more than sure she wanted Torrie to touch her inside and out, to love her body with tenderness and passion and even a bit of savagery. She wanted to both conquer and be conquered tonight in the very capable, caring arms of Torrie. As for the rest…as for her heart and Torrie's, well, those things would have to reveal themselves later. Right now her body cried out for solitary attention.

Torrie dropped to her knees, unzipped Grace's shorts, then slowly pulled them down her hips, her thighs, past her calves. Grace kicked them away. Torrie thumbed her thin cotton bikini briefs around the waistband, caressed her ass with her spanned fingers, then slid the panties down until they were around Grace's ankles.

Torrie's sharp intake of breath tickled her thighs. When she glanced down, Torrie was looking at her reverently, loving her body with her eyes.

"Oh, Torrie," Grace said shakily, her knees trembling and weak. Yes. She knew it would be like this with Torrie. So sweet.

Torrie stood, snaked her arm around Grace's waist and guided her to the double bed. "You are so beautiful, Grace. Even more beautiful than I imagined. And believe me, I spent lots of time imagining."

Grace laughed as they lay down side by side, facing each other. She was glad her body wasn't a disappointment to Torrie, who had probably made love to many young, nubile women over

176

the years. She too had spent many moments imagining what Torrie looked like naked, though she already could tell she would not be disappointed.

"You," Grace whispered. "I want your clothes off. I want to see you."

Torrie's grin was playful. She began pulling at her shirt, Grace helping her with her injured side. She left her tight, black boxer briefs on.

"Oh. My. God." Grace sucked in her breath, enthusiastically scrutinizing the tight, flinching muscles of Torrie's arms and shoulders and neck, the four-pack that was her stomach. Her breasts were small and firm, but curved gently to hardened, prominent nipples. She was like a sculpted goddess, and Grace felt suddenly unworthy. Every year of their age difference amplified her doubts now and made her hesitate a little.

Torrie must have sensed her insecurity. She began stroking Grace's face lovingly, and her eyes were a warm blue, like a hot, summer sky. "Don't be afraid, Grace."

Grace wanted to laugh. Afraid? What, like she was a virgin and this was her first time? What did Torrie mean, *don't be afraid?* And then it struck her that she was a little afraid. For the first time in...she couldn't even remember when, for she'd never been nervous like this with Aly. She couldn't even name what exactly she was afraid of. Complications? Someone getting hurt feelings? Of being inadequate? Of being disappointed? All of the above?

"Grace," Torrie whispered against her cheek, and she loved how her name sounded on Torrie's lips. "Grace. I want you so much."

She closed her eyes against the little kisses on her jaw and throat, then the side of her neck, the tip of her shoulder. Torrie was moving against her, half on top of her, her hips pressing against Grace's, her leg intertwining with Grace's. Torrie's hand gently cupped her breast, stroking the soft underside of it, and any doubts Grace had were incinerated in the heat of their mutual desire.

"I want you, Torrie." Grace's throat was sandpaper, and she

could hardly speak around her rampaging desire. As Torrie's fingers circled and stroked the stiff peak of her nipple, Grace thought how close she was to demanding Torrie enter her and answer her throbbing wetness with quick, full thrusts. Oh, how she wanted to be fucked. Fucked hard and fucked long by those strong hands, by that hard body.

Torrie's soft, wet mouth enveloped her nipple, gently sucking, lightly stroking. And then it was the other breast, and Grace arched up and deeper into Torrie's mouth. Oh, yes, it would be slow and deep and sweet with Torrie, not fast and hard and shallow, and Grace felt a whole new level of yearning inside. She was wetter than she had ever been for anyone and she pushed her hips against Torrie, her pelvis making gentle pleas.

"My, my." Torrie laughed, disengaging from a breast. "Are you forgetting we have all night?"

"That's what I'm afraid of."

Torrie laughed so hard, her body shook against Grace's, and Grace had the fleeting worry that they might both fall off the bed. "I wasn't even trying to be funny," Grace muttered.

Torrie kissed her hard on the mouth, her body still trembling with laughter. "Oh, Grace. You are so precious. God, I love you!"

Grace could only hear her own pounding heart as the rest of her body stilled. A sob rose quickly in her throat. She wished Torrie hadn't said those three words. They were the words that could have made this moment so perfect. Should have made this moment so perfect. "Oh, Torrie. Please don't."

Torrie smiled so benevolently that Grace was suddenly ashamed of herself and her inability to give herself fully to Torrie, who wanted nothing more than to love her.

"I'm sorry," Grace croaked, knowing full well the apology would do nothing to make her feel better.

"Don't be," Torrie soothed, a hand reaching down to stroke Grace's thigh. "I know I shouldn't have said it, but I couldn't help myself. It's true that I love you, but I don't want to make you uncomfortable."

In their three years together, Grace could count on one hand the number of times Aly had told her she loved her, and yet here was Torrie, whom she'd just met a little more than two weeks ago, professing her love for her. *God, it was so easy for Torrie.* And not just saying it, but delivering it with every stroke and every kiss. Grace had never been so wanted before. So cherished.

"No," Grace said, tears beginning to brim and spill over. As much as she ached for not being able to reciprocate, there was unmistakable joy in her heart too, as if Torrie's words had dislodged something heavy and cloying and poisonous in her. "Don't ever apologize for saying that. It's not your fault."

Torrie moved fully on top of Grace and began licking the tears from her cheeks. "I didn't mean to make you cry."

Grace smiled through her tears. "Do you know how long it's been since a woman has made me cry in a good way?"

Torrie shook her head and nuzzled Grace. "I'd rather make you scream."

Her breath left her lungs as Torrie's thigh began pushing against her in gentle pulses. The long, bulky muscles were hard and thick, and Grace clenched harder against them, increasing the pressure on her swollen, throbbing clitoris with her own answering thrusts. Her arms tightened around Torrie's strong back, and she struggled to remember which shoulder she should be careful with, until she spotted the angry slash of a scar. Her thoughts began to muddy even as her senses sharpened.

"You feel so good, Grace," Torrie said as she rocked against Grace, increasing the pace and pressure until they were both gasping for breath.

"Ohhh," Grace cried out, her eyes slamming shut against her pounding heart and rushing blood. She would need release. Soon.

"It's okay, baby."

Torrie's mouth moved to her breast again, and Grace bit her bottom lip to stifle another cry. Torrie's hand moved between them and Grace released a little to make room. She hoped, prayed, for Torrie to touch her now, for her fingers to relieve the burning ache that had already begun to consume her.

"I want to touch you, Grace."

"Oh, God. Yes. Please, Torrie."

Fingers danced over her slick, soft folds, tracing little patterns, flicking and stroking, tickling and rubbing, and it was driving Grace wild. She lifted her hips and pushed greedily into Torrie's fingers, trying to capture them, control them, but they were fast and light and moved to their own time. Her vision swam, her thoughts swirling incoherently but for one single, razor-like one—Torrie making her come. A palm pressed against her firmly and Grace opened her legs wider, inviting more from Torrie.

"Does that feel good?"

"Oh, yeah," Grace gasped.

A finger slipped inside her and Grace cried out.

"God, you're so wet, Grace."

"You make me wet, Torrie. Sooo wet." Grace feared she might slide right out from under her. Her chest heaved as she willed Torrie to take her higher and higher, further and further, and Torrie did, slipping a second finger in. They pumped together in a perfect, furious union of hips meeting thrusting fingers. When Torrie's other hand found her hardened clitoris, the onslaught of orgasm built to a painfully sweet climax, rushing toward her before crashing relentlessly onto her shores in endless, delicious waves. She cried Torrie's name as she pushed one last time against her hand, drawing every last bit of pleasure from her thrusts.

Torrie collapsed against her and they rolled until Grace was on top, her face hot and her breath still short.

"Torrie, that was amazing."

Torrie's eyes glinted with pleasure. She looked both sated and hungry at the same time. "You ain't seen nothing yet."

Grace giggled, feeling more alive than she had in years, and she credited it to the fact that this young, beautiful jock was looking at her like she wanted to eat her in one bite. And probably could. It was incredibly intoxicating. She began planting little kisses and licks on Torrie's throat, trying to tickle. She finally succeeded when she went after Torrie's stomach.

"Okay, that is so not fair," Torrie gasped.

"What?" Grace feigned innocence.

"Tickling is definitely hitting below the belt."

"You think so, do you?" Grace had her right where she wanted her. Her hand slid down to Torrie's cotton boxer briefs, and she cupped her firmly.

"Ohh!" Torrie moaned. "Okay, I was wrong. Oh, Jesus. Now that is definitely—"

"Below the belt?" Grace chimed wickedly.

"Yeah." Torrie grabbed Grace by the wrist. "You don't know what I do to naughty girls who tease."

Grace's eyebrows rose in challenge. "Make them your sex slave, I hope."

"How'd you guess?" Torrie plunged Grace's hands beneath the waistband of her briefs.

What greeted Grace there made her moan in pleasure and subconsciously lick her lips. Torrie was already so wet and swollen. "Mmmm, I like this, Torrie."

"Me too," Torrie whispered, her voice strained and her eyes foggy and half-lidded. "I'm so turned on, I had to stop myself from coming when you did." She moaned as Grace's hand moved rhythmically on her. "God, you're so beautiful when you come, Grace."

Grace kissed her, exploring Torrie's lips with her tongue and wondering what they would feel like on her. Down there. *Oh, God, I'm turned on again.* Would she not be able to get enough of this woman?

Torrie moved harder against her, her chest rapidly rising and falling. Grace knew Torrie was close to coming as she worked her, increasing the pace.

"I want to look at you when I come," Torrie breathed.

Grace smiled and held Torrie's feverish gaze as Torrie bucked a final time and came against her hand with a guttural cry. It was an incredible high to know she'd just given her such pleasure, and Grace kissed her again as the last tiny strains of orgasm ebbed.

"You're so damn beautiful, Grace," Torrie said between kisses, holding Grace in the crook of her good shoulder. "I don't know how I ever got so lucky."

"You," Grace said, "are good for my ego, Torrie Cannon."

"It's not your ego I care about, Grace Wellwood. Well, it is, but everything else too." She tenderly smoothed a lock of hair behind Grace's ear.

"Do you think your aunt would mind me being here like this?"

"Are you kidding me?" Torrie laughed deeply. "She'd love it. She's my biggest competition for you."

"She is not." Grace knew Torrie was just teasing her, but she didn't want to think about anyone else but the two of them right now. "Torrie." Grace could hardly catch her breath when she looked at Torrie. Especially at the way she looked back at her, so beautiful and sure of herself and exuding lust. And so much more. "You're so incredibly special. Do you know that?"

Torrie shrugged lightly, but she was beaming like she'd just won the biggest golf trophy ever. "It's you that makes me feel that way."

Grace wanted so badly to be able to love Torrie, to throw everything and everyone that had come before to the wind and let it scatter and be carried off forever. There were obstacles, for sure, not the least of which were their respective careers. And then. Of course, there was Grace's bruised heart that was still painfully shut. However much she wanted to let Torrie in, to take a chance again, something held her back. It was too soon, and she was too stubborn and afraid to completely relent. She just hoped Torrie understood.

"Torrie," Grace began slowly. "I can't make you any promises."

"I know." Torrie stroked Grace's face, and her touch was both electrifying and reassuring.

"I don't know what happens next." Grace swallowed. "If anything."

Torrie's smile was wistful, an indication that she was resigned to Grace's reticence. "I know. But I love you, Grace. And I'll wait for you for as long as you need."

Could love really be this simple? This uncomplicated? Grace doubted it, though it would be wonderful to believe, at least for a little while, that Torrie's love was enough for both of them—just as she'd once fooled herself that her love for Aly was enough to sustain the relationship.

Grace's heart skipped at least two beats. "But I don't—"

Torrie placed a finger over Grace's lips. "I know, Grace. Just love me now. Tonight. With your body."

Grace could only nod dumbly, afraid her voice would crack if she tried to speak again.

"Can you do that?" Torrie asked, smiling like she hadn't any other care in the world.

Grace nodded again.

"Good." Torrie was already sliding down the bed, sliding alongside Grace, planting little kisses on her stomach as she brushed past.

Torrie positioned herself between Grace's legs, sliding lower and lower.

Oh, God, she's going to... Grace grew unbearably wet again. She thrummed with this new round of desire, the tiny jolts shooting all the way down to her toes and back up to her chest. The thought of Torrie's mouth on her was almost too much. She was already on the edge, mere moments away.

"You're so incredibly beautiful," Torrie mumbled, staring at Grace's secret flesh, inhaling deeply, grinning wolfishly like a big plate of steak and potatoes had just been placed in front of her. She even licked her lips like an animal about to devour its prey, and Grace melted.

She cried out at the first touch of Torrie's tongue.

CHAPTER TWELVE

Catie and Trish looked every bit as exhausted and sexually hungover the next morning as Torrie and Grace. No one had to speak of it. They all had a pretty good idea about what had transpired at the two houses in the night.

The coffeemaker was working overtime as the two chefs prepared omelets and crisped up leftover hashed potatoes, yawning and stifling smiles while they worked.

"You look pretty happy this morning." Trish shot Grace an approving look over the stove.

Smugly, Grace replied, "I could say the same about you."

Trish shrugged, but she looked absurdly happy.

"Was it good?" Grace couldn't resist the urge to tease her, especially since her cheeks were turning a nice shade of pink.

Trish flipped the omelet, trying to look unconcerned. When she finally beamed at Grace, it could have melted a glacier. "Better than ever. How was Torrie?"

Grace was still hot liquid inside at the thought of what they'd done most of the night. They'd barely slept, so eager were they to touch and taste one another, over and over again. Even in the shower this morning, Torrie had snuggled in behind her, pressed her hard body against her while playing with her breasts. It was like they couldn't get enough of each other, and Grace couldn't help but make the inevitable comparisons with Aly. No, it had never been this consuming with Aly. This intense.

"Well?" Trish pressed.

Grace sparked with a new round of desire, even though her body was still exhausted and sore. "It was incredible," she said quietly, reflectively.

"Well, good. I'm glad for you, Grace. I really am."

"Thanks." Grace didn't want to talk about the wider implications yet of what sex with Torrie meant. "What about you. Are you okay? I mean, really?"

Trish leaned against the counter, her arms folded over her chest. She looked happy. "Yeah, I am. Catie's wonderful."

"Are you going to keep seeing her?"

"I think so. Yeah."

Grace pointed beyond the kitchen at Catie and Torrie on the deck, their heads together. "Think they're talking about us?"

Trish chuckled. "God, I hope so."

Grace breathed in deeply, happier than she'd been in months. Maybe years. She wished things could just stay like this forever— the four of them, hanging out like teenagers with nothing better to do. No pressures, no demands, no complications, just loving one another with simplicity.

"I don't know about you," Trish said, "but I could sure use some sleep today."

"God, me too."

"Why don't we send those two away for awhile after breakfast so we can have a nap?"

"What, you don't think we can nap with them?"

Trish rolled her eyes. "Not if we want to get any sleep."

"True." There was always tonight, anyway.

"Then I thought later this afternoon we could all take the ferry over to the mainland and have dinner at that new seafood restaurant. I'm dying to try it."

"Sure, that sounds great." Grace nodded at Torrie and Catie

on the deck. "Let's go break the news to them that they're going to be banished for a few hours."

The two couples shared two bottles of red wine over an orgy of lobster and mussels. The way Torrie kept looking at Grace, like she couldn't wait to get her back into bed, almost made Grace say to hell with dinner. Sex with Torrie wasn't just fun and exhilarating. It was quickly becoming the focal point of her existence.

They were a little tipsy when they returned to the island, but not drunk. Grace had no intention of getting drunk and jeopardizing another exceedingly hot night in bed with Torrie. She'd need all her energy to keep up with her. They walked the mile or so from the ferry dock to Trish's cottage as the last of the day's light vanished, Torrie and Grace holding hands, Trish and Catie doing the same. Grace idly wondered how many times over the years the two cousins had walked these roads with girlfriends clutched at their sides, back when they used to run around the island like they owned it. She wished she'd known Torrie then, but when Torrie was sixteen, Grace was twenty-six and already serious about her culinary career. Torrie would have struck her as some smart ass, cocky kid, and Grace would not have seen the woman Torrie would become.

A strange car was parked in Trish's driveway, and they stopped to stare for a moment. There was a long-haired, shadowed figure sitting statue-like in the driver's seat.

"Who the hell is that?" Trish whispered.

"I'll go see," Catie said.

Before Catie could move, the car door suddenly snapped open and two long, bare legs emerged. Even in the dark, Grace knew exactly who it was, and her stomach clenched. *Oh, Christ!*

It was Aly. She slammed the car door shut and stood stock-still, staring back at Grace, her expression unreadable in the dark.

Grace was frozen in place. Her body didn't seem to want to move, and her voice came out forced and strained. "Aly, what are you doing here?"

Torrie's hand tightened protectively around hers. Torrie's presence gave her more strength than she could have imagined, and she needed it now, in her ex-lover's unwelcome and unexpected presence.

"Grace," Aly answered weakly. She took a step forward. "Can I talk to you? Privately?"

There was a subtle pleading in Aly's voice, and Grace shifted uncomfortably. She knew the others were all staring at her, waiting for her next move. "I don't think so, Aly."

Aly took another step closer, and Grace could see that she was as beautiful as ever, in spite of her pained expression. Grace didn't think she had ever seen Aly this way before, looking so out of control, like a train wreck. "Please?"

Torrie looked at Grace as she moved between the two women. "Grace, you don't have to do this."

"I know," Grace said, quickly making her decision. "It's okay, Torrie." She glanced at her friends and registered the disapproval in Trish's face. "Really, it'll be fine. Why don't you guys go over to Connie's for a while? I'll come join you later."

Torrie put her hands on Grace's shoulders, looking both disappointed and worried. "Are you sure, Grace?"

"Yes." Grace swallowed, not sure at all. But if Aly wanted to talk—really wanted to understand what had happened between them and why—Grace would give her that. Then they could say good-bye properly and she wouldn't have to see Aly again.

Torrie bent her head and kissed her thoroughly and possessively, making it patently clear to Aly that she was Grace's past and that Torrie was the present and maybe—just maybe— her future as well. Grace had to admire Torrie's gumption.

Grace gave Torrie a final squeeze of assurance, then silently watched the three women disappear down the road. She almost called Torrie back.

"Okay." Grace glared at Aly. "I have to tell you that I'm not particularly thrilled that you've blindsided me like this."

"I'm sorry, Grace. I didn't see any other way."

Grace supposed Aly had a point. She'd done a pretty good job of exorcising Aly from her life so far. She'd given Aly every indication that she hadn't wanted to see or hear from her again, but that didn't mean Aly didn't need to talk. She had not given her that chance until now.

Grace sighed and invited Aly to follow her inside. She slipped off her sandals and clicked on a few lights. She was unsure whether she should offer Aly a drink, not wanting to seem too welcoming, but her manners got the best of her.

"Anything hard would be great," Aly said.

Remy came bounding out, and Aly recoiled in disgust. "Get away, you monster." She kept turning away from him, trying to shoo him away at the same time. Grace tried not to laugh, secretly urging Remy on. Aly didn't like dogs. They were too unpredictable with all their energy, not to mention dirty, she'd told Grace many times. She could never understand why Grace had a dog, and now Grace was glad it was another source of disagreement between them—another reason why they weren't meant for each other.

"Remy, go lie down," Grace finally said before retrieving a bottle of Jack Daniels. She poured herself a glass of water while Aly filled her glass with the Tennessee whiskey.

On the couch, Grace leaned forward on her elbows, wanting Aly to just get on with it and get the hell on her way. Thoughts of Torrie were making her more and more impatient to just be done with Aly and that part of her life.

In an adjacent chair, Aly said nothing for a long moment. She sipped her drink, sighing loudly every now and again, looking everywhere but at Grace. Grace couldn't quite read her emotions, but she looked like hell, as though she'd been drinking too much lately and not sleeping enough. She was rail thin and her complexion was shot.

"You look like crap, Aly."

"Well, you should know, darling. You did this to me."

Grace's anger sparked, then died just as quickly. It would be so easy to argue with Aly, to blame one another, but the idea of it was far too emotionally exhausting. "Look. This hasn't been easy for me, either."

"You're the one who left," Aly said accusingly. "It's always easier for the one who leaves."

"That's not true."

Aly's laughter was bitter, and it was as though Grace were really seeing her clearly for the first time. Her soul seemed only to be filled with blame and unqualified hurt. "I can see it didn't take you long to get over us. I just never thought you'd go so butch, Grace. Jesus, I suppose you're going to tell me she digs ditches for a living or something."

"Is this really why you came here, Aly? To insult me? Because if you did, you can leave right now."

"Oh, hell. Forget it." She raised defeated eyes to Grace. "Look, I'm sorry, okay? I just… I don't understand things, Grace. I don't understand why…" She dissolved into tears, and it occurred to Grace that she'd never seen Aly cry before.

Oh, shit. "Aly, it wasn't my intention to hurt you. Honestly."

"What did you think would happen, Grace?" Aly's voice hardened considerably, growing edgier with each syllable. "Did you really think you could just throw me away like a candy wrapper?"

Grace buried her face in her hands for a moment. She was frustrated that Aly still had no clue why it had ended. "It wasn't like that, Aly."

"Then what? Because I don't have a fucking clue."

"It wasn't working anymore, Aly."

"What? Of course it was working. We were fond of each other. We were good for each other. The sex was always fucking great. Christ, Grace, I could make you come like nobody else."

That part certainly wasn't true anymore, and Aly seemed to recognize her error, her expression turning from startled to angry as realization dawned.

"Look, Aly. It wasn't working for me anymore, okay?"

Aly guzzled the rest of her drink and refilled the glass. "Why didn't you fucking tell me? Why did you just wait like that to drop the bomb?"

Grace blew out an exasperated breath. She had tried to tell Aly many times—in the arguments about Tim, in the requests to slip out of town together, in the pleas to accompany her to appearances. But Aly wasn't capable of understanding. Or she didn't want to. She didn't even know why she should try, except that she'd been brought up to finish what she started. She wanted closure now, and Aly obviously needed it too. "It was pretty clear over those three years that nothing was going to change between us."

"What do you mean, change between us? I thought everything was great."

"That's the problem. It wasn't. Jesus, Aly, I wanted more. You know that. Why do you think I wanted you to leave Tim? Why do you think I kept bugging you to spend more time with me?"

Aly shook her head, resting her glass against her forehead like a pack of ice. She was being stubborn and choosing not to get it, just as she always did. "You knew what you were getting when you signed up with me, Grace."

"I didn't sign up for anything, Aly. Sure, it was just sex and fun early on. But it changed for me. I wanted more than that. You just couldn't give me more. That was why it was time for me to end it."

Aly was getting drunk. That was clear. She was drinking the whiskey like water and getting more sullen by the minute. "All right, so fucking string me up, why don't you? Christ, Grace. I miss you. I want you back, okay? What more can I say?"

"No," Grace said quietly. "It's too late."

"It's not too late. I'll do whatever you want."

Grace shook her head, feeling more pity for Aly than anything. Aly had made absolutely no progress in their time apart. If anything, she had regressed. "Aly, I said it's too late. There's nothing I want from you anymore."

Aly wiped a tear, and Grace almost felt sorry for her. But she would not forget that Aly was the architect of her own misery.

"Is it because of this woman you're with?"

This woman. No. Torrie hadn't driven them apart. The biggest issue was Aly's lack of commitment—had always been—and Grace told her so. Torrie had turned out to be the nice surprise in all this mess. More than a surprise. A gem.

"Do you want me to leave Tim? Give up my career? Is that really what you want?" Aly looked miserable but desperate, like she just might do it. She'd looked nearly that scared once before when Grace almost left her. But of course, Aly had never gone through with it and neither had Grace. She wondered now what she'd ever seen in Aly in the first place—other than her superficial beauty and her bold desire for Grace. Only a faint shadow of the appeal Aly once held for her was still evident.

"I don't want you to do anything, Aly. Don't you see that's the problem? I never wanted to force you into doing anything you didn't want to do. You never arrived at those conclusions yourself. You never wanted to make those changes yourself. And now I realize you're not capable of it, Aly. It's just not who you are."

Grace had been told many times by Aly that her marriage was crap, that she and Tim hardly talked or spent time together, that there was no sex. And yet Aly desperately hung on to her image of a perfect marriage, like an aging starlet who tries to look as she did in her heyday. It was all a cheap façade, but she just couldn't let go of her life and all its trappings. It was sad.

Aly began crying, quietly at first, then more wretchedly, like her insides were pouring out of her. It was distressing to watch. "I'm sorry, Aly," Grace said hollowly, not knowing what else to say.

Aly cried for a long time, still not convinced of what Grace was telling her—that it was too late for them, that Grace was no longer in love with Aly, if she ever really had been. It wasn't that Aly was evil, but she had a lot of limitations, and Grace no longer wanted to live with those limitations. She no longer had the patience or desire or energy to coax a relationship from Aly. It was clear Aly missed what they'd had, but there was still no love in her eyes, and certainly not in her motivation.

Grace reached over and stroked Aly's arm, trying to give what little comfort she could. "Are you okay?"

Aly shook her head futilely. She got up and wordlessly moved to the couch beside Grace. Once there, she snuggled into Grace, and Grace automatically slipped her arm around her shoulder.

"Is there any chance we can work this out?" Aly asked, her words slurring and crashing into one another, like bumper cars.

"No. I'm sorry, Aly."

"Then at least help me, Grace. You owe me that much."

Aly was wrong, Grace didn't owe her a thing. But Grace owed herself a chance to undo some of what she'd done the last three years. She owed it to herself to take responsibility, to shoulder at least half the blame. *Finally*.

It was going to be a long night.

Torrie hadn't been able to sleep. She'd paced the house like a nervous, caged animal, and ignored Catie's and Trish's pleas to calm down. She couldn't be calm, not when things were falling apart, she told them. And they were falling apart. She was sure of it. She'd finally sent them off to bed, wanting to be alone with her fears and concern for Grace. She couldn't understand what was taking so long, why Grace hadn't come over yet.

What the fuck are they doing over there? Was Grace okay, she wondered for about the millionth time. Should she go over and check? She'd stuck her head out the door a few times, but the neighborhood was quiet. It was a cowardly and powerless place for her. Aly's appearance on the island had shaken Torrie. More than she would have thought. She couldn't understand what Grace's ex-lover could possibly want. Okay. She could. Aly undoubtedly wanted Grace back, and it scared the shit out of her.

Finally, just after dawn broke, Torrie could no longer stand it. She marched over to Grace's, still clad in last night's clothes, determined to find out what was going on. And if Aly was still there, she decided she was going to throw her out on her ass. If Grace and Aly were going to get back together, it was damned well going to be somewhere other than on Torrie's beloved island.

Torrie's stomach knotted at the sight of Aly's rental car still in the driveway. Aly was still there, and the realization sent burning rockets of anger through her. Her imagination began to get the worst of her, thinking about Grace and Aly alone all these hours. She knew if it were her, she would do anything to get Grace back, including seduction and empty promises, if that was what it took. She had no doubt that Aly was the type of woman who would use anything in her arsenal to get Grace back. It made her panic.

Just as Torrie was deciding what to do, Aly emerged from the house, looking like she'd just walked off the pages of a Neiman Marcus catalog—her clothes immaculate, her purse and jewelry the perfect accessories. When she noticed Torrie, she smiled enigmatically, her red-rimmed eyes taking only a second or two to register who Torrie was. She smirked in an ugly, arrogant way that made Torrie instantly want to throttle her.

"You're a little late," Aly said, looking Torrie up and down. "A lot late, actually."

Torrie bristled, hating that she was getting drawn into a confrontation. Aly moved toward the car and Torrie automatically stepped away, the way one stepped away from a snake that was about to strike out.

"We're going to try to work things out, you know. Sorry for your luck." Aly opened the car door and tossed a withering look at Torrie. "She's free now if you want to say good-bye."

Torrie's fists clenched by her side, her chest so tight she could barely breathe. She wanted to pound this woman, kick the shit out of her. But the car was already backing out of the driveway, and Torrie just stood there helplessly, feeling angry and hurt and useless. It was the worst betrayal. The worst pain she could imagine. She was in love with Grace. She'd been ready to commit to Grace, and yet Grace had so easily tossed her aside for this heartless woman from her past. *How could you, Grace?*

Torrie shivered, rooted to where she stood. She was completely void inside, as though the life had just been sucked out of her.

The screen door creaked open. Grace stepped onto the

porch, looking exhausted.

"Hey," she said wearily. She looked drained. Maybe even a little guilty, Torrie imagined.

Torrie stared at Grace, wordless. It hurt too much to try to talk, and besides, there was nothing Grace could say that would make her feel better. *Nothing.*

Torrie turned and did the only thing that occurred to her. She bolted without a glance back.

CHAPTER THIRTEEN

Torrie hugged her knees to her chest against the chilling air. There was a front coming in, bringing colder air with it, and she was still in her shorts and T-shirt from last night. The tiny island, as usual, was all hers.

The bobbing of the orange Zodiac was intensifying a little more, the waves slapping harder against the rubber sides, and she thought vaguely that she would need to get back soon. At the same time, a part of her really didn't care if she got back. She'd lost Grace, and not much else mattered right now.

It had been hours, and yet the raw pain of her discovery was still so incredibly acute. The way Aly had looked, all smug and sneering. And her words...*We're going to try to work things out...* pierced Torrie all over again, making her want to scream. *Sorry for your luck.* Torrie tortured herself over and over, immersing herself in the awful sting of the words, wanting to remember this pain always so that she could avoid it in the future.

And she would avoid it. She would not be so stupid again. She'd made a fool of herself, falling for Grace the way she had. Worst of all, it wasn't even Grace's fault. It wasn't like Grace hadn't warned her she wasn't over this Aly creature yet, that she wasn't ready to give herself completely to Torrie. But no. Torrie had to barge ahead anyway and fall in love with her, and then confess her love.

God, she must think I'm an idiot.

Well, no more. No more reckless play on her part. *Course management, Torrie, course management.* It was how you won golf tournaments, playing course management. It meant playing smart, playing conservative and not letting the course get the best of you by taking risky chances. You controlled the course, made it yours, and you didn't panic about one bad shot or one bad lie. You certainly didn't go out on a limb and strand yourself, setting yourself up for failure. Exactly as she'd done with Grace.

Her cell phone vibrated in her pocket. She'd forgotten the damned thing was even there.

"Cannon," she answered tersely.

"Hey, Torrie." It was Catie. "Where the hell are you?"

"Smoke Island."

"Well, get your ass over here. The weather's coming on."

"Yeah, yeah. I'm coming."

"Good. I'll meet you at the dock."

"Look, you don't have—"

"I said I'm meeting you at the dock, Tor."

"Why?" The hair on the back of her neck bristled. "What's wrong?"

"I'll tell you when you get here."

Torrie slapped the phone shut and swore to herself. She couldn't get to the boat fast enough. Had something happened to Grace? Christ, she hoped not, but her heart pounded, and she feared the worst. She might have lost her to that snotty lawyer bitch, but she wasn't going to lose her to yet another force beyond her control.

Moments later, Catie helped her tie up the Zodiac.

"Is it Grace?" Torrie's empty stomach lurched. She thought she might be sick.

Catie shook her head, and Torrie stumbled with relief.

"Are you okay, Tor?"

"Yes, dammit." She bent over to catch her breath and to still her unsettled stomach. "Just tell me what the fuck is going on, would you?"

"It's Aunt Connie. Her friends she's staying with called me an hour ago. She broke her leg in two places yesterday. She was parasailing, of all things."

"What?" They hurried to the nearby ferry, which was just loading up its final few passengers. There was no time to load a car. They'd cab it to the hospital. "Is she fucking crazy? Parasailing?"

"I know, I know." Catie quickly paid their fare and they climbed aboard.

"Is she going to be okay?"

"Yeah. Eventually, I think. She won't be able to stay on the island for the rest of the summer, though."

They took a seat below decks in a quiet corner.

"Well, I for one am going to give her holy hell," Torrie grumbled.

"No, you're not. It's too late for that anyway."

Torrie sighed and stared out the window at the undulating, gray waves. They reminded her of Grace's eyes and the way Grace had looked on the porch this morning, sort of guilty and contrite. Tired too, like she hadn't slept. Maybe by now Grace realized she'd made a mistake letting Aly believe they might patch things up, but still Torrie couldn't fathom why Grace would even consider giving her ex another chance, especially after the night she and Torrie had shared. How could she think of going back to Aly, after Torrie had told her she loved her? It burned her, thinking of Grace with Aly, doing those exquisite things with Aly, letting Aly touch her in the very same places Torrie had. Aly loving her. It was beyond hurtful. It was shattering.

"What the hell is wrong with you anyway, Torrie?"

"Hmmm?"

"Why did you run off by yourself today? And Grace seems upset too. Trish is with her. Did you guys have a fight or something?"

Torrie just shrugged, wanting to be left alone with her misery.

Catie tapped her fingers impatiently on her lap. "Does it have to do with that Aly woman who showed up last night? I know I'd sure be pissed if Trish's ex just showed up like that."

"I don't want to talk about it, C."

Catie sighed and squirmed beside her, like she wanted to press Torrie, but didn't quite know what to say. Torrie was in no mood to indulge her. The diesel engines rumbled and the ferry chugged along. Torrie just wished like hell they were there already.

"Torrie," Catie said in her stern caddie voice, the one meant to get Torrie to focus on the task at hand.

"What?" Torrie knew Catie meant well, that she was just worried about her. On the golf course, she listened to Catie, and she tried to now, but it was halfhearted.

"Grace is crazy about you, you know. Even I can see that. She wouldn't do anything stupid."

Like hell, Torrie thought, but she didn't say it. Grace had made her choice, and it was abundantly clear that their time together was over before it had ever really even begun. It was the most disappointing loss Torrie had ever experienced. "Look, Catie. Sometimes things just..." Torrie drew a deep breath, corralling her strength. "...aren't meant to work out, you know?"

Catie looked at her with surprising disappointment. "It's not like you to be a quitter, Tor."

Torrie gave her a searing look. It wasn't a matter of quitting, but of cutting her losses. Of letting Grace sort out her life on her own time, not Torrie's.

The ferry give a light bump as it brushed its mooring station. Standing, Torrie shot Catie a warning look. "Don't you dare say anything about this to Aunt Connie."

Grace rushed from the cab to the hospital doors, afraid she wouldn't get to see Connie before visiting hours ended. She already knew she wouldn't make the final ferry back to the island, that she'd have to spend the night on the mainland. That was fine with her. Trish would look after Remy. As for Torrie, she didn't know what the hell her plans were, the way she'd run off this morning looking so angry and hurt, like Grace had committed some unforgivable mistake by inviting Aly in last night. Her behavior had been frustrating and hurtful, because Grace could have used Torrie's support and understanding, not her jealousy and fear.

She asked a receptionist for the room number and was about to turn toward the elevators when Torrie and Catie strode through the lobby.

Catie waved her over.

"You guys got my note?" Catie asked. She'd left a note for Grace and Trish explaining what had happened to Connie and saying that she was already on her way to the hospital.

"Yeah, thanks. Trish stayed behind, but I wanted to come over right away and see Connie." She didn't look at Torrie immediately. She wanted to, but if Torrie was still angry and hurt, a public confrontation held no appeal. "Is she going to be okay?"

"Yeah, she will be. We just came from her room. She'll be thrilled to see you."

"I'll be glad to see her too." Grace's emotions welled up without warning. She could use some of Connie's sage advice right about now, but she didn't want to burden her, especially with her injuries. It didn't help either that Torrie was her niece. "I've missed her."

Catie cleared her throat, looking from one to the other. "I want to give Trish a call. I'll be back in a few minutes."

Grace didn't know whether to bless Catie or curse her.

"Don't be long, or we won't make the ferry," Torrie called after her. She looked like she wanted to follow Catie.

It would be just like her to run again, Grace thought irritably. She put her arm on Torrie, deciding to get at the root of things. "Can we talk?"

Torrie grunted and Grace took it for a yes. She led her to a bank of vending machines in a corner.

"Look, Torrie, I didn't know Aly would just show up like that. And when she did, I felt like I couldn't just send her away without at least talking to her."

Torrie's eyes were strangely void, as though she'd walled herself off, and Grace's exasperation mounted. Torrie was being petulant and unreasonable, and Grace, frankly, didn't deserve it. She'd done nothing wrong.

"If she wanted to talk, it was the least I could do after three years together." Grace sighed heavily and leaned against a machine that offered twelve varieties of chocolate bars. She wouldn't apologize, but she could try to pacify. "Look, she was hurting and I felt bad for her, okay? Maybe I shouldn't, but I did."

"Is that why you want to get back together with her? Out of guilt? Was I just a revenge fuck?" Torrie's words were harsh and blunt, and the accusation hit Grace like a sledgehammer.

"What?"

Torrie's arms were crossed over her chest. She looked defiant, hurt and totally unforgiving. "Aly. She said…" Torrie looked away.

Grace was confused until the realization of what Aly must have told Torrie dawned on her with sickening force. Her first thought, when she could finally form one, was: *that fucking bitch*. Her second was: *oh, no*. She saw and keenly felt the damage that had been done by Aly's spite. *Perhaps irreversible damage*.

"Torrie," she gasped. She shook her head. "Whatever she said…you believed her?"

Torrie's eyes were on her Adidas runners, her hands jammed in her pockets. The rigidity of her posture was slowly abating, but not enough to satisfy Grace that she was ready to listen to reason. "I don't know."

"What do you mean you don't know?" Grace demanded.

"I'm sorry," Torrie said grudgingly. "I should be big enough to handle it, but I'm not."

"I don't understand. There's nothing to *handle*, Torrie."

"You mean you're not getting back together with her?"

Grace could hardly believe what a nightmare this was becoming. "Torrie, we need to talk. But not here."

Grace took her by the wrist and led her down a hall. She tried a door that was locked and kept going until she found one that was open. She tugged Torrie into the storage closet.

"You didn't answer my question," Torrie said petulantly.

Grace seethed. "Of course I didn't tell her I wanted to get back with her."

"Do you want to?"

"Torrie, how could you ask me that after our night together? Do you really think I would make love with you when what I really wanted to do was get back with Aly? How could you think that?"

For the first time, Grace felt a twinge of regret about her night with Torrie. She'd known, deep in her bones, that it was too soon for them. *Why didn't I listen to myself? Why couldn't Torrie and I have been stronger and waited?*

Torrie sat down hard on a metal step stool and slumped. "I don't know, Grace. I don't know what to think, okay? I mean, Jesus, she was there all night. What else could you be talking about all that time?"

"Torrie." Grace tried to stay calm, but Torrie was drifting away from her, one word at a time. "Aly hasn't dealt with the breakup very well, that's all."

"That's her problem, not yours."

"Yes, it is her problem. But it's my responsibility too. I've learned you don't just walk away from three years like they never happened. It's just not that black and white. Life isn't made up of seamless stages."

"It is to me," Torrie said stubbornly. "Because I don't think Aly's going to take no for an answer that easily, and I won't fight for you like you're some trophy to win, Grace."

"You told me you loved me," Grace roared, wanting Torrie's words to bite her in the ass. She was so tired of people telling her things they didn't mean.

"I do." Torrie looked stricken. "I didn't know it'd be this—"

"Hard? This much work?" Grace knew she sounded bitter, but she wanted so badly to inflict the same kind of pain she was feeling. "You thought making the declaration meant it was so? That that was all there was to it?"

Torrie shook her head slowly. She began to cry softly. "I don't know what I thought." She was nearly inaudible.

"Oh, Torrie." A flood of emotions washed over Grace, drowning her almost. She wanted to kick Torrie in the ass, but she also wanted to hold her tightly and tell her everything was going to be all right. That they'd get through this. That she just needed more time.

"I was stupid to fall for you so quickly, Grace." Torrie was muttering, rambling, her words making Grace reel back on her heels. "It's not like you didn't warn me you weren't ready to move on. You never told me you loved me back. I was stupid. So stupid. I'm sorry."

Grace's mouth went dry with disbelief. Not only was Torrie slipping away, she wanted to negate what had happened between them. "That's it? You're throwing in the towel?"

Torrie simply shrugged and it was several anguished seconds before she spoke. "I thought I could do this relationship thing, Grace. But I'm a failure at it. It's not you. It's not your fault, okay? I just can't fucking do this. I guess I can't be normal and do relationships like everyone else."

Grace was astounded. This was the woman she thought she was falling in love with? This, this coward, this child who shrank so quickly from a challenge? Well. Let Torrie choke on her words. Let her run off to her golf and her girls and her carefree—careless—lifestyle.

"Fine," Grace finally said, her voice grating, like broken glass. "I won't hold you back. I just hope that someday you'll learn that when you tell someone you love them, you actually mean it."

She turned before Torrie could say anything more and made her exit, her legs somehow functioning. She was trying to stay afloat with nothing to grab onto but her own anger and pain.

"Torrie's gone, you know."

"Well, that's a helluva greeting."

"She left first thing this morning. Catie said she packed all her stuff and was heading back home."

Grace threw her keys and bag on a nearby table. It had been a long, sleepless night at the motel near the hospital. She was not in the mood for an argument with Trish, especially where Torrie was concerned.

"To Arizona," Trish continued.

Grace flopped down on the couch, threw her head back and closed her eyes. Christ, this just kept getting worse and worse. "It's not my fault, Trish. I'm not responsible for Torrie going to Arizona or wherever. She's a big girl."

Grace opened her eyes in time to see Trish shoot her an admonishing look. Really, did Trish think she was supposed to chase after Torrie, hunt her down in Arizona and beg her to come back? It was Torrie who'd made it plain she was giving up on them. It was Torrie who needed to grow up, needed to show some trust and patience. Grace gave Remy, who'd waddled over to her, some loving pats on the head and turned away from his stinky dog breath. "What's Aunt Trish been feeding you, Remy? Dead fish? Yuk."

Trish stood before her with her hands on her hips. "All right. Who is this cold, heartless woman and what have you done with Grace?"

"Why don't you just spit it out already? Tell me I'm a heartless bitch because I broke Torrie's heart or something. Isn't that what you're really trying to say?"

"Well, did you break her heart?"

"I don't know, Trish. And frankly, I'm a little too pissed right now to care."

"Why?"

Grace still burned with the memory of her argument with Torrie. Torrie believing Aly over her. Torrie taking the coward's way out. "Because Torrie thinks I'm being too nice to Aly and that I secretly want to go back to her or something."

Trish's eyes widened. "Do you?"

"No! Christ, not you too."

Trish shrugged apologetically. "Sorry. I just thought... Shit. I know break-ups are seldom tidy. That sometimes it's two steps back for every step forward."

"Is that why you and Scott kept separating and getting back together for awhile?"

"Even when you know it's not right, there's something comforting about familiarity, you know?"

"Yeah, well, there's nothing comforting about the idea of getting back with Aly." Grace would not slide backward. But she didn't want any blurred lines before she fully committed to Torrie or anyone else. Everything in her life had to be in its place, just like her mise en place...the chopped herbs in their own bowl, the diced onions in theirs, the garlic in its own little pile, the spices proportioned out. Aly needed to be firmly and cleanly in her past before she could fully turn to the future. She knew that now.

"Look, you can't blame Torrie for jumping to conclusions." Trish plopped down beside Grace, stretching her legs on the coffee table.

"Yes, I can. She doesn't trust me."

"She doesn't know you well enough, that's all."

"She knows me well enough to tell me she loves me," Grace said. As soon as the words were out, she began to tremble. She tucked her hands under her thighs to still them.

"Oh, no."

Grace nodded, wanting to cry. "I thought she was telling the truth about that, Trish. I was wrong."

Trish moved beside her, touching shoulders. "Trust. Love. They're new to her. And even if they weren't, those two things are never easy. You know that."

Grace supposed so. She hardly knew much about them herself. "I don't want to be anybody's Guinea pig."

"Can't you give her some time, Grace? Give her a chance?"

Grace squeezed her eyes shut, annoyed that Trish was so quick to take Torrie's side. "I'm the one who needs some time here, because you know what? I think I've had it with women right now."

Trish laughed, caught the look on Grace's face and quickly sobered. "You're not serious are you? Are you going straight?" She shook her head and began to mumble. "Figures. Just when I'm going gay, you're going straight."

Grace blew out an exasperated breath. "No, I'm not going straight. But I don't want a relationship right now. With anyone."

"You like Torrie, don't you? I mean, two days ago you were on cloud nine."

It was true, she had been after that incredible night with Torrie. Before that, even. Torrie made her feel so special—cherished and desired, respected, loved. She was nothing like Aly. She was sweet and honest and genuine. Someone you could dream with, build things with. Maybe even make a life with. And yeah, Torrie wasn't an expert at relationships or handling her emotions. She would make mistakes, just like Grace would. And maybe making those mistakes together was better than being miserable apart. *Maybe, but it's too late now, anyway. She's gone, and there's nothing I can do about that.*

Grace allowed the weight of sadness and loss and that familiar sense of futility to press on her like an invisible weight. "Trish, when are you going back to Boston?"

"In a couple of days. Catie has to go back on the Tour, and I need to get back to work."

Grace nodded sharply. "I'm going with you." She was already an island. She didn't need to spend any more time alone on a real one.

CHAPTER FOURTEEN

It didn't take Aunt Connie long to raise her concerns about Torrie and her seeming fixation on punishing herself. That was her aunt—never one to keep her strong opinions to herself, especially where her loved ones were concerned. The only thing that made the habit annoying was the fact she was so often right.

After spending a week in the hospital and another week convalescing with her friends on the mainland, Aunt Connie had flown out to Arizona to stay with Torrie and her parents. The pain had aged her, but she was as feisty as ever. She had graduated to crutches, but the family didn't trust her to look after herself for at least a couple more weeks. They were happy to help look after her, and now, as she sat on the covered patio of the Cannons' Spanish-style, sprawling bungalow, her broken leg elevated on a footstool, her eyes intently followed Torrie as she repeatedly swung a golf club in the backyard.

"Isn't it a little soon to be swinging golf clubs?"

"Nope." Torrie swung again, harder this time, not connecting with anything, but just trying to get the timing of the motion back. She still didn't have her full backswing, or her power. It would be at least a couple more weeks before she could start practicing for real.

"You're pale and you're wincing, Torrie. Aren't you going to make things worse?"

"I'm fine. My physio said I could start swinging a club."

Aunt Connie snorted. "She probably meant putting. Not a full swing."

Torrie knew her aunt was just being overly protective. "I'm fine. Really."

Torrie wasn't fine and she knew it. In the mirror, she'd seen the shadows beneath her eyes, the slightly haunted look on her face. The pounds had been melting off, and not just because of the endless miles of jogging and trips to the gym nearly every day. Much of her notorious appetite had deserted her, and she knew exactly why.

Aunt Connie sighed impatiently. "Torrie, honey, come and sit down for a minute. Take a break."

Torrie swung the club a few more times. It could make her forget things for a while, but now the pain was sharp. She wiped the sweat from her face with the hand towel she'd stuffed into her back pocket. "All right." She relented and dropped into a chair, her body more exhausted than she wanted to admit. Her shoulder throbbed dully, like a persistent toothache.

"Are you going to tell me what happened between you and Grace?" The question was posed as matter-of-factly as asking about the price of gasoline.

"What?" Torrie was momentarily stunned. Had Grace said something to her aunt? Catie perhaps? "What makes you think anything happened?"

"Oh, Torrie." A gnarly hand reached over and patted her knee affectionately. "Haven't you realized by now how well I know you?"

Torrie smiled at that. In some ways, her aunt knew her better than anyone in the family. Her mother knew what drove Torrie, knew her strengths and weaknesses and had an uncanny ability to perceive what her daughter needed to become stronger, better, happier. But it was Aunt Connie who had a unique grasp of Torrie's deepest, most intimate self. Aunt Connie had always known when she was struggling with some inner demon, or some elusive desire. She understood her private pain. She seemed to understand things about Torrie before Torrie even acknowledged them to herself. It was inevitable that Aunt Connie would figure things out, she supposed.

"We got to know each other better after you left," Torrie said.

A single gray eyebrow arched. "Did you tell her how you felt?"

Torrie's throat closed up. "Yeah," she rasped. She'd laid her heart bare to Grace in a way she'd never done with anyone before. Grace had been so gracious, accepting of Torrie's love, even though she couldn't fully reciprocate. Torrie would give anything to have that one, precious night back. It had been almost perfect, and she'd been so sure then that Grace would have returned her love with just a little more time. Grace did care for her, even if she couldn't say the words. It was expressed in the way she responded to Torrie's touch, in the way she looked at Torrie. It was in the way she arched back and called Torrie's name at the moment when the body collides with the soul in perfect, blissful synchronicity.

"Judging by the way you've been acting, I'd say it went badly?"

"No." Torrie shook her head and gazed off into the distance, immersed in the fleeting joy of their night together. "It was wonderful. I had the best night of my life, Aunt Connie."

Aunt Connie whistled low and long, then smiled broadly. "Well, that's wonderful, dear. You don't know how happy I am to hear that." Her expression turned to worry. "But what went so terribly wrong?"

Torrie didn't speak for a long time. She wanted to be composed first. She'd cried privately enough times over Grace, but she couldn't be sure there weren't still more tears.

"What is it, dear?" Aunt Connie pressed gently.

Torrie had felt a certain measure of destiny with Grace. Now she wasn't sure of anything anymore, except that she was alone and more lost than at any time in her life. She thought returning home would help, but it hadn't. Maybe rejoining the Tour would. "She told me she wasn't ready to commit herself to me, that she wasn't ready to love me. She was just coming out of a relationship."

Aunt Connie nodded thoughtfully. "I see. I'd suspected as much."

"You did?"

"She hadn't told me specifically, but it seemed that way to me from things she'd hinted at. I gathered it wasn't a very good relationship."

"It wasn't."

"I can understand why she needs time, Torrie. Are you not patient enough to give her that time?"

"It's more complicated than that."

Aunt Connie looked puzzled. "I don't understand, dear."

"You see, right after we..." Torrie faltered, hesitant about discussing sex with her aunt.

Aunt Connie smiled knowingly. "It's okay. I get it, Torrie. After a night of mad, passionate love."

Torrie warmed at the sweet memory of Grace beneath her, Grace moving rhythmically on top of her, their bodies fused together in a utopian blend of fiery want and patient need. Then her heart clamped shut at the memory of Aly showing up and wanting to claim Grace. She'd succeeded in making Torrie feel that Grace would never really be hers, and for that, she would never forgive Aly. "Her ex showed up unexpectedly," Torrie said roughly. "She wants Grace back."

Emotions flickered across her aunt's face. First surprise and then doubt. "What does Grace want?"

Torrie shrugged. "She feels some sort of duty to help..." that bitch, she wanted to say, "her ex through the breakup."

"Well, don't you think it's better to fall in love with someone kind like that than someone who's coldhearted?"

209

"I don't think it's better to fall in love at all."

"Oh, Torrie. You can't mean that."

"I can and I do, Aunt Connie." It was simpler on her own, immersing herself in her career. Golf would be her refuge. It would fill her loneliness—that and perhaps a good-looking woman every now and again. Golf and meaningless flings had always been enough, and they would be again. "I'm not cut out for that kind of life, Aunt Connie."

"Bullshit."

Torrie had rarely heard her aunt swear before. It gave her a jolt.

"You're afraid because this isn't coming easy to you," Aunt Connie continued. "Oh, love can come easily enough, but to keep it, Torrie, takes guts. And hard work. And commitment."

Torrie's anger spontaneously hardened her jaw. "I know about guts and hard work and commitment. I wouldn't be on the Tour this long if I didn't."

"But golf came easy to you, Torrie. It always did, right from the get-go, and that's my point. You can't be spectacular at everything right away. You can't be perfect at everything you do. Some things take time, and sometimes you have to fall down before you succeed."

Torrie sometimes hated these little nuggets of wisdom from her aunt, particularly now. She was thirty years old. She could make her own way, make her own decisions. She didn't need her aunt's guiding hand anymore.

"I know that, Aunt Connie. I really do." Torrie drew hard on her patience. It was the kind of patience that let her persevere against windy, stormy conditions on the golf course or a swing that was just off. "And I know you're trying to help me. I appreciate that. But I think it's just as well, the way things turned out."

Aunt Connie shook her head lightly. "How can you be sure?"

"It's not meant to be." Torrie said the words with a finality that eluded her, but for now, it was what she wanted to believe. "We both have our careers, Aunt Connie. She's in Boston and

I'm not. And if her ex wants to try to get her back, well, I can't stop her."

"You can overcome geographical distances, Torrie."

"I know that. But I can't put something I have no confidence in above my career. It's a gamble I'm not able to take right now. Golf is my present and my future. Grace... I'm not so sure."

Disapproval poured from her aunt just as surely as if she'd given voice to it. She knew Aunt Connie thought she was making a mistake, but if she was—and it was a big if—then it was hers to make. "I need to work at getting back on the Tour," she said softly. "This is my time now. And being reminded that I failed with Grace is not what I need right now."

Her aunt looked at her with more love than criticism. They clasped hands on the glass tabletop.

The weeks since Grace had left Sheridan Island had brought about changes, not the least of which was her appearance. She'd decided on impulse to cut her hair short. Once cut, it was naturally thick and wavy, and she'd had it highlighted. She had to agree with Trish and James. It made her look years younger. Better yet, she hoped it signaled a fresh start in other facets of her life too.

Torrie hadn't contacted her, and while Torrie's silence hurt, Grace struggled to move on from the brief affair that had been another addition to her list of mistakes. She tried to take it easy, going for lots of walks with Remy, reading novels, hitting the gym regularly. She eased herself back into work, unsure of how much of her old way of life she wanted to resume. The pace of work she'd once endured was grueling and that, she now knew, was at the root of her problems. If she was going to make positive changes in her life, she knew she needed to take more time out for herself and slow the crazy pace that had consumed her life the last few years. She needed to dial back the clock somehow.

It was a Friday afternoon, hot and sticky and typical of early August in Boston. Grace wanted to work a shift on the line at Sheridan's. She hadn't actually cooked on the line in months, her role revolving into a more supervisory one over the past year, and most of it at arm's length while they filmed their television show and toured with their cookbook. She and Trish would go over the books regularly, meet with the executive chef once a week to talk about the menu, staff, supplies. Her managerial relationship with her restaurant had become boring and unsatisfying, and now she yearned to get her hands dirty, get back in the trenches for a night or two. It just might help her remember why she was in this business and find what she still wanted from it. She was toying with the idea of scaling back, finding her niche again, and there was nothing like a hot, frenetic, bustling kitchen on a busy Friday night to do just that.

Trish was there too. They started the afternoon by inspecting each of the chefs' stations under the guidance of their executive chef, a short, stocky, African-American woman who was one of the best chefs on the eastern seaboard. Liz was fussy and ran her motley crew with the precision of a battle-hardened general.

Several of the line chefs were busy getting their mise en place ready—chopping onions, peppers, garlic, chives and other herbs. The chatter was relaxed and nothing like the brusque, rude commands and vulgar language that would leave the air blue once the dinner rush started. Music was an assortment of hip-hop and urban, just loud enough and pounding enough to work up everyone's energy. Grace and Trish moved on to where a tall, Latino chef was boning a leg of veal. He smiled and nodded in their direction without taking his eyes off his work. He had already separated the skinned leg into different muscles: top round, bottom round, top knuckle, top sirloin and shank. He was trimming each of the cuts. It was a meticulous process, but he went about it quickly and adeptly.

Another cook was cleaning fish, and at the sauce station, chicken and beef stocks were on a low simmer in large iron pots. A third pot was a béchamel. Grace knew that a slight variation in seasoning, viscosity, reduction or cooking time could make the difference between an average and an extraordinary sauce. Stocks and sauces were the backbone of a successful kitchen. They were the main thickening or flavoring agent and were usually the essential but nearly invisible element behind a great dish.

Each chef had a territory, an area of expertise, and the kitchen had begun to take on a rhythm that would escalate as the dinner hour approached. Grace liked the unspoken inclusion in a restaurant kitchen. It didn't matter what your religion or sexual preference was, whether you had a criminal record or an addiction. What mattered was that you worked quickly and efficiently, took orders and worked as a team. She missed the camaraderie, the hard work under pressure, the praise for a job well done.

Tonight, Grace would prepare a large vat of New England clam chowder. She set to work on chopping and frying bacon, then chopping and sautéing onions. She was a little rusty with her knife work, but only a little. It didn't take her long to work up her speed so that she could almost do it without looking. Chopping, scraping, chopping, scraping. Her hands danced across the cutting board—fluid, decisive, smooth. She chopped clam meat then diced some red potatoes. The repetitive work was a nice break. She didn't have to think, and it was exactly what she needed after almost three months of doing nothing but thinking. Thinking and, too often, agonizing.

Customers had begun arriving for dinner. Soon the constant sizzling of steak or pork being tossed in a pan or on a grill sliced through the music and chatter. Liver was being sautéed, pork was being seared, a large pan of beef tenderloin was pulled from an oven. Orders were shouted out. "Where's my fucking tuna steak!" the sous-chef yelled. "Did you run out and catch the bloody thing yourself?"

"Coming," someone called back. Potatoes were spooned up, sauces were drizzled. Grace moved to the pasta station to help out. She poured olive oil into a pan and began sautéing paper thin garlic slices and crushed red peppers, artichoke hearts, vegetables, olives. Thankfully, the music had changed to Ella Fitzgerald, then Frank Sinatra, and she started humming, even sang a few bars of "That's Life."

She mixed the concoction into a bowl of cooked penne,

threw some fresh basil and grated parmesan on top, spun and slid the plate the length of the counter, putting a little English on it. "Number five ready," she yelled and started another. The assembly line was in high gear now and Grace's body responded to the rush. Adrenaline pumped and she began shuffling her feet and swaying her hips to the music. Oh yeah. This was fun!

As the evening progressed and the pace eventually slowed, exhaustion began to seep in. By midnight, the restaurant was empty and the chefs had cleaned their stations. The tradition was to hit last call at a pub to soak up the final fragments of leftover energy and to hash over the night's events. A group of them cabbed it to a pub in Harvard Square, where Trish handed Grace a vodka and orange juice. She downed half of it in one gulp.

"Thirsty?" Trish teased.

Grace stretched her neck, hearing the fine bones click. "God, I haven't worked that hard in a while. My feet are killing me, and my hands feel like they're the size of oven mitts."

Trish laughed wearily. "Believe me. I know what you mean."

Jayla, a new hire at Sheridan's, sidled up to them and leaned against the bar, a frothy glass of beer in one hand. Her skin was the color of milky coffee and her eyes were as dark as cocoa. She smiled at Grace, her perfect white teeth a dazzling contrast to the dull lighting of the pub. "You were awesome, Grace. I really enjoyed working with you tonight."

Surprised for an instant, Grace returned the smile and tipped her glass. "Thank you, Jayla. I enjoyed working with you too."

"I like how you're so calm and cool in there. Like when Juan burned his hand? You never missed a step, taking over his station the way you did." She stepped closer and laid a hand softly next to Grace's. "Truthfully? You work faster than Juan. And…" Her eyes quickly shot up and down the length of Grace's body as her smile lengthened. "You're much nicer to look at."

A twinge of pleasure caught Grace off guard. It was nice having someone flirt with her, but she certainly had no intention of taking it further. Her thoughts still drifted to Torrie more often than she wanted. She didn't want to think about her because

Torrie was in the past, and there was no chance of a future. They'd had a brief moment where Grace thought something meaningful was developing between them, perhaps even something lasting. But she'd learned the painful way that Torrie wasn't truly serious about her, that at the first sign of trouble, she had bolted. Torrie was no more ready for a serious relationship right now than Grace was. Perhaps even less so.

More of the restaurant's workers drifted over to the trio. They were boisterous, on their second drinks and laughing about a waiter's dumped plate of spaghetti earlier in the evening.

Grace collected her second vodka and orange juice and Trish led her to a private table in a corner. Jayla looked disappointed by their departure.

"How'd it feel tonight?" Trish asked.

Grace sat down and sipped her drink, slowly this time. "Great. I've missed the cooking part, Trish. It seems like we've been busier being celebrities lately than being actual chefs."

Trish nodded dolefully. "I've been thinking the same thing."

"It's hard not to though, isn't it? You start having some success, and more and more opportunities seem to open up, and people urge you to take them. And then they demand you take them, so you do, and it just leads to more. I don't know...We've gotten so far removed from where we started."

Trish smiled nostalgically. "Remember the little bistro we started together eight years ago? Just the two of us?"

"Yeah." It was their first restaurant together, so small it only seated two dozen people. They'd specialized in French cuisine, and they'd worked like dogs to make it a success, learning quickly from their mistakes. "It was fun, wasn't it?"

"The best."

They sat in silence, nursing their drinks, immersed in their own thoughts. Grace could feel Jayla's eyes on her back, not uncomfortably so.

"What killed your marriage with Scott?" Grace suddenly asked.

Trish popped a peanut into her mouth, thoughtful for a

moment. "Never seeing each other for one thing. Never having had a solid base of friendship for another."

"Friendship and spending time together." Grace winked. "The secret ingredients?"

"Hell, I'm no authority on it, but it makes sense to me. I didn't have those things with Scott. You didn't have them with Aly, and now look at us."

"Yeah." Grace laughed. "Lonely old maids. Or at least I am."

Trish didn't laugh. "You could have had those things with Torrie."

Grace was disgusted by the tears pooling suddenly. Damn Torrie for still making her hurt like this when she least expected it. Twenty days. That's all Torrie had been in her life, but those twenty days still made her quiver with regret. Still made her heart desolate in a way she'd never experienced before. It was like finally discovering a taste for something and having it permanently taken away.

"I'm sorry, Grace. You haven't talked much about Torrie and I wish you would."

Grace swallowed her unshed tears and took another drink. "What's to say? You know the story."

"Yeah, but I don't think I know how it ends yet."

Grace laughed bitterly. "Yes you do. It's over. Torrie will be back on the Tour any day now, and she's made it clear by her very loud silence that she wants nothing more to do with me."

"Catie says Torrie's not herself. That she's hurting too."

Grace drained her drink and set the empty glass down with an angry thud. "Torrie is the engineer of her own unhappiness. What the hell do you want me to say, Trish?"

Trish gave her a look of gentle understanding. "That it's not all her fault, Grace. That maybe some of it's your responsibility too."

Responsibility. Grace had thought a lot about that word over the last three months. It was why Torrie's leaving filled her with more regret than anger. Yes, Trish was right. It would be simpler if she could just blame everything on everybody else. Except she couldn't anymore. She was the one responsible for her own life and for whether she was happy or not.

"I know, Trish." Grace rubbed her temples wearily. "I wasn't ready for Torrie."

"Torrie, or anyone?"

"Anyone," Grace said. "When Torrie came into my life, I wanted it to be the right time. I really did, but it wasn't. I think, honestly, it was probably for the best that she walked out."

Trish shrugged. "I don't know about that. Maybe you two could have worked on things. Have you thought about getting in touch with her?"

Grace had never been serious about the idea. "No. There's no point. I don't think we'd be any further ahead than where we were."

"You know, I've been thinking a lot about things too lately."

"Catie?"

"Yeah."

"Are you in love with her?"

Trish shrugged, but she couldn't quite keep the smile off her face. "I like her, Grace. A lot. We're trying to see each other every couple of weeks, but it's not enough."

"What are you going to do about it?"

Trish studied the wooden tabletop scratched and maimed by years of use. "Like I said, you can't make a relationship work if you don't spend time together."

"And like I said, what are you going to do about it?"

Trish raised slightly desperate eyes. "I don't know, Grace. We'll be starting to tape a new season of shows soon. We've got the Manhattan restaurant opening for Christmas. We're going to be so socked in soon, we won't know which way is up."

"What if we weren't?"

"What?"

"Socked in." Grace's voice took on new life. "What if we just said fuck it?"

Trish's eyebrows nearly jumped off her forehead. Then she laughed long and hard, right from the belly. "You can't be serious,

Gracie."

"Maybe I am." Grace was deadly serious. More serious about anything than she'd ever been. "I'm not sure we'll ever get what we need in our lives if we keep up this pace."

Trish had gone a little pale, but she wasn't dismissing Grace's suggestion. "Do you think we actually could scale back? I mean, just go back to running Sheridan's?"

Grace was growing excited by the idea. They could, if they wanted to. They'd always been able to do anything they wanted. "Why not? We'll be finished taping all our shows by early December. Our contract is only for a season at a time, so we don't have to renew it."

"What about the new restaurant?"

That was a little more serious. "There'll be penalties with the contractor. We're probably on the hook for the lease for a year. We'll lose a bit, but James can work his charm."

Trish smiled widely, then leaned over and kissed Grace on the cheek. "Let's do it, Grace."

"Yeah," Grace said with conviction. "Let's do it."

They ordered another drink to celebrate their impulsive decision. It was scary, unraveling their plans. But it was necessary, and Grace knew it was right.

Trish was looking past her. "You do realize Jayla's been trying to hit on you?"

Grace spun her glass around in her hand, her other hand playing with the straw. "She's a nice woman, but I'm not interested."

"It could be fun."

Grace shot Trish a look that told her to knock it off. Jayla could, no doubt, provide a few hours of fun and distraction, but it was the furthest thing from Grace's mind right now.

Before leaving, she spun around and flicked a brief, apologetic glance at Jayla that told her there was no hope.

Torrie's shoulder hurt with every swing of the club. By the third day of the four-day tournament—her first back on the

Tour—it began to hurt even when she wasn't swinging. The rounds and the punishing practice hours the last few days had taken a painful toll. Ice and ibuprofen were her temporary liberators, but by bedtime, Torrie would curl up and bite back a sob. One more day, she told herself. She was in sixth position, a marvelous and surprising showing after her months-long layoff. She was only five strokes off the lead, which, in past tournaments, was nothing for Torrie. Five strokes she could practically make up in her sleep. Then. Now, it struck her that those five strokes meant five fewer painful swings of her club, which sounded heavenly, but seemed nearly insurmountable.

It was early, barely ten o'clock, but Torrie was exhausted. She would have to be up by seven in the morning for the final round. She'd eat no later than eight, giving herself enough time for her breakfast to settle before she would start warming up on the range and the practice green. Two hours of that and she would be ready for her noon tee time.

In her mind, Torrie ran through tomorrow's routine. It would be precise and the same as always. She would eat the same thing she always ate on tournament day—bacon, eggs, potatoes, fruit. She would meet Catie, and they would go through all the equipment in her bag. She would pack power drinks, power bars and bananas, extra socks. She'd go over their notes on the course, page by page. They'd look at the weather forecast and check the wind. Her clothing was already set out. Routine was important because once she started practicing for the round, she wanted nothing on her mind but the task at hand. And by the time she made her way to the first tee box, she would be completely focused, totally unconcerned about how the other golfers were doing. It would be like walking through a tunnel.

Torrie tried to visualize that tunnel, dark on all sides, nothing but sunshine and green grass at the end. There was only herself, walking toward it, feeling the heat on her face the closer she got. Her breathing was calm, regular. She was almost there, at the opening, where a field of green awaited. Three more steps. Two more. One. *Grace! Oh, God, it's Grace.* She was there suddenly, waiting at the opening to the field, her arms outstretched, a gentle smile on her face. Her eyes were not angry, only forgiving.

Torrie sucked in a deep breath tightly, as though she were drawing it in through a straw. Tomorrow would be her biggest day in months and yet there was Grace. Torrie had not been able to expel her from her thoughts, from her very being. She was the one Torrie talked to in her mind every day. *I'm having a good shoulder day today, Grace. You should see how much farther I was hitting the ball today, Grace. It felt so good. The e-mail Aunt Connie sent me today was a real laugh, Grace, because she talked about actually getting a dog of her own and that it was all your fault. Grace, this meal I had last night would have been right up your alley, though you probably could have cooked it better. Grace, did you hear that new song on the radio, "I Kissed a Girl?" Man, it's wild, isn't it?*

She had conversations in her head like that all the time, but tonight and tomorrow, she did not want Grace in her head. She had no time for the tiny tremble in her limbs whenever she thought of Grace, or the little tickle in her stomach, or the tightness in her chest. *This is not the time for you, Grace. Go away.*

With effort, Torrie pushed Grace out. When she awoke in the morning she felt rested, and thankfully, calm. She would be in control today, she decided. She would be in absolute control of her body and her mind. Today would be hers. She would make up those five shots, no matter what anyone else did. Five shots. The thought—the goal—was all that mattered.

She and Catie didn't talk a lot. Catie instinctively knew it was not a day where Torrie needed any sort of bolstering or helpful distractions, so she let Torrie retreat into herself. To focus.

Torrie's friend Diana was her playing partner today, a luck of the draw that Torrie welcomed. Torrie knew Diana was secretly pulling for her to do well, even though Diana was a shot ahead of her. They would both focus on climbing ahead of the pack, but not climbing on each other's backs to do it like some did. Players played their own game, but there were head games too sometimes, like walking through someone's line of sight or stepping on their putting line with an artificial oops, I'm sorry.

Or it might be walking away before the opponent strikes her ball, or whispering too loudly to a caddie or Tour official nearby. There would be no such nonsense between Torrie and Diana. They respected one another too much.

Diana gave her an encouraging nod just before her first drive. Torrie gasped a little from the pain as her club struck the ball, sending it powerfully into the air. She watched it arc neatly and nearly disappear in the almost white light of the noon sky. They matched each other shot for shot, slowly overtaking the field, with Diana remaining a stroke ahead of Torrie.

"How's the shoulder?" Diana asked midway through the round.

"Manageable, I guess." With anyone else, Torrie might have lied and said it felt great.

Diana nodded in sympathy. They didn't speak much the rest of the way as they jockeyed for top position on the leader board. Back and forth they went, a birdie for Torrie sending her into a tie with Diana. They both parred the next hole, and on the par-three seventeenth, Diana's eight-iron drive plopped down smoothly, mere inches from the hole. Torrie, who had to go up a club because of her weakened shoulder, couldn't harness enough spin. Her ball landed several feet from the hole and above it, which would make for a difficult putt. Diana was pretty much guaranteed to pull ahead of Torrie again, with one hole left to play. Torrie's birdie attempt veered wide. Diana's thunked into the cup.

On the final tee box, Torrie calculated her chances. She was playing her own game, playing against herself, but she could not pretend she didn't want to win this one. She did want it. Badly. It would send a powerful message to her rivals and her fans that she was back in the biggest way possible. She'd need a birdie just to tie Diana and force a playoff. If Diana birdied as well, the win would be hers.

Torrie sent her drive out well beyond two hundred and sixty yards—a strong drive considering her shoulder felt like an elephant was sitting on it. But it sliced a little, and Torrie winced more from the pain of the ball's direction than from her shoulder. She swore to herself, because Diana's ball was nicely in the middle and her own sat just on the gluey edge of the fairway and the dense rough.

Torrie would hit first. She and Catie quickly discussed the line to the hole and which club to use. She knew what she had to do—lock her wrists and power through the edge of the deep rough that would try to hang on to her ball and mess with its trajectory. Torrie took a deep breath, lined herself up to the ball and cleared her mind. Between shots she often let a song run through her head—nothing more complex than that. Always a catchy tune too, nothing with deep lyrics or a doleful melody. Just before taking her shot, however, her mind always went completely blank. She was beyond thinking about what she needed to do, and she was beyond visualizing it. It was time to trust the mechanics of her swing and the plan she was about to put in motion. The repetitiveness and the muscle memory of years of playing told her it was just like any of the other millions of shots she'd taken. In her backswing, she knew the shot would hurt. On the downswing she knew it would hurt significantly. On impact, it hurt like bloody hell. She grunted loudly and doubled over in a flash of pain.

"Jesus, Torrie." Catie rushed to her side. "Are you okay?"

Torrie nodded, unable to speak. She would have to be okay. She would have to make at least one, maybe two more shots. She had yet to look at where her ball had gone.

"You did good, Tor."

Torrie finally glanced up. The pain had caused her to take something off the ball, and instead of being on the green, it lay just at the edge. It would mean a chip and a put for par. An up and down, unless she could pull magic out of her hat and sink her chip shot.

Her shoulder throbbing wildly, Torrie strode ahead, hoping for the best, thinking the worst. She had to make that chip. What's more, she had to believe she would. She knew how it worked. Doubt was for losers. But these were special circumstances and her shoulder was a very real impediment. It occurred to her for the first time in these four days that maybe she'd come back to the Tour too soon.

She stood over her chip shot, catching an encouraging wink from Diana, but barely, for the first time in years, feeling any confidence. She knew it was a crappy shot before the ball even left her club. She and Catie shared a look of frustration and resignation as the ball wobbled and stopped three feet before the hole. Diana did not miss her four-foot birdie putt, just as Torrie knew she wouldn't. The win was hers, and Torrie felt instant relief that the ordeal was over.

"Congratulations, Diana." Torrie gave her a tight hug and a kiss on both cheeks.

"Thanks, hon." Diana gave her an extra squeeze. "You were awesome this week, Torrie. I'm sorry I spoiled your comeback."

Torrie smiled and meant it. "You didn't spoil anything. You deserved this. But next time I plan to make it much tougher for you."

Diana laughed. "I expect nothing less, my friend." She winked once more and walked toward the waiting arms of her girlfriend.

Torrie's parents, meanwhile, stood on the sidelines, and Torrie smiled and nodded at them. She could see by their wide smiles that they were thrilled with her results. Her dad, always one to embarrass her, gave her two thumbs up and yelled her name.

God, she thought. What a loser I am. *A thirty-year-old woman with no one but her parents waiting at the end for her.* Grace's absence hit her devastatingly hard just then. Every day she'd felt it for the last months, but not like this. This was every bit as piercing as her damaged shoulder. This was what caused her now to gasp for air, to stumble a step. Grace should be here, with her loving eyes and her understanding smile, her tender embraces and soothing words. Grace was the only one she really wanted here. Grace, she realized, was the only one she would ever really want in her corner, waiting at the end for her, above anyone else.

Fuck. Tears welled and Torrie had to swallow them back.

Crying over spilled milk was what her aunt always scolded her about as a kid. Well, tough. She was going to damn well cry over that spilled milk now and everyone else be damned.

The championship dinner had long ago been consumed and most of the night's participants had drifted off to their hotel rooms or to the airport. Torrie and Diana sat together at a corner table over glasses of wine, Torrie needing Diana's company tonight. Her partner, Becky, had left for their room moments ago.

"Wanna tell me what's going on?" Diana asked in that way she had—curious without being judgmental.

Torrie didn't try to deny her need to talk. Months ago, she might have, but she was different now. She was beginning to see, or at least feel, the collateral damage of keeping things bottled up. When her emotions welled, as they did now, they would spill eventually, and it was better if she directed where they went. She was no expert, but she was at least beginning to learn that her feelings were real and they ran deep and they were a part of her.

She told Diana all about Grace and all that had happened between them. Diana let Torrie talk. She nodded in reply and sipped her wine, her eyes riveted on Torrie.

"So what are you going to do about it, Torrie?" It was just like Diana to zero in on the one question that needed asking. She was good at distilling an issue, no matter how complicated it was.

Torrie had to do something, because she could not get Grace out of her heart. Getting back on the Tour hadn't put any distance between them. In fact, it only made missing Grace worse. Her need for Grace was like a gaping hole in her soul. She took a sip of wine, no closer to an answer after stalling for a few minutes. "I'm not sure, Diana."

"You know, my grandma always told me that it's often the simplest answer that's the right one."

"And the simple answer would be to go after her," Torrie said without hesitation.

"So why haven't you?"

Yes. Why hadn't she? At first she was angry, disappointed,

wanting to stew in her own self-pity and pessimism. She'd thought of all the reasons why she and Grace couldn't be together. Thought of all her shortcomings, and Grace's too, and realized they didn't add up to a workable relationship. But with time, the obstacles and arguments in her mind dulled a little, the way any pain did after awhile. Now there was just an emptiness and a regret for what might have been.

"Well?" Diana gently prodded.

Whatever she said would sound lame, even to her own ears. "I don't know the first clue about how to make a real relationship work, Diana."

"Well, here's a secret, my friend. Most of us don't. Once we're in it, we just hang on for the ride and hope that love and respect and hard work are enough."

Torrie shook her head. "I don't like jumping into something without being prepared. Without being ready to do my very best."

"Oh, Torrie. She'll forgive you for not being an expert at it, you know. Love forgives a lot of things."

Torrie supposed that was so, or at least she hoped it was. But would she be able to forgive herself too, for not scoring an ace every day in a life with Grace? What if she disappointed Grace? Made a mistake? What if she wasn't a good partner?

"You won't have the answers to your doubts unless you try, Torrie."

"I know that, Diana." The question remained. Did she even have a chance with Grace anymore? Had Grace found someone else by now? Had she written Torrie off completely? More to the point, could Torrie swallow her pride and her insecurities and just go for it?

Torrie finished the last of her wine and reached for her wallet.

"I got it, Torrie."

"Hey," Torrie said breezily. "You won today. I wanted drinks to be on me."

Diana rewarded her with a conspiratorial smile. "I have a

feeling you're about to win something much bigger, my friend."

After a heartfelt hug, Torrie retrieved her cell phone from her room and dialed Catie's number. She would need her and Trish's help.

CHAPTER FIFTEEN

"Well, that was fun. Not!" Trish exclaimed as the waitress took away the remnants of their lunch. She looked exhausted and relieved and a touch nervous.

They'd spent the morning with their business manager, James, trying to iron out plans to scale back their work. He'd been shocked and incredulous and more than a little perturbed when they first announced their wishes. He was their friend and pledged to do everything he could to get them out of their long-term contracts, but he didn't pretend to understand. Trish joked that he'd obviously never been in love, and James reluctantly admitted as much, saying the only thing he was in love with was money.

"He'll get over it," Grace said, not entirely sure he would.

"You'd think it was a major catastrophe, the way he went on about how much money it's going to cost us to get out of the new restaurant."

It was true. The penalties of reneging on their contracts in Manhattan were going to cost them a bundle, but Trish and Grace both agreed it was still worth it.

"James will just have to find someone else to hitch his wagon to, that's all. He'll still love us, though."

"You're right. He will. Who else would put up with him?" Trish's expression grew pained. "It's going to be really busy for us the next few months before things slow down. Are you sure you're up to it?"

Grace smiled, wanting to reassure her. They would tape all twenty-six of their television show episodes in October and November and do a small book signing tour before that. By December, she hoped to be able to breathe again. "I'll be fine. I'm not as fragile as you think."

"I know you're not, Grace. You're the strongest woman I know. I just worry about you, that's all."

"Why? Because I don't have anyone to go home to at the end of the day?"

Trish averted her eyes. "I guess I worry about you being alone."

"Oh, hell, Trish. I've been alone for years."

"All right. I meant happy."

Happy was something Grace couldn't casually guarantee, and Trish knew it. Grace still replayed in her mind her last moments with Torrie, still questioned whether she'd done the right thing in not going after her. In letting her get away so easily. She'd had her doubts, and Trish was certainly keen to remind her that she'd made a catastrophic mistake in not going after Torrie. In fact, Grace had heard nothing but that the last few weeks.

"Trish, I'm fine. Really," she muttered, trying to turn up the bullshit factor. She wasn't fine because she missed Torrie. But she would be fine again one day.

Trish looked doubtful but stood to go, signaling her desire to let the topic drop. Grace knew from years of experience that Trish never truly let anything drop. The other shoe was still to fall, she was sure.

"So I'll meet you at the concert tonight?" Grace asked.

"I might be a bit late, so don't wait out front for me, okay? I've got my ticket, so I'll see you inside."

"Don't be too late. We might never see Herbie Hancock and

Diana Krall together again."

Trish grinned. "You just want to watch Diana Krall all night and get all hot for her. Are you even going to be listening to the music?"

Grace swatted Trish. "Don't try to push your little fantasies onto me."

Trish laughed before hugging Grace good-bye.

The concert started off vigorously, with Herbie Hancock playing a couple of raucous tunes on the ivories, his fingers moving with grace and astonishing adeptness. Diana Krall joined him on stage, and they performed a couple of swing songs, then settled into "East of the Sun" and "Let's Fall In Love." The crowd was loving it, and Grace tried to let Diana's deep, sultry voice send her into a mellow, dreamy state, as it usually did when she listened to her music. But Trish still hadn't shown up, and Grace was worried.

At intermission, Grace bolted for the lobby and dialed Trish's cell phone number. It went immediately into voice mail. There was no answer at her house either. Her mind thought of a hundred excuses that might be keeping the usually punctual Trish from the concert. After she raced through all the morbid reasons, she decided to stay positive, thinking Catie had perhaps arrived in town unexpectedly.

Grace slipped back into her seat and vowed that if Trish didn't show or leave her a phone message by the third song of the second set, she would leave and try to track her down. She settled back as the lights dimmed, feeling uneasy.

Torrie cursed the traffic for the hundredth time, then cursed herself for cutting the timing so close. She practically leaped from the taxi before it even halted in front of the concert hall. She rushed in and flashed her ticket to an usher. The auditorium was dim, all the lighting focused brightly on the stage and on the blond singer holding the microphone like a torch. Ungracefully, Torrie made her way down the aisle, trying not to draw attention to herself, but she felt like a blind person, going by feel.

Finally, in the shadows, she saw Grace, or someone she thought was Grace. The profile looked the same, with the strong nose and cheekbones, but her hair was short. Softly, Torrie sat down. She couldn't decide whether she was relieved or disappointed that Grace didn't notice her right away.

Trying to take up as little space as she could, she watched the concert and tried to concentrate on the duet "Dream a Little Dream of Me." Her palms were sweating, and when she felt Grace's eyes burning into her and heard the sharp intake of breath, she froze. Her heart pounding loudly in her ears, Torrie briefly considered fleeing. She thought she was prepared to see Grace again, but now she wasn't so sure.

"Torrie?" came a strangled whisper. "What are you doing here?"

Torrie forced a smile that felt like torture and turned to Grace. She wanted to touch her but didn't dare, and instead tried to find a way past her sudden lack of coherent thought. She'd rehearsed what she would say, how she would act. Now all she had was a blank slate. "Can we talk?"

Grace stared at her for a long moment, her face unreadable in the dim light. Hastily, she stood and, clutching her small purse to her hip, made her way through the narrow aisle crowded with knees and feet. Torrie followed, and several muttered apologies later, they were in the bright lobby, the sounds of the concert faint like a whisper.

"Where's Trish?" Grace sounded worried.

"She's fine." Torrie was relieved to find her voice again. "She and I arranged this a while back. I have her ticket." She pulled the crumpled stub from her pocket like it was a winning lottery ticket. "I wanted to surprise you, but the traffic from Logan to here was crazy."

Tiny frown lines had formed around Grace's mouth and between her eyes. Torrie wanted nothing more than to kiss them away, and then they suddenly smoothed out, like the stilling of water. "I didn't think I'd ever see you again."

Grace's tone was neutral, and Torrie still couldn't tell whether Grace was happy to see her or not. She braced herself for disappointment. "Can we go somewhere? To talk?"

Grace's eyes flicked to the door and back. "The hotel across the street has a nice bar."

"No." Torrie shook her head. She was adamant about wanting to be alone with Grace. She'd waited this long to see her, and she didn't want a hasty, public meeting. She was too afraid it would make it easy for Grace to dismiss her. "I want us to talk. In private."

Grace considered for a long moment. "My place is only a few blocks away. Near Bunker Hill. Would you like to walk?"

Torrie happily agreed and was even happier when Grace automatically took her arm. It was a warm, humid night, a slight haze covering the stars, like gauze. "I'm sorry about missing the rest of the concert. We could have stayed, you know."

Grace gave her a sideways glance. "I don't think that would have been a good idea."

Was this a good idea, going to Grace's? Torrie couldn't be sure. She felt as though a big, yawning crevasse was opening in front of her, about to swallow her up. Yet she was compelled to keep moving forward, to keep plunging on, to go one more round with Grace in the hopes of winning her back. It was like starting out a golf tournament with a bogey or two and battling back, and she wanted this battle. She was more sure than ever how she felt about Grace. She knew in her depths that this woman was most definitely worth the fight.

"I like your haircut, by the way." Actually, Torrie loved it. It made Grace look youthful and fun, and best of all, it showcased her beautiful face.

"Thanks. How's your shoulder?"

They rounded the corner of one hilly, narrow street to another, and Grace pointed to a five-story white, stonewashed building just ahead. It was majestic and looked a century old, with wide marble steps leading up to it.

"Hurt like a bugger in last week's tournament, but I

managed."

Grace slid a card into a security scanner to unlock the front door. "I heard you did really well, Torrie. Congratulations."

"I didn't win."

"I know."

Grace was playing it so cool. Did she even care that Torrie had gone back to the Tour? Did she care that she had just fallen short of a win? Did she care that she was here now?

In the elevator, Grace punched a special code into the keypad. "I have the fifth floor to myself."

"Nice." Torrie was looking forward to seeing Grace's private sanctuary. She had a feeling it would be both tasteful and cozy.

When the elevator door opened onto the top floor, Grace used a key to unlock a fancy iron gate before they could exit. Then they were suddenly standing in her foyer, with its fourteen-foot vaulted ceiling, crystal chandelier and marble floor.

"Wow, Grace! This is spectacular."

Remy came barreling into the foyer at the sound of their voices, his tail a wagging blur.

"Hey, buddy," Torrie said, dropping to the floor to let him give her sloppy kisses.

"He missed you."

"I missed you too, Remy. Have you been a good boy?"

She hugged him one last time and jumped to her feet. "Sorry."

"It's okay. I'm happy you two like each other."

"You are?"

Grace smiled. The ice was definitely melting. "Anyway, the rest of the place is not as formal as this. Come on. I'll take you on a tour."

She led Torrie into the living room first, where the high ceilings continued. The floors were oak, the fireplace marble, and the windows were at least twelve feet high and spanned an entire wall. A thick, rich area rug of red and gold made the room instantly cozy, and the chocolate brown furniture was inviting. The kitchen was just as impressive, with its white oak cupboards, black granite counters and ceramic tiled floor.

Grace pointed out the six-burner, stainless steel gas range. "That little baby is my pride and joy."

"Do you do a lot of cooking at home?"

"I usually try out new recipes here. Especially when we're researching for a cookbook or our TV show." She pulled open the large, double-door stainless steel fridge and retrieved a bottle of white wine. "Would you like a glass? I know I could sure use one."

"Sure," Torrie said, not quite knowing how to take Grace's comment about needing a drink. It occurred to her that Grace was as nervous as she was. They were being civil, friendly even, and that, at least, was encouraging.

Glasses in hand, Grace led Torrie to the master bedroom. Torrie couldn't take her eyes off the king-sized bed with its sage green duvet and oversized pillows. She wondered what it would be like to wake up with Grace in this room every morning, to start their day together right here with a soft kiss and a final snuggle before the day's demands began to crowd in on them. The light caught a framed photo on the nightstand beside the bed, and Torrie stepped closer to look at it. She felt a flutter of excitement when she realized it was the picture of her and Grace with Catie and Trish posing beside the cake at the golf tournament in Hartford.

Grace must have caught her grinning and staring at the photo because she shifted uncomfortably and began chattering nervously. Torrie resisted the invitation to see the guest bedroom and the third bedroom, which, Grace explained, was her office.

Torrie put her hand softly on Grace's arm. "Why don't we go to the living room and talk?"

She noticed immediately the nervous catch in her voice when Grace replied, "Okay."

Torrie bravely chose the couch—a subtle challenge to see whether Grace would sit beside her. Grace didn't, instead choosing an adjacent matching chair. She looked lovely—the wine infusing a hint of rosiness in her cheeks, her nervous energy giving her a bit of an edge.

"Are you happy to see me, Grace?"

Assorted emotions flickered instantly across Grace's face—anguish, fear, excitement. "I don't quite know what to think, Torrie. We didn't exactly part on good terms."

"It's my fault." Torrie unexpectedly felt her eyes moisten. "I should have believed you. I should have trusted you and given us more time. I wanted to. I guess I was afraid. I thought I would lose you, that you might pick her over me." Torrie was rambling, but she had to get it all out. "I was afraid I wasn't deserving of you. I didn't believe in myself enough. I didn't believe in us enough."

Grace only nodded, slow and deliberate, like a professor grading an oral presentation from her student. "And now you do?"

Torrie moved to the edge of the seat cushion. "Yes. Yes, Grace. I do."

"I haven't heard from you in months. I thought you were okay with how we left things. That you didn't want to see me again. Why did you wait all this time?"

Torrie was relieved at the slight tremor in Grace's voice. It meant she was every bit as scared and nervous as Torrie. "I always wanted to see you again, baby. Every day." She had to take a sip of wine to quench the desert her mouth had become.

"Then why didn't you..." Grace's voice dropped off. She looked hurt and confused.

"I wanted to be sure that I was in this for the long haul. That I would fight for you. For us. That I didn't want you like you were some trophy to win and put up on a shelf. I needed time. I'm sorry it took me so long. And now I'm hoping like hell it's not too late."

Impulsively, Torrie slid off the couch and dropped to her knees in front of Grace. She felt a sudden sob rise in her chest. "Grace," she said thickly. "I love you so much." She laid her head in Grace's lap and allowed herself to cry, her shoulders heaving with every sob. Grace's hands softly stroked her head. Fingers wound gently through her hair.

"It's okay," Grace soothed, and Torrie believed her. "You're here with me now."

"I don't want to go through life without you, Grace."

Grace's hands cupped her head and tilted her tear-stained face up. Torrie was surprised to see tears shimmering on Grace's cheeks.

"I'm so sorry too, Torrie. I shouldn't have let you go the way I did. I didn't think you knew how to love." She swallowed visibly. "I thought I'd made a mistake again choosing you, like I did with Aly."

Torrie pulled Grace to her and kissed her lips delicately, as though she were afraid to come on too fast, too strong. Though she wanted so much to make up for lost time, she knew she needed to know how Grace felt, and whether Grace was about to put the brakes on. She didn't think her heart could go through the wringer again.

She pulled back and watched as Grace's wet eyelashes fluttered and her eyes slowly opened. They were like puddles of gray and green. "Grace," Torrie said softly. "I need to know how you feel. I need to know if there's a future for us, because all I want to do is spend my life loving you."

Grace's mouth curled up into a shadow of a smile. "I would love a future for us, Torrie."

"You would?" Torrie's heart danced. She pulled Grace to her and kissed her with complete abandon. She felt Grace's mouth respond with its own brand of impatience. They pressed hard into one another, almost like the crashing together of waves on rock in a wild, pounding surf. Lips parted and tongues roughly explored one another—first the outline of lips, and then they fought a duel of playful passion. Grace moaned from deep within, and Torrie disengaged enough to look into Grace's eyes again.

"Grace, I want you to know I'm not just asking for tonight." She was slightly breathless and more than a little nervous with the anticipation of what she would say next. She tried to settle her pounding heart. "I'm asking for every night, Grace. I'm asking for a life with you."

Grace looked thoughtful. "We both have pretty crazy lives, you know. It wouldn't be easy."

"I know, and I don't care how hard it is. I'll do anything it takes, Grace."

A pale eyebrow quirked teasingly. "Anything?"

Torrie laughed, and it was cleansing like a good spring rain. "Yes. Anything."

Grace smiled brightly, then kissed the tip of Torrie's nose. "I love you, Torrie Cannon. And if you don't take me to bed this minute, I'm going to combust. And it wouldn't be a pretty sight."

"No, we definitely wouldn't want that to happen." Torrie stood and extended her hand invitingly. "I do believe I remember where the bedroom is."

Grace winked slowly. "Take our glasses and I'll meet you there with the bottle."

Torrie was waiting naked for her beneath the cool Egyptian cotton sheets with their high thread count. She propped herself up on an elbow to allow Grace to fill her wineglass. Grace sat down on the edge of the bed with her glass and sipped, in no hurry. Torrie was in a hurry, but this was nice too.

"Are you okay?" Torrie asked tentatively.

"I'm more than okay." Grace beamed. "I missed you like crazy these last months, Torrie. I was getting downright pissed that you hadn't ridden into town on your white steed to sweep me off my feet. Luckily you finally did, and just in time."

"You can't rush these chivalrous things and ruin the mystique, you know." A question rose in Torrie's mind, and she felt a little roguish. "What would you have done if I hadn't?"

"Oh, probably pined for another few months and then maybe taken up with…hmm…let's see…a professional tennis player?" She laughed so that Torrie would know she was teasing.

"Come here," Torrie said, suddenly more turned on than she could stand.

Grace sank into her and they kissed, Torrie's fingers finding the first button to her crisp white blouse, then the next. She rolled Grace onto her back beside her, halting with the buttons long enough to trace a finger along Grace's cheek.

"I can't believe I almost let you go," Torrie whispered, her breath suddenly catching in her throat.

Grace bit her bottom lip, looking like she might cry again. "I can't believe I was almost stubborn enough to let it happen."

Torrie's fingers resumed their quest with the buttons. She liked the way the smooth cotton of the blouse molded around Grace's shapely breasts and liked it even better when the material fell away with the unfastening of each button. "I will never make that mistake again." Torrie's lips brushed the newly exposed skin of Grace's chest.

"Good." Grace's breath was growing more halting with each kiss.

Torrie parted the blouse, then unhinged the lacy white bra, enjoying the momentary feel of the fabric between her thumb and forefinger. She liked Grace's femininity. These weren't things that she would ever wear herself, but on Grace, they were beautiful.

"You're beautiful, Grace." Torrie pushed the bra aside and marveled at Grace's round breasts, white and creamy next to her tanned chest and stomach. "So incredibly beautiful."

"Oh, Torrie. You make me feel beautiful."

Grace stroked her face, but Torrie couldn't take her eyes off the rosy stiff peaks of Grace's nipples. Impulsively, she moved her mouth to one, flicked her tongue over it. It felt hard, like a pebble, but soft too. She sucked a little, flicked faster with her tongue, and felt Grace squirm beneath her. She would make love to this woman every night for the rest of her life if she could.

"I want you so much, Torrie." Grace's voice sounded far away and strained with passion. "I've never stopped wanting you."

Torrie moved her mouth to Grace's, and she kissed her tenderly at first, her hand cupping a breast and squeezing gently. She tugged and nipped and sucked roughly on Grace's lips, knowing she would probably leave them swollen and bruised the next day, but she didn't care right now. Besides, Grace was giving every bit as good as she was getting. She was not fragile. She was pressing her body into Torrie's, demanding friction and release.

"You don't mind if we get these pants off, do you?" Torrie teased.

"Ha, mind? I'm about to rip them to shreds if you don't hurry."

Torrie laughed and fumbled with the zipper. "Has anyone told you that you can be bossy sometimes?"

"Of course. I'm an executive chef, remember? Bossy is my middle name."

"How could I forget?" Torrie began to slide the slacks and bikini underwear down, Grace helping by finally kicking them off the rest of the way. "As someone who usually does the cooking, I hope you don't mind being the main course this time."

Grace's eyes widened with desire. "If it means you're going to devour me, I'm all for it."

Torrie's laugh was deep and low. She wanted nothing more than to devour Grace, but a little mischief was too tempting. "Can I write a review afterward? Say, rate you on a five-star system?"

Grace swatted Torrie's bare shoulder. "Only if I can score your performance. How does it work...an ace is the best, right? And then an eagle. Is birdie next?"

"You can rest assured, my love, that I will come in well under par."

"Ooh, I can hardly wait."

"You won't have to, darling." Torrie thrust her hand between Grace's legs. She kissed Grace again, moved down to kiss her breasts, her hand moving in slow circles against the wetness between her thighs. "You're so warm and wet," she muttered against Grace's breasts. She felt like the luckiest woman in the world.

Grace pushed up into her hand, moaning from deep in her throat. At the same time, she arched further back into the pillow, her neck a smooth, graceful, curving line. Torrie squeezed and stroked the soft, velvety folds, then slipped two fingers inside. She felt herself grow impossibly wet at the thrill of being inside Grace, of being accepted deeper and deeper into the hot, welcoming depths of her lover. She pumped quicker, heard Grace's breathing quicken, felt her pelvis greedily meet each thrust. With her other hand, Torrie palmed her, quickening her pace to match the plunging fingers. Grace squealed and stiffened, thrusting herself against Torrie one final time, then shuddered with a loud gasp.

Torrie clutched Grace to her, kissing her neck tenderly as the final tremors died. She felt a tear drip onto her face. She was surprised Grace was crying.

"Are you okay, sweetheart?"

Grace's smile was watery. "I'm stupidly happy, Torrie. You're the best thing that's ever happened to me."

Torrie licked a tear away. "Promise me you won't ever doubt my love for you again."

"I promise you that, Torrie."

Relieved, Torrie resumed her kisses. Without looking at her, she knew Grace was smiling happily. She felt Grace's joy in her own core, and it was the most wonderful feeling she'd ever known. She wanted to share everything with Grace, make every sacrifice for her. She rolled onto her side and propped herself up on an elbow.

"I meant what I said earlier, Grace. About doing anything it takes to make this work."

"I appreciate that, Torrie, but I don't want you to have to do anything drastic."

"You mean with my career?"

"Yes."

"Hell, I'll be a stay-at-home wife if you want me to."

Grace laughed and impulsively kissed Torrie on the lips. "Somehow, I can't quite picture that."

"What, being the queen of domesticity?"

Giggling, Grace said, "Do you even know what that means, my sweet?"

"Of course. I took home economics for a year."

"Great, so you know how to sew and cook and clean, be a hostess at parties, iron my clothes. Hmmm, what else could we have you do?"

"How about make love to you every day? That I would much prefer!" She rolled on top of Grace again, pushing her hard center against Grace's. "I'd be a lot better at that part anyway."

"I'll bet you would."

Lightly, Torrie clasped Grace around the wrists and pressed them into the mattress. "Want me to show you?"

Growing breathless, Grace said, "I thought you just did."

Torrie nibbled her throat. "I'm not sure I quite got the point across. That was just the appetizer."

Grace chuckled throatily. "Oh, I see. I can hardly wait for the other courses then."

Torrie pulsed into Grace, hard and rhythmically, until her own breath was being sucked out of her chest. The friction made her so wet, and she throbbed achingly as she felt Grace grow excited too. She continued to push against her, still pinning her wrists, caught up in her own fierce desire with each thrust of her pelvis. "Oh, yeah," she said thickly. "Oh, Grace. You make me want to come so hard."

"Yes, baby," Grace cooed between breaths. "I want you to come for me."

"Ohh!" Torrie yelled, and with a final thrust, she came, collapsing on Grace. Trembling, she let go of Grace and Grace's arms enclosed her. Grace softly kissed her temple, soothing her, loving her, and Torrie felt her own tears surface.

"I love you so much, Torrie. I'm never going to let you go again, my beautiful, beautiful lover."

Torrie couldn't speak, even though she wanted to express her love for Grace again, her mouth wouldn't work, and even if it could, she wouldn't have been able to find her voice. Grace seemed to sense it, and she held her tighter.

They stayed that way for a long time. Vaguely, Torrie knew it must be getting late, but she didn't care. She fully expected to stay up all night, talking with Grace, making endless love to her. There was no sense in pacing herself now, not when she'd waited all her life for this.

She kissed Grace, then rolled onto her back and let Grace nestle into the crook of her shoulder. "I'm so incredibly happy, Grace."

"Me too." She looked at the ceiling, unblinking. "I never thought I'd find this, Torrie. I never thought I'd find you." She turned her head to look at Torrie and the smile reached all the way to her eyes. "There's so many things I want to do with you."

"Really? Didn't we get off to a good start already?"

Grace blushed a little. "The best. But there are other things too."

"Not laundry, I hope."

Grace laughed shortly. "You're off the hook for laundry, but I want to do stuff like, I don't know, go to concerts together and stay for the whole thing next time!"

"Agreed."

"And go on trips together, and read out loud to each other in bed. Maybe even get our own place together on Sheridan Island."

"That would be awesome," Torrie said. "Aunt Connie would love that."

"She would, wouldn't she? I'd love it too." Her eyes flashed with a revelation. "Torrie, I'm going to teach you how to cook."

A surge of panic rose through Torrie. "Are you sure you want to take that project on?"

"I'll bet you'd be a wonderful student."

"Only if I get to be the teacher's pet."

"I can most certainly promise you that."

"Whew. I don't have to waste my time bringing you an apple."

Grace shook her head, laughing. "I love your sense of humor, Torrie."

"Good, because we'll need that sense of humor when I teach you to golf."

"What?"

"Oh, yes." Torrie narrowed her eyes playfully. "If you get to teach me how to cook, then I get to teach you how to golf!"

Grace leaned over and nipped at her throat playfully. "I don't think that's a fair tradeoff."

"It sounds perfectly fair to me."

"You know," Grace said before planting a kiss on her chin. "We could call it a draw and take up tennis or skiing."

"Kiss me and we'll negotiate."

Grace crawled fully on top of her and kissed her spiritedly. "If I do more than kiss you, will you let me choose our new hobby?"

Torrie looked into Grace's eyes, enjoying the playfulness in them. "All right. Just as long as you don't choose knitting."

Grace kissed her again, the spark in her eyes bright when she looked at Torrie and said, "Okay, I've got it."

"Oh, no." Torrie feigned concern. "What?"

"Dancing!"

"What?"

"Ballroom dancing! God, I would love to do that with you, Torrie. We could take lessons and be just like the people on *Dancing With The Stars*. It would so much fun!"

"Are you serious?"

"I am, actually."

Torrie laughed, feeling surprisingly exultant. Being in a relationship was so incredibly different from the way she'd been living her life, where she had only to think of herself and plan for herself. Her house now had so many more rooms. She was a part of something so much bigger, and she loved it. She would go anywhere with Grace, do anything with her. "I'd love to whirl you around the dance floor. But only if we can call it *Dancing With The Dykes*."

Grace laughed and looked pleased. "It's a deal."

"Now, how about those things you were going to do to me since I let you choose dancing?"

"Hmmm, let me think. I could give your hair a trim. Or, let's see. I could give you a manicure."

Torrie's brow furrowed. "Do I look like the kind of person who wants a manicure?"

"Okay." Grace grinned. "How about a massage then?"

"Only if it's a certain kind of massage."

"You're a picky customer."

"Yes, and don't you forget it." She grabbed Grace's hand and pressed it between her legs. She only meant to tease, but… Oh! It felt so good when Grace touched her. She could not get enough of Grace, even wrapped tightly in her arms like this. The sudden, skilled stroking of Grace's fingers was rapidly pushing her to the edge once again—almost too quickly. "Oh, honey. You don't know what you do to me." Her voice sounded rough and gravelly to her ears.

"I think I do," Grace burred. "Judging by how wet you are."

"I just want you so much." Air came thinly into her lungs now. Her chest heaved. She felt Grace sliding down her body, kissing her way down, and Torrie had to use all her concentration and effort to stop herself from coming just at the thought of Grace going down on her. "Grace," she said hoarsely, trying to warn Grace she was barely holding on, but it was too late. Grace's mouth was on her and Torrie felt the center of her world expand and burst into a kaleidoscope of colors and shapes. And then it all collapsed into itself, like a house of cards, and she came harder than she'd ever come before.

Gently, she pulled a protesting Grace up.

"I was only getting started, you know."

Torrie kissed the disappointment from her fair eyebrows. "Sorry, but when you touch me like that…"

"I'll just have to go slower next time. Torture you a little."

"Don't you dare!" Torrie let Grace nestle into the crook of her arm again. It felt so natural, like the fit of her favorite pair of boots. Only much nicer. "Just remember. I have plenty of ways in which to torture you too, my love."

"I can't wait for anything you can dish out."

"Oh, really?" Torrie turned on her and began tickling Grace relentlessly under the arms, down her sides and across her stomach. She squirmed and giggled, finally squealing and begging Torrie to stop.

"That was pretty cocky of you to dare me like that." Torrie kissed her nose, then her lips.

"Maybe I was testing you to see if you really would."

"I'm a woman of my word, Grace."

"So I see." Grace's smile faded and she looked earnestly at Torrie. "I shouldn't have had such little faith in you before."

"I shouldn't have had such little faith in you, Grace. In us." Torrie sighed heavily, feeling ashamed again. She hadn't entirely forgiven herself for thinking Grace had wanted to get back with her ex.

"All right," Grace said with authority. "Let's agree to stop beating ourselves up about what happened. Tonight is a fresh start."

Torrie sat up and reached for their wineglasses, handing one to Grace. She topped them both with the wine that was no longer chilled. "It's more than just a fresh start. Tonight is about the rest of our lives."

Grace clinked her glass with Torrie's. "I'll drink to that, sweetheart."

Later, when the bottle was nearly empty and the time on the digital clock slipped into the new day, Grace told Torrie that she was scaling back her work. She explained how both she and Trish had come to the conclusion that they wanted time for other things in their lives, so they were nixing the Manhattan plans, and once they'd taped all their television show episodes, they could close the chapter on that too.

"Grace," Torrie said solemnly, knowing she was about to make an equally big sacrifice. "I can quit the Tour."

Grace looked unsure. "Do you want to?"

"I want to be with you."

"That's not what I asked."

Oh, crap. Torrie wanted nothing more than to spend her time with Grace, being alternately lazy and doing things together. Grace was her priority now, but she still felt the undeniable pull of her career. "You're right. I'm sorry." Torrie wanted only honesty between them. "I do still want to golf, but I don't want it

244

to consume my life like it did before. I don't want that life again. That life without you."

"What will make you happy, Torrie?"

"You make me happy."

"What else?"

"Having you in my life but still golfing for a few more years, anyway."

"You are rather young to retire."

"I don't feel young. I feel like one of the old vets on the Tour."

Grace laughed. "I forget that in the world of sports, you're old at thirty."

"Grace," Torrie said, feeling a little scared that she might be asking too much. "I don't want to do anything that's going to jeopardize us."

"You won't." Grace began tracing a finger along Torrie's jawline, and it was both tender and sexy. "I'll support you in whatever you want to do, Torrie."

"What if I cut my schedule in half? Just do a dozen tournaments a year?"

"Will that be enough?"

Torrie knew with certainty that it would be. "Yes."

"You're sure?"

"I've never been more sure of anything in my life."

Grace kissed the smile from her face. "I love you, Torrie."

"I love you, Grace." Torrie feigned seriousness. "There is one more thing."

"What?"

Torrie stretched, arching her feet. "Do we ever have to get out of this bed?"

Grace purred against her throat. "God, I wish we didn't have to. But I think Remy might have something to say about that."

As if on cue, the chocolate Lab bounded into the room and leapt onto the bed, causing Grace and Torrie to immediately protect their vulnerable areas from the big paws and the exuberant body they were attached to.

"Poor boy." Grace laughed. "Are you feeling ignored?"

Torrie swung her legs over the side of the bed. "Come on, Remy. Do you have to go out for a pee?"

"Already, you're leaving me for another," Grace clucked.

"Only temporarily, sweetheart. Will you keep the bed warm?"

"Need you ask?"

EPILOGUE

Grace carried the breakfast tray to the bedroom, nudging the door open with her foot. She stood for a long moment, balancing the dishes, while she admired the sight of her sleeping lover. Streaks of sun slashed across Torrie's sprawled nude body, the sheet scattered across her waist. It was the body of a beautiful young, hard warrior, although battle-scarred. She knew Torrie's bad shoulder still ached on damp days.

Torrie stirred as Grace set the clattering tray onto the bed.

"Good morning," Grace said eagerly, bending to kiss Torrie. They'd barely seen each other last night. Torrie had flown in late and gone straight to sleep. Grace had felt her body next to hers in the night, but that was about it.

"Yes, it is a good morning." Torrie smiled sleepily. "The best morning in the last eleven days, now that I'm here with you."

Grace raised an eyebrow. "I see you were counting our days apart."

"Days? I was counting the hours, honey." Torrie sat up, her compact, firm breasts and muscular shoulders exposed, and Grace had to restrain herself from moving the tray to the floor and throwing herself on the bed. It would be a wonderful way to celebrate Valentine's Day, except Grace had other things on her mind. Or one other thing, at least.

"Are you hungry?"

"Starving." Torrie grinned provocatively at her. "But not for food. Come here."

"Not yet," Grace answered coyly. She nodded at the scrambled eggs with their fresh ground mint, fine chopped tomatoes and goat cheese, the bacon that was quickly cooling, and the toast with blueberry jam. "I want you to get your strength up first."

Torrie looked from Grace to the food and back, and Grace laughed at the torment she'd forced on Torrie, making her choose between sex and food.

"Well, okay," Torrie said reluctantly. "First this wonderful breakfast." She winked at Grace, and Grace felt a shiver of excitement. "And then I'm going to ravage you."

"God, I hope so." Grace kissed Torrie again, slower and deeper this time, then set the tray between them on the bed.

"This looks awesome," Torrie said, her eyes already devouring the food.

"Hope you don't mind me letting you sleep while I worked in the kitchen."

"Mind? I love you for it!"

They ate the food together, Torrie ravenously, Grace more conservatively. She felt a faint wave of nausea, though not enough to stop her from eating. They caught each other up on their time apart, Torrie having gone down to Florida to spend some time with her swing coach and to practice with her friend Diana to get ready for the Tour's first tournament of the year in two weeks. Grace smiled at Torrie, knowing she'd probably done her ritual of holding the babies at the hospital down there, but she'd faithfully kept Diana's secret.

As much as Grace would have enjoyed spending the eleven days with Torrie, especially in a warm climate, she had stayed behind to putter in her restaurant. Grace had appointments she didn't want to miss and there had been plans to make. Torrie's family was flying in to Boston later today. They were gathering for a private dinner at Sheridan's for Torrie and Grace's engagement announcement. So far, it had miraculously remained a secret.

"I can't wait to see everyone's faces tonight when we tell them." Torrie grinned, looking like she might burst from her pride and excitement. "I'll bet you fifty bucks Aunt Connie's going to faint."

Grace smiled. She knew Aunt Connie would be thrilled to death having her officially join the family, just as Grace was thrilled to be joining it. "I'll bet you the fifty bucks that I'm going to cry when I ask her to give me away."

"Don't worry. She'll be bawling too."

"Just bring lots of Kleenexes."

"Do you think Trish and Catie will agree to stand up for us?"

"Of course they will. They'd be pissed off if we didn't ask them."

"Yeah. I suppose you're right." Torrie looked thoughtful for a moment. "Do you think they'll make their own announcement one of these days?"

"Jesus, I hope so. Wouldn't it be awesome if they announced it at our wedding?"

"Yeah. If there's one thing I would allow to steal the spotlight from us for a few minutes, that would be it!"

"And then we could stand up for them."

Torrie cast her an impatient look. "I think we're getting one wedding ahead of ourselves. And now, sweetheart, since you've filled my stomach, I want to fill my hands and my mouth with something else!" She reached out for her.

Grace set the tray on the night table and crawled into Torrie's arms. She'd been wanting to tell Torrie her news for two days, but not over the phone. Now she couldn't wait any longer. A tiny bit of nervousness—the good kind—pricked at her. "You know, honey, there is one more announcement we're going to have to make tonight."

"There is?"

Grace couldn't keep the bliss from her voice. "Um. What are

you doing in September?"

"There's a tournament in Arizona I want to do. Home field advantage and all that."

"Hmm. That might just work."

"What might work?" Torrie looked puzzled, and Grace softly smoothed the worry lines from her forehead.

"Having the baby born near your—"

"What?" Torrie's eyes were so wide, Grace thought they might pop out of her head. It was like something out of a movie, and Grace had to stifle a giggle. "The baby? You're…?"

Grace nodded and watched the emotions stampede across Torrie's face. Elation quickly pushed aside all else. Torrie was breathless, her chest heaving a little, her cheeks pink with excitement.

"Holy shit! We're going to have a baby?"

Again, Grace nodded, and Torrie wrapped her so tight in a bear hug, Grace thought she might squeeze the tiny embryo right out of her. "Careful, now."

"Oh, God, I'm sorry. Are you okay?"

Grace kissed Torrie on the lips. "Yes, I'm fine. I'm great."

"Me too. Oh, my God, Grace." Torrie was shaking her head, looking astonished and pleased. She placed the palm of her hand gently on Grace's stomach and gazed into her eyes reverently. "You're having our baby! I can't believe it worked out so perfectly."

"We'll have to start calling your brother One-Shot Wonder."

Torrie laughed. "He'd like that."

They'd wanted to start a family, and with Grace turning forty-one in a few months, she hadn't wanted to wait much longer. Torrie's youngest brother Dan had quickly agreed to be the donor when they approached him at Thanksgiving. He was the only one of Torrie's three brothers who was unattached. He was also gay.

"I hope she has your eyes, Grace."

"I hope she has your height. And your athletic ability."

Torrie's hand moved up to Grace's breast, which she cupped gingerly. She licked her lips. "I guess these are going to get bigger, huh?"

"Don't look so happy about it!"

"Sorry. You know I'm a bit of a boob woman." She gave another squeeze, more intense this time. "Not that you don't already have a nice set."

"Shut up and kiss me."

Torrie was happy to do as she was told. "Is it all right if we… you know?"

"God, it better be!"

Torrie giggled against her throat. "How about we do a test run now?"

Grace laughed and turned into Torrie. "I thought you'd never ask." She kissed Torrie deeply, reveling in the heat of Torrie's body, the feel of Torrie's lips against hers, then the soft, wet tip of Torrie's tongue brushing her lips. The feel of Torrie, whether it was her skin, her mouth, her lips, her tongue, her hands, electrified Grace beyond measure. "Torrie," Grace whispered, disengaging and looking into Torrie's eyes. "You don't think we're rushing things, do you?" It all had happened rather quickly, their coming together and then the baby. And while Torrie seemed genuinely pleased and excited by the news, Grace wanted to be sure.

Torrie smiled at her, traced her finger along Grace's cheek and down her jaw, then her throat. "Of course we're rushing it. I want to rush everything with you, Grace. I want our whole life together. Now."

Grace melted into Torrie's embrace and planted little kisses on her neck. "God, I love you, Torrie."

"I love you, Grace. And I'm going to love that little baby you're carrying more than anything else in the world."

Grace pulled her head up and kissed Torrie thoroughly. She had it now, finally…the perfect recipe for her life.

**Publications from
Bella Books, Inc.**
The best in contemporary lesbian fiction

**P.O. Box 10543, Tallahassee, FL 32302
Phone: 800-729-4992
www.bellabooks.com**

WITHOUT WARNING: Book one in the Shaken series by KG MacGregor. *Without Warning* is the story of their courageous journey through adversity, and their promise of steadfast love.
ISBN: 978-1-59493-120-8
$13.95

THE CANDIDATE by Tracey Richardson. Presidential candidate Jane Kincaid had always expected the road to the White House would exact a high personal toll. She just never knew how high until forced to choose between her heart and her political destiny.
ISBN: 978-1-59493-133-8
$13.95

TALL IN THE SADDLE by Karin Kallmaker, Barbara Johnson, Therese Szymanski and Julia Watts. The playful quartet that penned the acclaimed *Once Upon A Dyke* and *Stake Through the Heart* are back and now turning to the Wild (and Very Hot) West to bring you another collection of erotically charged, action-packed, tales.
ISBN: 978-1-59493-106-2
$15.95

IN THE NAME OF THE FATHER by Gerri Hill. In this highly anticipated sequel to *Hunter's Way*, Dallas Homicide Detectives Tori Hunter and Samantha Kennedy investigate the murder of a Catholic priest who is found naked and strangled to death.
ISBN: 978-1-59493-108-6
$13.95